People in Season
Copyright © 2016 by Simon Fay

All rights reserved. No part of this book may be reproduced in any form by any electronic or mechanical means including photocopying, recording, or information storage and retrieval without permission in writing from the author.

ISBN-13: 978-1539307709
ISBN-10: 1539307700

www.simonfayauthor.com
twitter.com/SimonFayAuthor

Say hi sometime <3
simonfay@live.ie

First Edition

NOTE FROM THE AUTHOR

If you enjoy People in Season and would like to learn about my other books then make sure to subscribe to my newsletter or add me on Twitter. Information on both can be found at www.simonfayauthor.com.

Not everybody who writes a book can find an audience so I won't take it for granted if you count yourself among mine. As always I've had a huge amount of support from family and friends throughout the writing process. To my parents and brother, thanks for being there. To the other guys – Eoin Barclay, Matthew Dunne and Michael Plummer – keep up the good work.

Cheers,
Simon @simonfayauthor

PEOPLE IN SEASON

SIMON FAY

# 1

What you need to understand about smiles is that, on the whole, they're peculiar things. In the flash of a person's teeth might be love, polite tolerance, friendly greeting, or just as likely, a sharpened knife. When his head is clear Francis Mullen knows as much. He knows people can lie with smiles and more often than not do exactly that. The protection that comes with this awareness is supposed to be comforting. In truth, it numbs him.

He's observing his landlord, whose tongue rests on a dull canine. The thin curving lips, brown from a lifetime of tobacco and stout, move to say, 'Watch the cards.'

The landlord's hands twitch purposefully about a deck and flick suits in turn onto the coffee table. Perched on a wooden chair, he deals cards from the bottom while making a show of taking them from the top. Between two glasses of wine a king appears, a queen, a joker. And the numbers. Francis is sunk helplessly into the couch cushions, his shirt bunched up to his ears and his loose tie, forgotten after a long day of prep work, falls this way across his chest. He shifts his attention to the hands which move independent of any thought. When the deck is done, Francis looks up at the old man's smiling mouth, now a yawning soggy hole that seems to pull him in. The teeth have disappeared.

'Amazing,' Francis laughs. 'Where did they go?'

Giddy, the landlord smacks his gums together and lisps, 'You'd know if you were watching my mouth, wouldn't you? Figure it out and I'll let you live, rent free.'

'You told me to watch the cards.'

The chair his landlord sits on, dragged conspicuously from the kitchen, had been in place when Francis arrived, a stage seat which a hand at his back led him around. Francis had planned on a walk to tire himself out but when there was news of a flash riot in the city he decided not to risk the evening amble. Though the road he resides on is miles from most of that, the rash of public disturbances has been plaguing the country long enough to make him cautious. Their damp townhouse on a grey strait by Phoenix Park serves as shelter from any ornery teenagers that might want to take advantage of the ongoing panic to look tough and get away with it. Sometimes Francis hates Dublin. Sometimes he hates his landlord. It's not very convenient when the two feelings converge. Downstairs is his cluttered bedsit where a moth bangs its head against the bare light bulb and a single dish waits dirtied in the sink. Worst of all, his laptop, stuffed to the brim and dripping over the sides with pornography, remains cold. He needs to stop using it to masturbate and has designated one night a week when he's allowed the privilege. Easier said than done. Sitting in his flat is not an option. Trapped in the couch cushion folds, he decides it isn't worth the effort moving, and finally, he stops squirming to allow them to swallow him whole.

'Am I wearing a sheriff badge? You've got your own mind, Francis. Now look over there. I can't put them back in without giving the trick away,' the landlord says. 'Yet.'

Francis makes a point of not turning his head before he decides that they don't need to suffer the old man's lisp for the rest of the night, and doesn't face him again until the teeth have clamped together once more.

'You know how to spot a real magician, Francis?'

'The tux is usually a give-away.'

'With an amateur, you can see it in his eyes. He has marks to hit, lines to arrive at, diversions to set up. Like we're watching him put a jig-saw together on stage. A real one makes you feel like he's just a particularly charming friend who wants to tell a good story. Fearless–'

'Then he tricks you.'

The wine tastes bitter as Francis considers the theory. They've emptied a bottle together, though he just now realises that he's drunk most of it himself, and as his banter has become playful, the landlord's has become more of a lecture. They're used to the routine. The old man likes to talk, not listen, and if Francis ever begrudges him it, he need only remind himself that enjoying people as television shows, something to be watched through a sheet of glass, isn't much of a higher ground to stand on. Francis has this habit of criticising himself when thinking ill of somebody else. But anyway, it's a tidy arrangement, the bartering of entertainment for a patient ear.

'Stack them,' the landlord commands. 'Practice.'

If they didn't have tricks to talk about they'd have nothing, so, with a great amount of effort, Francis leans forward and gathers the spread of upturned cards. The old man monitors him carefully as they're dealt and collected and dealt and collected. Francis takes the lack of commentary as encouragement. Eventually the old man bores of just supervising and, smacking his teeth around his mouth, launches into a monologue to accompany his acolyte's task.

'I grew up out near Boyle. A small crop of buildings down the road you could barely call a village.' The old man is from the country, Francis from the city. A pause allows them a moment to picture the foreign land, a huddle of buildings with docile eyes crowded together like cows in rain. 'There's a small mountain nearby with an obelisk built in the middle of its woods. The woods, they're the farmed kind, a barcode forest planted and felled every couple of years, trees stuck in the ground like lines of lampposts. The obelisk, some resident Englishman back in the day had raised it for his young wife. That's young by his times standards, not ours, right? She'd died giving birth and he'd decided that making a monument to her would create some much needed work for the community of haggard farmers. I suppose he was a philanthropist. Not that it mattered. They all thought of themselves that way back then, didn't they? That's neither here nor there. To us, the obelisk was known as Devil's Cross. Go to Devil's Cross, walk around it three times backward and the Devil appears to grant your wish. Friendly fella, that Devil. Children we were. Used to camp out by the woods in the summer and every now and again one of us would pluck up the courage to go out by the obelisk and try our luck.

Kids would come back with stories – He had hooves, laughed like a Cork hyena, smelled like manure. Nobody believed it of course. Without a wish granted it was just water spilling between our fingers. You can't believe in Santa unless he brings you presents, can you? We'd try to drink, to believe, but it would only last a few drops.

'Now,' the landlord declares as if he's had to interrupt himself. 'Who knows where all this came from, or how it grew to what it did, but that's superstition for you. Eventually the lot of us had the idea that if you met the Devil you'd come back with blood dripping from your eyes. That's a convenient little catch, isn't it? The Devil was out there if you wanted to meet him but if you returned in good health we'd know you were lying, and besides, what child in their right mind would want to chance proving it?

'Danny. We didn't count on that lad. One way or another, that little runt of the litter, Danny Keane was going to have his wish granted. He had a hard time of it, Danny, pushed around by his older cousin, a dense thug called Badger on account of his sloping forehead and dark hair. We could well imagine what Danny wanted the night he went out there. He'd arrived at the campsite with his arm in a cast and Badger trailing behind him, a smug grin on the bully's face at that. We pestered Danny about it, but his lips were sealed, and Badger, his smile got smugger the more we went at them. A few knowing glances get passed around. We were kids, but we weren't stupid. Everyone knew-sure. That Badger.

'Danny was quiet all day and hadn't set up his tent with the rest of us. When night was coming he said he'd camp out at the obelisk. At Devil's Cross. He got his fair share of jeering and cajoling, everyone saying he didn't have the guts. To be perfectly honest, we all knew he did and didn't like that a kid almost half our age was happy to skip along where none of us would dare. The boy knew it as well. He took the slags quietly for as long as they lasted and disappeared into the black between the pines when night came, Badger laughing at him louder than any of us. Well, Badger was never popular himself. Why would he be? Just a thick with a strong punch who none of us really liked. That's why Danny got it all from him, I suppose. When the eegit was left alone with us the only way he got into the group would be by pushing people around. We didn't like it, and really, neither did he. So the night goes on and he's getting more and more isolated and bulling to take it out on somebody, but Danny, his target of choice, is away with the fairies.

Eventually the clouds break a little and the moon gives us a wee bit of light, which gives Badger the courage he needs to traipse off on his own. That's when he announces he's going to find Danny at the obelisk. Knowing looks pass around again, heavier ones this time-mind. What was he going to do? He'd already broken the boy's arm. None of us could stop him, could we? Maybe if somebody had spoke up the group of us could have held him back, but-sure, nobody wanted to be that first voice, myself included. And anyway, when do children ever get together to stop a bully? Sure if he'd been a little more popular we'd probably have been ganging up with him. Children are savages, truly. He wouldn't be gone long, Badger said, and he was bringing Danny back with him – one way or another.'

The landlord sucks on his teeth as a means to delay the end of the story. Francis endures the wait by shuffling the deck of cards.

'We were tucked into our sleeping bags when we heard the scream. Spooked us a bit, in a giddy kind of way, still, we left them out there. Fifteen minutes go by. Badger stumbles back into the campsite with Danny in tow. Danny's t-shirt red now, blood pouring from his eyes.'

Francis interjects with an astonished, 'No.'

'I don't remember which one of us did it, but someone called Danny's parents and we sat and waited for them. That boy, Danny, eyes squinted shut, blood all over his face, rocking himself back and forth. Badger, pale as a ghost, not a word to be gotten out of him. We were screaming at them to tell us what happened and screaming at each other to figure it out when the Dad found us, took the two of them away, and said that our parents would be up for us soon. Oh, it was lonely out there, left in the woods with nothing but questions.'

The landlord gives a long practiced shrug that seems to make his joints ache.

'Badger could do that to his own cousin,' Francis drops a card. 'I've met a lot of untouched people in my time. Some of them real sickos, you know? The childhood stories still get under my skin.'

'The thing about being a kid in a bogger-town like that is, no matter what happens, everybody sees each other again at school on Monday. Not this time. Near sight of Badger. Didn't see the dolt for a week. We didn't know it but his folks were mulling over sending him to live somewhere else until the buzz died down. He stayed as it happens.

The only psychologist in the town was a marriage counsellor. I think she had a course or two in child therapy under her belt. Anyway, it was enough for his parents. He was condemned to her sofa for a few weeks and everything went back to normal. She must have done something right though, because he never bullied Danny again.'

The old man leaves a question hanging in the air for Francis to grab at.

'What about Danny? What'd he say about it all?'

'Danny,' the landlord says. 'Danny said he met the Devil.'

'The Devil,' Francis repeats.

'Said he got his wish.'

'His wish?' Francis fumbles the deck of cards nervously. 'What did he wish for?'

'That poor little boy,' the landlord shakes his head, sympathetic words dipped and presented in aged sarcasm. 'Bullied his whole life. Who could blame him? Danny Keane, he just wished he could be anything he wanted to be, that he could turn into a monster and gobble up anybody he didn't like. And he said nobody was going to bully him anymore, nobody, least of all his eegit of a cousin, Badger.'

With that, the old man wipes his hands to signal the end of the story and stares at Francis, waiting to see him light up in shock. It's like the landlord has his fingers on a dimmer switch. It was dark before, but now the young fellow sees.

'He did it to himself,' Francis says. 'Danny made his own eyes bleed.'

The landlord smacks his knee, delighted at witnessing the realisation.

'How?' Francis asks, the cards in his hands forgotten.

'In the light of day it was obvious to anyone who wanted to know. There were two tiny slits in the brow above his eyes. Scabs first, then white little scars, and eventually gone altogether. A craft blade would be my guess. Must have stung bad, slitting his own skin.'

'What age was he?'

'Old enough for long division? Nah. Young enough to get away with it? Just about.'

Outside, a dog growls across their cracked road, another yelp echoes in response, and an owner shouts a command, probably dragging the animal away by the lead, further into the juxtaposed landscape of dustbins and trees.

'You must be good at your job,' the landlord compliments Francis. 'I usually have to spell it out a bit clearer. It took me a few years to cop-on, and even then I thought I was the only one who'd figured it out. The only one who knew Danny could do something like that. But-sure, you'd hear comments. You see the way people acted around him. Some were ignorant, others just kept their heads down. You know what the funny thing is? Once I realised what he'd done – what he was – I thought back on that night, to when Badger pulled him out of the woods, and I think every single one of us, from the youngest to the oldest, knew exactly what had happened, and we stood there gobsmacked and let him fool us anyway.'

'Dreadful,' Francis shakes his head, lets the story brew in him, and feeling something bubble to the surface he bursts into an embarrassed laugh. 'That poor fecker Badger sent to a marriage counsellor.'

'She was a divorced marriage counsellor.'

'You're joking.'

'Divorced and kept living with her ex-husband. They'd built an extension onto the house and he'd moved into it. Always trying to win her back too. Some mad eegit.'

'And the loony giving people relationship advice.'

'Never-mind that, imagine what kind of loony you'd have to be to actually go to her.'

Francis tries to set the deck of cards onto the table but in his fit of laughter finds himself so deeply set into the couch that he has to clutch them to his chest instead. Cackling, his landlord falls forward, sides gripped before going into a throaty cough. When they both quiet down, they notice how sad the mood in the sparse room actually is.

'You stopped shuffling,' the landlord says, and they just now realise that he's hit his mark.

Francis takes note of his stalled hands, 'I guess I'm just not a magician.'

'I wouldn't have let you in here if you were,' the old man replies. 'I hope you're careful out there, Francis. You're good at your job but they're better at what they do. It's their existence. Don't let them dazzle you. Suspect everything, but never let them see it. If they do,' he draws a dotted line across his throat. 'Practice your shuffling. Don't stop for anything, and always keep up a front.'

Used to being patronised by the old man like this, Francis smiles, nodding, 'I know,' while thinking to himself – If only it were that easy. But this is why he comes here. The landlord's certainty, and the zeal that comes with it, is something he doesn't have in himself. He borrows it in cupfuls like sugar for his tea. Picturing his cold bed in the flat underneath their feet, he struggles to climb out of the cushions.

'We need to upgrade from this cheap Tesco wine. What time is it? I'm up early tomorrow. There's a whole media organisation of potential UPD to process.'

'A perilous trek to where the obelisk stands.' The landlord rises and claps his hand into his tenant's to pull him up.

'Do you think there's a lot of them working for ChatterFive?'

'I could pick five just browsing their website,' he brags.

'I've got a few suspects myself, but I'm going to have to put that aside. It should be easy enough. This isn't a government office where their jobs depend on them acting untouched, right?'

'Huh.'

'Then again, maybe your creepy Danny friend will be working there. Something tells me he'd make a fine columnist. Whatever happened to him?'

Francis holds the wine to his lips while he awaits an answer.

'I couldn't say. Once people leave that town they disappear for good. God knows I did. And don't be so hard on him. Maybe he did meet the Devil. His wish came true didn't it?'

Francis, looking at the dark pool in the bottom of his glass, inhales the scent as he considers the words and swallows what's left of his drink along with any superstitious misgivings he might have. 'I suppose,' he says, and dips to the low end of a seesaw.

'Well,' the landlord opens the three locks on his door, a chub, a key and a chain, in that order. 'Go on.'

Francis wobbles over, tipping left and right as he returns the deck of cards.

'You have to try harder,' the old man places his hands over the tenant's, pushing the deck away. 'Don't forget what I said, watch out for yourself.'

'I've got a pack downstairs,' Francis says, ignoring the warning.

'You need a fresh one. They're useless once the edges are frayed. Keep them. Practice always. Get another deck in a week.'

'Thank you,' Francis accepts, knowing the landlord won't let go until he does.

'Don't thank me, I'll add it to your rent.'

As he steps through the door, another idea lights up in Francis, that he should check his landlord's eyes to see if there's a hint of any scar tissue in the brow, but by the time he decides to turn the door is already closed and three locks are sounding from the other side. Untouched? It wouldn't be the first time he's had such a thought. It's a fairly regular one at that. There are occasions when he can read more from the back of the man's head than he can from his face, a sure sign if ever there was one. But he's a lonely man, Francis, and chats with the old man help hone him – he has done good work and tomorrow in ChatterFive, scalpel sharp, he will do some more.

2

In the untouched personality, we are dealing with a disparate collection of individuals who stand among us, but remain separate. This sounds vague. You think it's a description that could be applied to yourself. I'm sure you don't feel especially attached to your colleagues when you chat over rushed espressos each morning. But you are. There's a sense we share, a network which they are not connected to, that exists to help us grow organically as one group. Empathy, the ability to understand and share the feelings of another, is completely lacking in the UPD. Impaired in this regard the signals they send and receive are mere facsimiles. A mouth drawn downward becomes a tool to demonstrate sadness, while pinched eyes are only an approximation of what you and I would call being happy. You might wonder what it's like to exist in such a way. To that I will suggest, in the same manner a computer can scan the expression on your face and alter the lighting and music in your home to suit your mood, so the untouched understand us. There is simply no value attached to their read of our features other than how they should react. It is this critical fault that defines them. Ethics, morality, law, love... they're only known to the UPD as abstract ideas that make about as much sense as the fear of a black cat crossing their path...' On the fifth floor of an office block overlooking the edge of Dublin city, a grey sky is pressed firmly against the glass. Suffering his way through a hangover, Francis Mullen takes a deep breath to salvage these lines he's rehearsed in front of the mirror so many times.

Before him are the forms from which he will have to decipher distinct personalities. Set to social agent mode, he peels his tongue from the roof of his mouth and goes on. 'The truth is, a dying man on the bus seat next to the UPD is as moving to him as a minus number in a math problem. At most, you and I are something for the untouched to pity. Since they're unable to form strong emotional bonds with others and lack any guilt and anxiety, what else could we be but pawns to them?'

A crop of listless heads sprout above their cubicle walls to note the tabloid sentiment. Francis has been talking for the past twenty minutes, but only now piqued the newsroom's curiosity. Painfully aware that he had been tuned out long ago, the mechanical typing of journalists at work and the ringtones of incoming calls have been interrupting him since he began. At first he politely halted his lecture, allowing whoever it was to quickly end their conversation, but soon he realised with a deferential laugh that he was just going to have to talk into the thrum. The lesson he has learned is this: The news slows for no man. Right now, as he's getting to the point of his introductory speech, a particularly frightful woman is firing a string of profanity at her screen. Frustrated with the argument, she hangs up and looks about in search of another target. When she connects with the social agent, Francis gives her an aching expression that begs for an apology, but the woman only offers a spiteful look of contempt until he leaves her, opens a button on his jacket and closes it again, then looks to the editor of ChatterFive for support – Joanne Victoria, she's hardly been a help so far. Stationed outside her office, the editor taps her e-smoke as though there were actual ash to be flicked off, and surveys the room to note whose heads are poking out of their cubicles, like soldiers from trenches, and whose are buried safely in their work. Her gaze stops on the Englishman, Barry Danger. Ankles and socks stretched out of pant legs, his lanky arms are folded while he ignores an alert from his screen. On catching the intense warning his editor directs, Barry nods his gaunt face in friendly greeting before giving his attention back to the presentation, only, Francis is frozen, watching as Joanne's eyes abandon the daft man and continue around the maze of cubicles, past the cautionary posters that each advise, 'Remember The Children,' and land on his own once more.

Francis is framed by a slide of the human brain, an organic mass bunched up like a load of laundry in need of ironing that hangs over everything he has to say.

'Coupled with the illusion they present of being fully connected to our collective reality, the intelligent UPD are masters of mimicry. In part, their manipulative processes come so naturally because they've had to develop them from childhood just to fit in. As such, their use of lies and deceit is not a choice, more a compulsive state of behaviour that was crystallised in a severe detachment from consequences. The unintelligent are just as ruthless, but the threat both embody is their drive to get what they want removed from any deep emotions. Opportunistic, this is their most dangerous feature. If the brief moment we let our guard down happens to correspond with the realisation that they can get something desirable, they will take full advantage with no doubt, no qualms, and no mercy. You may think I'm being unduly malicious,' Francis pauses and coughs to hide a nervous smirk. 'You may even enjoy an occasional glass of wine with one of them. After all, the qualities you admire and want to cultivate in yourself are often those they choose to dress themselves in. It's fair to say some untouched you've known may actually have been the most charming individuals you've met. Well, I'm sure I don't have to tell a room full of journalists what the dark subtext to the word charm is in this instance.'

That's a joke.

Francis was chuffed when he pencilled it in and imagined a round of friendly chuckles from his audience. He would even have settled for a sympathetic smile. Instead, the quip goes unappreciated and he wipes his forehead while searching for an absent bottle of water.

'This personality that you might have met is a fictional construction written by two people. The UPD and its interaction with you. If you see one, if you're friends with one – remember – in the case of the untouched, the person you think you know is only a fantasy, and whatever benefits you gain from allowing them their disguise is a detriment to somebody else. For years those who held power were encouraged to act untouched, with UPD employees not only surviving within the folds, but thriving in the mix. Any attempts to regulate behaviour were simply cases of plugging a finger in the hole of a leaky dam.

Today I'm here to say the dam has burst, folks. Acknowledging the problem isn't pessimistic. It's an opportunity to make things better. We should not consider present social organisation natural just because it's what we've arrived at thus far. The UPD reforms are a declaration that we want to live in a world where people consider each other's interests, not just their own.'

'Pish-posh,' the editor takes a drag on her e-smoke.

So far as Francis can tell, the woman hasn't let her lips go without the plastic tube since he arrived. Something about the situation must be bothering her, but then, in the way she's glancing around the room it's more like she's searching for a missing piece of furniture. Whatever it is that has her nervous, the nicotine seems to offer her little relief. Francis can sympathise. Stood quietly at the top of the office, he's dismally aware that the busy journalists are still ignoring him as he's telling them that they care. In an effort to regroup, he makes a show of going through his ragged notes and manages to convince himself that he's flopping on stage because of the wine he had last night, a choice he momentarily blames his landlord for, but after a beat he's back to chiding himself for letting the time go by.

'Listen!' Discarding his script, he elicits the rise of a few more heads. 'We've all had to take car keys off a drunk friend. They're not inhuman. Even within the untouched scale it's a narrow margin of people that are of concern. Remember, it isn't a crime to be who they are. We can't and shouldn't punish them because they're able to pass as functional members of society. In a phrase, just because with their disability they might do us harm, it does not mean that we should do intentional harm onto them. And it is a disability. Not just a pattern of behaviour we've imagined and labelled for bureaucratic purposes. It is a physical problem within the brain. The image you see behind me highlights at least seven regions that can lead to problems when damaged. If you got a bonk on the head with a mallet and suffered long term consequences, god forbid, you'd want your disability recognised. The standard UPD is no different, except that the development of their problem stems from birth, the conditions of which are made better or worse by the life they're thrust. This term we categorise them with, UPD, it's an unfortunate necessity to guard sections of the community where they could do wrong.

The government has been cleared and, shocked as we all were, the majority were safe...' Another joke that dies. 'Now it's the media's turn. If there are any untouched in this office they can be identified with a simple neural examination. There are those that think this to be invasive. I have no desire to trample over your rights. That means not all of you will be put through the procedure. Over the course of the next two weeks I will be overseeing self-report tests and interviewing everyone in the office, from the interns to the editor. Only those I deem to be potential risks will go on to be scanned. Any information you have that might help in selecting people for further processing could be invaluable. If you make sure that you're completely honest when we get a chance to talk, I'll make sure that you aren't put under any more pressure than necessary.'

'Utter pish-posh,' Joanne hisses down the length plastic cigarette and somebody huffs at the idea that this sheepish man could apply any pressure at all.

'I understand how examining your colleagues could make you uncomfortable, that being put under scrutiny yourself may feel a little claustrophobic, but I'd like each of you to take it as an indication of how important the work you do is, and how critical it is for your environment and the stories produced from it to be free of untouched contamination. Over the next two weeks, I've got the car keys. It's my job to assure the environment you speak from is clean.' Francis takes a deep breath. He's at the end of his spiel and ready to go out with a bang. Charging himself for one last jab at his audience's funny bone, he puffs up his chest and nurses a twinkle in his eye – this one's a killer. 'And if that isn't enough motivation, just think about the headlines you could make if you found a UPD at the top of your own media organisation.'

Winking at Joanne, he chuckles loudly. Once again though, he has to retreat when he notices the e-smoke is so tightly clamped between her teeth that she could almost snap in two.

He's supposed to end the talk by calling to mind the disaster which created the law. It's standard protocol, but he can never bring himself to do it. The tragedy that drove the reforms into effect and all those ruined people, now just fodder for leaflets, they feel too important to use in such a cheap way. However, if it means he can avoid another floundering joke next time, it might be worth exchanging some of his principals for.

With this in mind, he waves a hand of surrender, his face a red beacon that announces to the editor he's finished his introduction, and taps a button on his pocket projector to switch it off. No flowers thrown on stage, only the meek performer left to tidy his equipment away. Barry Danger applauds methodically as the diagram of the wrinkled brain disappears from the air and Francis nods his gratitude, convinced that his efforts weren't a total disaster. Besides, the slideshow is only procedure, any panache he puts into his attempt at showmanship is just a challenge he sets for himself. His real work in flushing out UPD will start later.

Joanne Victoria is still struggling to swallow his attempt at humour when she appears to discover what's missing. A corner desk, notable among the unkempt neighbours for its economy of space, is lacking an occupant. A gap in her defensive lines. It's the contributing assistant editor. She hasn't shown up for work. Joanne squints through her glasses to confirm the time and looks oddly panicked when she can't find the clock. The woman is about to snag a wandering girl to demand its whereabouts, but before she can ask a thing an alarm blasts and overwhelms the room with its metallic racket. The alarm, it's a warning that they should all get out while they can.

•

Startled under the bell, Francis jumps to cover his ears.

'Fire?!' he shouts at the staff as they return to work. The editor is about to scream for the alarm to be silenced when the social agent shouts over it, 'Is there a fire?!'

Feeling a headache come on, and aware that this is what it's to be like operating as a cell under the microscope, Joanne reluctantly agrees.

'Fire,' standing from her doorway, she rubs a temple and calls upon her childhood speech and drama lessons to give the words a dramatic flair, 'Fire drill everybody!' With a clap of her hands, the dithering heads slowly rise and turn to her. This is when it dawns on them that the presence of a social agent is actually going to affect the day to day events of their workplace. The realisation rolls over them like a stench has drifted through the room. 'Don't just look at me like a bunch of roadside cattle, head for the emergency exit! Come on Barry, lead us out, you don't seem too busy anyway!'

Taking in a view of the place emptying, Francis watches as they jostle about for the retreat. The newsroom so far has not been what he expected. The public image of ChatterFive is spirited and energetic, it's veneer polished to represent a collection of young, bright people gathered together to change the world through the exchange of information. He had envisioned a room with brand name graffiti spread across the brickwork and a coffee bar-come-break room with fruit smoothie options attached. Instead, he has discovered this, an office like any other. It's even a little old-fashioned compared to most. The cubicles, though their walls are low, are a far cry from the open plans he has found in so many other places. The employees too, wearied rather than frantic in the clamber to meet deadlines, aren't up to the romantic standard. Though their job is the distribution of facts and opinion, they seem to be nothing more than labourers under the thumb of the short tempered boss who torments them with unrealistic quota demands. From countless wires, data streams and social networks, they dig for veins of untapped material, spurred on by the knowledge that an errant fact which has not been written up may yield weeks of material if spun correctly. Indeed, journalist seems an antiquated word, the slang newsminer more fitting. With the clangourous alarm, they've received some relief from their heavy work load. Barry Danger, demonstrating a taste for the ridiculous, shakes his head and snickers as they leave in a cluttered line, while Francis finds himself in a growing vacuum of space when he joins the bustle. The people in front of him can feel his stare, and he in turn can feel a hole being bored into the back of his skull.

'Have you heard from Ava today?' Joanne has latched onto a girl whose name she doesn't know so that she won't have to interact with the social agent.

There is giggling and cursing, and grumbles at being interrupted, but mostly it's as though the alarm going off has reminded the staff of a bell at the end of a school day. As they descend the first staircase, bumping into one another and talking louder when they pass alarms, they're joined by stragglers from the office below who pass comments like, 'ChatterFive? Joanne actually let you leave your desks?' and, 'There really must be a fire. It'd want to have destroyed half the building for her to let you guys out.'

Everybody laughs except Joanne, who looks about self-consciously for the social agent, hopeful that the comments about her management style go unnoticed. 'Ava!' she calls again, not expecting to find the assistant editor, but wanting to remind those present that she is not to be a topic of conversation. The corridor is, after all, an incubator in which they are being studied. Relieved when they reach the ground floor, she approaches the security guard, shouting, 'Where's this goddamn fire? I'll put it out myself if that's what it takes to get these people back at their desks.'

Directing her across the lobby, the security guard says, 'I was on the second floor when the panel broke. Seems like some dope's idea of a prank to me.'

Joanne plants her feet into the ground and bites down on her e-smoke. Around her, the crowd splits in two, flow by, and join again on the other side where they're conveyed into the grey by the force of their own momentum.

'A prank? Does that mean we can go back?'

'We have to do a headcount and check the building.'

'Give me strength.'

'The rules aren't for me to break,' says the guard.

'Nor for me,' Joanne says as the social agent passes by. 'Who on earth set the alarm off though?'

'Somebody who works here I reckon.' He points to a camera in the corner, thrilled by the rare excitement in his monotonous job. 'It's a mystery. They knew we were refitting the system today so there's no chance of catching them on video.'

For their part, Joanne's subordinates comment that it'll at least make good fodder on the live feed. Joking about what headlines they could use, Barry takes out a camera and begins to record the scene.

'Sabotage At ChatterFive – The Untouched Are Undercover.'

'That's dry as sandpaper,' goes the voice of a critic.

'Alright,' Barry suggests, 'The Untouched Strike Back,' his cumbersome London accent making punches of the vowel sounds. 'Nah,' he says, 'Disaster At Five! No Smoke Without Fire! Have it take up the homepage, make them click through for the story.'

There's a few snickers, but people squirm as they notice the sober grimace on Francis. The journalists are reading suspicion in his scrunched up nose.

This social agent, who they ignored for the length of his stuttered presentation, now has their future in his hands. The thought spreads telepathically from one person to the next as he slinks about the place, on the watch for clues. After sneering at a colleague's warning to pipe down, Barry Danger pans his camera over the bundle of nervous suspects. 'Susan, you've always had a mischievous bent, haven't you? Derek, don't think I've trusted you in years.' But he pans the opposite direction as Joanne comes into frame. The man has been pushing his luck today and clocking the grinding of her jaw, is smart enough to walk away. Francis knows that he should follow him. With the chattering crowd dispersing among the vehicles to become collections of private whispers, he could use any entry point he can get. Flushed with anxiety though, he's pained to do anything except try to remain calm.

Somebody has triggered a false alarm. This has happened on his first day in the office. Coincidences in his job are not something to be glossed over. It is a perfect situation to get a feel for the people he'll be examining over the course of the next few weeks. Right now in particular, whoever smashed that panel is of considerable interest. Francis has an image in mind. A thin glowing point filed away like stock in a photo archive, he concentrates on it to clear his head.

At his side, Joanne slips her e-smoke into its case and replaces the thing almost immediately with a real cigarette. Touching the stick perched on her lips with the flame of her gold plated lighter, she's the first to spot the woman sectioned off in the smoker's area. Pale, lithe and dressed in a wool coat, Francis mistakes the stranger's shy greeting to Joanne as a signal to him. When she drops a packet of cigarettes, he falls forward to pick them up, and as his fingers graze hers the thin glowing point he so delicately brought to the fore disappears – her porcelain features overwhelm its place like a flash of lighting in the sky. At the same time, somewhere between a Merc and a Fiat, Barry's camera now rests on the striking woman. Capturing the assistant editor in his lens, he says her name with wary clarity.

'Ava O'Dwyer.'

3

The newsroom's building occupies a business district nestled into the Dublin mountains, and the car park, set into the hillside where a slice had been taken out for it, is bleak and windy. Ava O'Dwyer's colleagues spilled into the lot before her, a procession of jabbering faces, flat in her eyes, which like two cups of coffee sit on a pair of slick white saucers. The man who'd come to her aid almost tripped over in his haste to return the cigarettes she dropped, but steadies now, fidgety hand pocketed on one side. Poised with the composure of a marionette on display, Ava comes to life with a smirk and just as suddenly brushes past him, leaving the man two steps behind and smelling her perfume thinly weaved with the trail of her smoke. She's late. What little concern she has about it disappears as Joanne rushes toward her, the woman's face aghast between a green blazer and dry straw hair bunched atop her head. She judges her editor's moods by the clothes she wears and choosing a word for her now, she settles on distraught. In a sea of confusion, Ava, her face balanced on either side by slight rectangular earrings, offers Joanne a life preserver.

'You won't believe this,' Ava says in a stage whisper.

'Good news or bad?' Joanne takes a drag on her cigarette.

'Bad news sells good news, doesn't it?'

Her editor brightens, hungry for a fix of scandal. 'What have you got?'

'I was in a riot.'

'My god,' the gauche man has sidled over, 'are you alright?'

Ava jumps at the sound of his voice, blatantly surprised, and looks through him as if he were invisible and had spoken to frighten her. Without replying, she turns to Joanne for explanation.

'Ava, this is our new friend, Agent Mullen. He'll be taking staff members for interview, and ultimately, selecting people to be scanned.' Irritated, Joanne adds, 'I'm sure you knew he was starting today.'

'Oh, that's right.' The man becomes solid now that he's earned a name. After registering the drippy suit, Ava lets her eyes settle on his. 'Nice to meet you. A social agent, is it? Hefty title. I'm sure you have a nicer name we could use. You'll be poking around our heads after all.'

'Francis,' he nods, caught in her gaze.

'Don't be too rough with us, we might seem thick skinned but it's only bravado.'

'Not many will get to the scanning stage, really, I can't imagine most of your days will be interfered with at all.'

'That's a relief, I'd hate to have to suffer through the electric shock process,' she nudges her editor and gives Francis a cheeky smile to entrap him in the joke.

'Electric shock?!'

The huddle of journalists about them feel a jolt at Joanne's cry. All ears prick up to hear the social agent's response.

'It's not that bad.' Wriggling free of Ava, Francis attempts to reassure them, 'I promise it's not. Read one of the leaflets, it covers everything you need to know. I'll go through it with you all later.'

'It doesn't sound like nothing,' Joanne rubs her arms. 'I had an aunt who went through three rounds of shock therapy. Her roots were never the same again.'

The image the editor provides overwhelms the social agent's reassurances in the eavesdroppers around them. Francis is about to insist that it isn't anything remotely like electric shock therapy when Ava speaks over him.

'Joanne, the riot.'

'Yes-yes, the riot!'

'I think I heard something about that last night,' says Francis.

'So it's not an exclusive,' Joanne's excitement fades as quickly as it came. 'Agent Mullen, do you mind if I have a few minutes alone with my assistant editor? There are plenty of other people standing around for you to inspect and I think Ava here might be traumatised. She seems a tad confused, thinking I should be excited by old news.'

'I have full access to ChatterFive,' Francis declares authoritatively. The change in character is so abrupt that they're left standing quietly in response. Embarrassed by the women's reaction, he rubs the length of his tie and stops when he notices himself doing it. 'The conversations that take place during work hours are completely within my purview and open for...'

Growling, Joanne rolls her eyes and pulls her assistant editor toward their building. With the social agent abandoned to an empty car space, Ava scrunches up her face in sympathy, but makes no effort to help him in any way.

'Don't waste my time on this Ava, tell me you've got a spin on it.'

The security guard taps their shoulders for a head count as he passes by.

'Of course I do, I was there.'

Cigarette a stub between her fingers, Joanne spins her hand around impatiently.

'On Grafton street, late night shopping, you know what Thursday's are like.' Ava paints a picture of it, the preoccupied people jostling between lines of crammed buildings, then the next moment, 'Somebody flicked a switch. This school of picketers came through like they were trying to escape a net, passing some horrible fit of anger from one face to the next, and in a heartbeat they were looting. I was knocked to the ground, as much from the shock of it as anything else. Really, I don't remember being pushed or even the fall, just finding myself on the concrete looking at peoples' filthy shoes go by. Then I saw it. A button must have ripped off my coat. I was crawling to pick it up when somebody pulled me into an alcove. It was like waiting under a tree for a storm to pass. I suppose it was silly of me to be so caught up in finding a button, but I'd have been pulled along with the current if only for it. It was monstrous. All those people flared up and acting like they only had one mind between them. A savage one at that. I felt like the only sane person for miles.'

'Bollocks,' Barry points his camera at Ava as they push into the building. 'You've made all that up.'

'Get that out of my face,' Ava sighs, 'you were probably caught up in it too, egging it all on, I bet.'

'Her coat isn't ripped and it's got all the buttons.'

'Tell him to put the camera away, I'm not working on a reality show.'

Barry catches a stern look from Joanne and flicks his phone shut, 'Go on then.'

'Let's take the lift.' Ignoring a protest from the security guard, Joanne nudges her way through the crowd while Francis, following in their wake, is tugged back by the sleeve and stops to talk his way past security rather than just pushing. The elevator is long shut before he can.

'I picked up a new coat after.'

'I saw you wearing that one yesterday.'

'I bought the same one again,' she says as if to a child. 'Wool's in fashion. Some of us make an effort for work, right Joanne? Though I do hate the stink of it when it rains.'

'The riot, Ava, the riot.'

'A car parked down the way was a charred skeleton of itself. It must have exploded. I didn't even notice that my hearing was gone until it came back, you know, it sounded like an alarm at first and then real alarms were ringing and the sound of somebody crying out. The ground was covered in tiny pieces of smashed glass like sweets from a piñata. When I tried to walk my heel was loose on my left foot, and well, you should see the cut I got.'

'Oh do show us your little scratch.'

'Did anybody die?' asks Joanne.

'No, I don't think so,' Ava admits the fault in her sales pitch. By way of making up for it she adds, 'The guy who helped me might have took a hit to the head. I hope he was alright.'

'This isn't a story,' Barry snorts. 'This is a blog entry.'

'Do you know how many flash riots we've ignored the past six months, Ava?'

'Not really,' she mutters.

'Neither do I,' Joanne Victoria arches her eyebrows, 'because nobody cares. You said it yourself, they're like spots of rain, best left to the weather pages.'

Stepping ahead of them, Barry's long arm reaches for the conference room's doorknob. Opening it and begging them to enter, he is a parody of a gentleman. 'At least you got a new coat out of it, sweetheart.'

At once, all looks go to the projection at the far end of the room. A photo of a man's face dominates the wall. He seems to have been carved and sanded especially for the image. Though the picture is one from a photo booth, for a passport or driver's licence, he is no less attractive for it. The sanguine expression he wears could be that of a statesman, or better yet, a man who could play one in Hollywood. Both women stop to absorb the beauty, one choosing a guarded expression, the other visibly salivating.

Not missing a beat, Barry jeers, 'Don't fight over him just yet, ladies.'

'Who on earth is he?' asks Joanne.

'That arresting youth, is Doctor Alistair Evans.'

'He's gorgeous,' breathless, she falls into her chair at the head of the table. 'Such a virtuous smile.'

'Yeah, I wonder who he stole it from. He has, after all, only just dodged charges of malpractice, relating to four women who he sent to intensive care in a north London hospital last year. All a bit mundane until you take his history into account, a colourful CV with a sprinkling of sexual harassment claims and also happens to include a dropped manslaughter charge.'

'My God.' Hand pressed against chest, Joanne declares, 'I'm in love.'

'And it's exclusive to us for now.'

'Barry, I take back everything I said about you. Close the door, let's hammer this out and get it online.'

'I don't know,' Ava says, cautious. She's gotten a sniff of something she likes and, as is her habit, goes to doing what she can to get it without giving a thought to the how or why. 'This is an English story. Why should we be breaking it?'

Joanne, exasperated, explains, 'He's beautiful and he murders people.'

Barry sits, arms lazily folded. 'Besides, he's Irish.'

'One of us,' Joanne swoons. 'Take us through it. Who are these patients he hurt?'

Tapping a display, Barry brings up information on the doctor's background to recite. 'Working with subjects in early stage testing of a potential new medicine for inflammatory diseases, the worst of them reportedly had extreme breathing difficulties within three hours of taking the drug.

One ended up in a coma for fifteen days. Loss of blood to her limbs during the ordeal resulted in dry gangrene – that's mummification of toes, leaving them like stone. Gruesome, but why is it the good doctor's fault? He didn't develop the product. Here's the suss part. In animal studies, delivery of the drug had been carried out over a period of an hour. In the human trial this was reduced to six minutes. Apparently that's a big deal. On top of that, there'd been concerns that a patient, who'd been prescribed an antibiotic the week previous, would react badly. Two red flags that both needed signatures for them to be overlooked, and our beautiful man,' Barry gestures to the screen, 'is the bloke who did the signing.'

'Medical trial gone wrong doesn't exactly make him Doctor Death,' Ava tuts.

The doubt is ignored. Her colleagues put it down to a competitive streak she's grown with Barry.

'Where's this manslaughter charge?'

Barry winces, 'More a suspicion really.'

'Go on.'

'Working for the same company, SimperP, an American business in the top ten big pharma, he was based at their Jersey labs overseeing yet another medical trial when a woman died from an aneurism. There was a suspicion that trace amounts of cytokine would be found in her system but it's not explained why. Hours passed by the time she got to autopsy, which is suss in itself, and that's not even taking into account that any trace might have left her system by then.'

'That's it?' Ava's voice sinks dubiously. 'They brought him up on charges for that?'

'Tell me they stuck,' Joanne begs.

'No, they were dropped soon after and he left the island. He dossed around Belgium for a while after, but I couldn't dig anything up on him there. One problem is that a doctor can amass a malpractice record in one country, but pack up and move to another, get licensed and begin again with a clean slate. Malpractice in one place doesn't appear on the new licensing record. Our doctor has moved around more than your average parish priest. A story about this guy is a story about the whole mess of a system. It's big. After Belgium he went to England where his latest troubles went down, and now he's back home, running a trial for the same company just off Dublin Two.'

'So what do we have here?' Joanne is trying to bunch the details into a presentable bouquet. 'Oodles of allegations that didn't stick, laws that don't work, and a sinister man who wriggled his way wherever he liked because of it.' She tap-taps her finger on the table, examining the model-like features of the projected man. 'A face for the failed system. More a tagline than a headline isn't it?'

'There's no grammar mistakes,' Ava smirks. 'Who got this together for you, Barry?'

'One of the interns found it on the community pages. It's not big yet. If a couple more people come out of the woodwork to press charges against him it could be a hit though. We have his face, but none for the victims since they've all settled. If a pretty girl comes out with something, a struggling mother maybe – we need to get on this before somebody else breaks it.'

'Nobody will break it.'

'Look at him Ava!' Joanna waves at the screen.

'Who's representing him?'

'Tracy and Co.' Barry smiles sourly, as though the fact is a lemon he's bitten into.

'Tracy and Co.' Ava repeats, the sound of triumph clear in her voice.

'I am tired of only publishing what their PR give us. What did we lead with yesterday? Some scandalised minister defending taxi drivers rights to nap on the job?'

'You want something interesting, this is it.'

'I'm parched for a drink and you've just teased me with water before spilling it down the drain.'

Sensing her editor's headache, Ava throws a bottle of painkillers that she keeps on hand, watches Joanne dry swallow one, and catches them as they're thrown back. 'There's an electric fence around this guy. Anything you say about him that isn't good publicity is libel. That's why nobody else has picked it up. The best we can hope for is for it to go viral, let the community break it and report on the reporting.'

'Ah, just have some balls for once, Joanne,' Barry says, petulant. 'We're supposed to be journalists.'

The editor buries her head in her arms, lamenting, 'He was so beautiful.'

'Give me the homepage,' Ava grins.

'Honey, your flash riot is barely a story.'

Replacing the image of the doctor, Ava flicks a photo from her phone to the screen. It's a picture of a featureless young girl standing under a pillar of smoke which billows from a destroyed car.

'Picture of the year?'

Barry squints an eye, 'It's alright.'

'Give me the homepage and I will write a story so steeped in personal experience that it will wake everybody up to the fact that flash riots aren't going away until we deal with them. That it's our responsibility to do as much.'

'Why'd this riot spark up anyway? You're a bit short on details.'

'Why?' Ava grins and types on the table panel so the words appear over the photo. 'Why did this happen? A little girl's question to you.'

Joanne is tonguing the side of her cheek. 'That could work. Do we know who she is?' Neither Barry or Ava fill the gap she leaves at the end of this question. 'Do we need to find out?'

'Don't be silly, that's not our job. Worst comes to worst, people will lose interest in two weeks and the cop's rep will be tarnished for a day. The little girl? She's our daughter – everybody's daughter – faceless. Nameless.'

Joanne lets this sink in. 'It'd be nice if we had something to direct the outrage at, put it into context... but the public. They can pin it on anyone really. It's universal. Everyone has somebody they want to blame for something, right? Let them choose and then we can run with it.' Looking to her writers to confirm the reasoning, Barry is only able to offer her a noncommittal shrug while Ava, straight-faced, is quiet with confidence. 'Type it up. Get that photo over to the fixers, I want her coat at least twice as bright. Is that oil leaking from the car? Make it look like blood. Have it all online in the next twenty minutes.'

Barry groans in protest and Ava allows herself a victory yelp, but as they notice Joanne's face overcome with a sudden frost, they turn to see where the cold snap has come from.

Social Agent Mullen is standing at the door.

'So that's how the news is made at ChatterFive.'

They thought they'd locked him out of their transactions.

Seeing him stand there is like finding out an adult has discovered them indulging in a game they're far too young to be playing. Having weighed the merit of each story by the emotional content and initial impact against possible libel, only now, under the gaze of the social agent do they notice how untouched it could all seem. Their reactions to the realisation are noted one by one in the mind of Francis.

Joanne, feathers ruffled, removes her glasses. 'That's how the news is made everywhere, Agent Mullen. I thought we'd closed that door.'

'It was, eh, left open a little.'

She stiffens at his explanation, Ava smiles, somewhat titillated, and Barry winks to him knowingly.

'There you have it, ladies and gentleman,' Joanne sours. 'If you leave a crack open, anybody can work their way in. Even the unassuming Agent Mullen.'

'It's not like that,' he says, flustered.

'Don't worry about it mate,' Barry pats him on the shoulder as he leaves the room. 'I look forward to the interview. Got a few suspects myself.'

Ava follows her colleague, but stops as she passes the social agent to reach out and adjust his crooked tie. 'Keep up the good work, Francis. Let me know if you need anything.' As he gulps to find an answer for her, she's already dashed away. Having performed one sleight of hand, she's intent on executing her next.

For his part, the social agent only finds himself wondering how she knew his name. He's chastising himself for it when, like a punch to the chest, he realises that he can't remember if he told her and scrambles to retrace his steps back to the car pack. There's no mistaking it, Francis Mullen has been dazzled. Left with the man, Joanne Victoria keels forward to touch her forehead against the cool of the table.

'Agent Mullen, can you turn the light off on your way out?' And as Francis obliges the request, she says, 'Thank you, Agent Mullen.'

4

In a window on the second to top floor of her building, Ava, framed by a set of undrawn curtains, reclines, half naked as music rolls over her to pump faintly against the glass. At a still point in time the window is a painting, then, as though Ava's forgotten to check something, she hunches toward her laptop, face a vacant cast as she taps at the keyboard to bring up the details of the night ahead. Seemingly pleased, she sits back, crosses her leg and watches it bounce, then stands and closes over the glowing screen. Draped on the couch is a knee length stretch satin dress. Gathering it, she guides a foot through the slip and pours herself into the material for it to hug her curves. As she leaves the window, it becomes a landscape without reference – her apartment is empty but for the necessities of life and a few pictures strategically placed to cover bare walls. Ava is of the type who searches for entertainment outside her home rather than in it. Sometimes she feels like she only exists if other people's attentions are on her. When she returns a minute later, heels and a silver necklace have been added to her outfit. Stood at the glass, it's as though she's struck with wonder by the web of people who populate the city sprawl, but as she fixes the necklace against her chest, pulls down the dress a little on one side and flicks back her neck length hair, it's apparent that she's only looking at her own reflection. Turning now, she bunches a scarf and handbag under her arm, stops at the door, looks in another mirror and sprays a mist of perfume to walk through as she exits the apartment.

The music continues to play and the lights remain on when she's gone, but as they're set to do, turn off after five minutes of her absence.

Ava is on her way to meet Doctor Alistair Evans.

When she left the conference room earlier that day you might have set a timer to count down. She had a mission in mind, and her article on the riot, satisfied as she was to get her way, became something to be dealt with rather than indulged. What she wanted was to track down the intern who had brought the doctor's story to Barry Danger, so once her piece was typed up she went about her business of compiling a list of those currently employed. Finding the one who helped Barry had been as easy as finding a soup stain on the boorish man's suit. She'd first divided the interns into two categories, the few names she knew and the many she didn't, then on learning them, the many Barry would like to sleep with and the few he wouldn't. Of nine interns, five were female, and of those, three were overweight. Between the remaining suspects, one was well out of Barry's league and, so far as Ava could tell, completely unaware of the English mug's existence. The other was pretty enough to get his attention and just timid enough for him to feel like he might have a chance. Once she found the girl's name she decided to talk to her privately. Email is a medium for cutting ties rather than creating them. Conversation, where buttons are revealed in expression, tone and body language, was the mode Ava chose. And besides, Agent Mullen was about. Even though he seemed set on avoiding her for the rest of the afternoon, he was stuck in the corner of her vision like an eyelash she couldn't rub away. When she found the girl she decided she had to talk to her somewhere out of the social agent's sight. With that, she leaned back to get an angle on the intern's desk and staked it out until she saw her heading for the bathroom. Like the kickback from a sniper rifle, Ava's chair was left spinning as she chased the girl into the stalls.

'Nice shoes, Susan.'

The intern Susan Ward had stood a heartbeat, surprised that the glamorous assistant editor was not just talking to her, but giving her a compliment too. Ava noticed the girl's suppressed giddiness and realised she had a better shot at getting into her pants than Barry did.

'These things? They were on sale,' she said, and not wanting the talk with Ava to end at that, added, 'I love your blouse.'

Lipstick uncapped to spread across her mouth, Ava allowed a silence for the girl to fill.

'Your articles got me through college.' Her voice bounced off the bathroom walls as she routed nervously through her handbag. 'I was such a tomboy before I found your stuff.'

Turning to review Susan, Ava noted the skirt the intern was wearing – past her knees but a long way short of her ankles – the frumpy cardigan, faux pearl necklace and finally, the thinly framed glasses that made her face seem rounder than it was. And that hair. Was that supposed to be red? She decided not to take it as a fault of her writing, but as the girls inability to learn, that she was dressed so badly.

'Please Susan, you'll make me feel old. Next thing you know I'll be puffing on an e-smoke all day and screaming that I have a headache at anybody who coughs.'

Susan, startled by the jab at their boss, laughed, and without thinking about it sensed the invitation to create a bond. 'She is a bit scary. Some days I'm glad she can't remember my name. Usually if she grabs onto me for something she's forgotten what she asked by the time she's stormed off. Less pressure on me that way at least.'

It was a kiss on the cheek, the shared joke, all the more powerful for how close the intern knew Ava was to Joanne. With the link created, Ava felt free to move around the girl, sniffing for information and eventually, poking for it. She passed comments about the complications of office politics, the little respect Joanne had for Barry, and how if you wanted a story out there, it was best to find another route. As they walked back to their desks Susan turned to look at Ava, who wrinkled her nose and smirked in response. By lunch she'd received an email from the girl detailing everything she had learned about the doctor, including the formalwear auction he would be attending that night. She explained that she knew Ava was busy with the torrent of replies on her riot article, but she felt the story of the doctor really needed to see the light of day and that maybe Ava could push it where Barry Danger had failed. It was everything Ava needed and more. She responded with two dots and a curve and let her awareness of Susan recede to the back of her mind as Alistair came to the front – she was zoning in, observing him in a wide circle that was shrinking as evening approached.

The fact of the matter, so far as she saw it, was that the man belonged to her. She need only collect the prize.

Behind Ava now, on a knot of roads at the edge of Dublin, her apartment building disappears into the orange night sky. In a taxi heading for the auction, its driver is asleep at the wheel. The car is navigating its own way. Usually this would bother Ava, but tonight she's focused in one direction. The roads are trails and buildings at either side sweep by in a blur. The doctor spends the twenty minute drive stuck like a splinter in her mind. When they arrive, she inserts her card and pin, deciding to tip the driver generously as a reward for not bothering her on the trip, and leaves a note in the comment box, thanking him for not snoring.

As she exits the cab, bulbous lights drape toward her. They're hanging on wires between the steeples and pillars. The building itself, St. Patrick's Cathedral, is a fortress scooped of its innards and stuffed with well dressed drunks, sauced up to pay more money at auction. Climbing the courtly steps, Ava the invader trots at a steady pace, passing women who hold their heels in hands and have their husbands lift the trains of their dresses. Into a crowd of well dressed biddies, she goes unnoticed until the clammy palm of an usher closes around her arm.

'Sorry, Miss...?'

'That's ok,' she smiles and walks away from his sticky grip.

'Your ticket?' the usher cringes.

'My husband has it inside.'

The excuse offered is a painful one for the usher to accept. She isn't even wearing a wedding ring. As he searches around for help, he finds his colleague is busy with a crowd. Left to decide for himself, Ava, of all people, is the one to reassure him.

'It's alright, I'm supposed to be here.'

Stealing a glance at her tight skirt he finds it hard to disagree. She walks and dresses and talks and holds herself like she's never had to question a choice in her life. The usher is still taking her measurements when she nonchalantly plucks a glass of wine from a passing waiters tray to complete the picture of expected guest. Sniffing at it contentedly, she takes a sip, 'Mm, you should sneak yourself a glass of this.'

Charmed, the usher bows in begrudged acceptance. 'Alright,' he says, embarrassed to be letting her away with it. 'Not like there's anything in there worth stealing.'

And without correcting him, she takes her leave.

The church hall is empty of pews and fitted with round tables laid out in a checker board pattern. It had been bought and desanctified in the hopes of establishing it as five star restaurant. Tonight the art it held, it's spiritual worth all but gone, is being sold for its kitsch to help fund it. A crush of voices wash over Ava as she enters the room and become a murmuring wall as they echo off the arched ceiling. Stationed between two pillars overlooking the floor, she's surrounded by tables decorated with candles and littered with gaudy handbags. Everyone in the room is golden, bathing in the light of a newly fitted chandelier that smoothes their faces like water over stone. At the front, on an altar where the absent auctioneers stand is set, an elderly gentleman has been dusted off to eke out a stilted dribble of piano notes. Ava allows a group of revellers to pass by, find their tables and clink glasses together when they do. In search of Alistair, she walks the length of the hall, clicking her heels loudly to be noticed. He's hidden in this sea of black suits somewhere. Biting her lower lip, she wonders if she should fake a choking fit – Is there a doctor in the house? – and briefly considers doing so before deciding it would cause too much of a scene.

It doesn't take much effort to find him anyway.

The women about, classless phonies that they are, do their best to hide the glances his direction, but they betray enough desire for Ava to spot the object of their affection before long. It's the man from the picture alright. Sat at a table by the confession box-come-bar, brought to life and no less attractive, he's as striking in the soft lighting as he is in any other. Heart quickened in expectation, Ava is about to cross the hall to take her seat with him until she sees the arm of his date, presumably, wrapped around his as she gushes over whatever he said. The young woman is wearing a long Gucci dress and has it mismatched with an Armani handbag. Noticing her overbite, Ava is somewhat disappointed that the doctor didn't select a better companion for himself and doesn't blame him when he fidgets away from her grip. Like a badly chosen tie, the woman is making him look cheap. Ava only means to mask her pity for her as she comes between the two, but in a blink they catch each other, Alistair and Ava, and like magnets drawn close neither can look away.

The doctor has been waiting impatiently for something interesting to happen and seeing Ava now, he realises he's found it. Their dark eyes sink into one another's and Ava nods. Granting him a smile, she tips her glass of wine before making a show of leaving it on the table at her side. Slinking toward the bar, her invitation is clear.

Alistair, catlike in his observation, savours her with a deep breath as she walks by. She can feel his desire. Replaying the image of the woman holding his arm she decides that they haven't been together long and that if they're a new couple, he won't be interested in her anymore – not that it would matter. He had, after all, been squirming restlessly in his seat when she found him.

At the bar, she orders another glass of wine, and when the barman stands waiting for payment, she informs him that the man she's with will take care of it. Spoken like a spell, these words summon Doctor Alistair Evans to her side.

'Jameson, ice.'

He lays his wallet on the bar, but it drops to the ground seemingly without his notice.

Ava doesn't tilt her head and so far as she can tell, he hasn't done so himself, but when the wallet hits the ground, she grins, teeth bared, knowing the gambit well. Bending at the knees, she picks it up, and slowly rising, hands it to him in ritualistic calm. He doesn't pass comment as he pockets the wallet once more.

'I'd like a cigarette,' she informs him.

'I'll join you,' he says, leaving money on the bar.

Somewhere behind them, the woman Alistair was with is trembling, nervous as a rabbit who all of a sudden realises how far away she is from her hutch. His hand fitted into the small of Ava's back, heads turn when they walk through the mill of people, the strangers admiring this enchanting sparkle that doesn't often pass them by.

Under the shivering bulbs outside, Ava lights a cigarette and waits for Alistair to say something.

He obliges with, 'Those things will kill you.'

'I'm sure something far more interesting than that will get me in the end.'

They each take the time to evaluate the other. Ava approves of his choice of tux but reads from it that he's compensating for something, working class roots perhaps. She begins to plan how she'd like him to dress and how she'd go about applying it.

Her throat tingles as she does so and she swallows, feeling him circle her as she had circled him. She knows what they're doing and so does he, the only question is, who will take the first bite?

Afraid that it won't be the doctor, Ava is about to open her mouth when he takes a step forward. Looking down, coquettish, she exhales a cloud of smoke that he leans through to speak in her ear. With a shiver sent down her spine, she feels the words more than she hears them.

'Let's pretend we're untouched.'

5

'So,' she twiddles a link on her silver necklace, 'why don't you start by telling me your name?'

'James,' he answers, square jaw set.

The trite pub they've found, decorated with antique farm equipment, rusted tools hung among photos of Dublin past, and replica placards for drinks and tobacco that are no longer sold, creeks around them. It wouldn't have been her first choice if she'd cared to plan the evening, but it was the most convenient. The only purpose they need served by a location is privacy to conduct their interviews. They're talking conspicuously, cautious of being found in the booth nestled at the back of the room. Only for being engrossed in their game they'd have copped that they can't be missed. In elegant evening wear, the pair look like royalty in a barn. The barman leaning against his counter sneezes and they glance at him to confirm he's just an extra in their scene, present only to serve them drinks. He wipes a towel down a drooping moustache, his attention absorbed by a screen that hangs above him, which warns that another flash riot is likely in the wake of the coverage Ava provided to the nights previous. But that's of no concern to them now. The world could be gone and humanity with it for all they care. They'd abandoned it when they left the auction. That building and the people who populated it were mere props to be cleared, and the pub they saw across the road just another stage to be entered.

Ava's glass fogs as she holds it at her lips, the wine touching her tongue to make her mouth ache. She drinks and repeats, 'James.' Stretching it out, she's feeling the name, passing it from one hand to the other like a piece of clay, trying to shape it into something recognisable. 'James, you're missing your auction.'

'Maybe I couldn't bid on what I wanted.'

'What do you want?' She squeezes the false name again, 'James.'

He draws a gold pen from his breast pocket and holds it in his fist, its nib directed toward Ava as he sharpens his smile. 'Maybe I'd like to run the tip of this into your oesophagus, slowly, and watch you gurgle underneath me as you stiffen and go limp.'

Ava arches her eyebrows, more irritated by his change in form than she is shocked by the vivid description he had at hand. 'That's stupid.'

'I don't see what's so stupid about it,' he goes sullen.

'Just because you're untouched it doesn't mean that you're a murderer and sadist.'

He pockets the pen for later use. 'It doesn't mean I'm not either.'

The doctor likes games. He'd seen one when he found Ava, prowling the aisles of the church. As a man who thrives in chaos, he has a taste for the unpredictable and craves it in the company he keeps. When he pushes, he appreciates a woman who can push back. The proposition he set, to talk as though they were untouched, one UPD to another, was enjoyable for its taboo, so she humoured him with it, but it's clear she has a singular direction in mind and resumes working the man toward it.

'Back to the beginning,' she says.

'Ask me again.'

'Ask what? Your name?'

The doctor stares blankly until she takes her cue and mouths the words widely, fully expecting to hear an honest answer this time.

'What is your name?'

'James,' he repeats, mimicking her wide mouth.

Ava had hidden her curiosity when he lied the first time and realises it probably means that he knows that she knows his name already, along with his colourful list of legal problems. The tease about stabbing her throat confirmed it, surely? He's playing up to his almost-public-persona.

The man who gets his kicks from death. How banal. Joanne was right in assuming he'd be perfect for capturing the public imagination though. He's aware of his magnetism too, and playing on it, pushing and pulling at whim to see what he can get. There's a childishness to him that she doesn't like, hidden under the mature face, though she decides to put up with it, supposing that the foolishness is a part of his charm. He could tell you his blood covered hands were actually soaked in paint and you'd give him the benefit of the doubt, only because of his boyish smile. He's the perfect news story embodied in a human being – a nightmare posing as a dream. Ava though, is already tired of the cat and mouse antics – who's the cat and who's the mouse? – and ends them abruptly.

'You're not a very good liar, Alistair,' she underlines his real name with a deeper tone.

Grinning, his hands go up in surrender. Ava follows them, feeling for a second how it was to have them touch her. Under the table, she uncrosses a leg and folds the other over, barely brushing her foot against him as she does. She's enjoying having him in front of her, charged with the knowledge of what's going to happen, admiring him like something she's about to buy.

'You're well informed,' he says. 'Maybe you can tell me, am I really untouched?'

His hands are always moving, leading from one thought, one sentence, to the next. Later, she knows, one will close around her waist as the other grips the dark hair at her neck, pulling her close by the hip and drawing her back to feel her lips on his. The hands, they'll move along her body clinging to her as they go. She'll move away from him and stand in full view to pull down her slip so she's stood in her underwear, a strap of her lace bra loose on her shoulder like an untied ribbon. He'll stand coolly, pursing his lips in approval as he waits for her to come back. Lifting a toe out of the dress bunched on the floor, she'll loosen his tie with a flick or two of her wrist, open his shirt one button at a time, and making sure he keeps his hand at his side, she'll take her time to examine him, his hard chest heaving slowly, his flat, ripped stomach, tensing as she runs her palm along the muscles. When she indicates her approval, they'll slip out of their last items of clothing and into the thin sheets of the bed, her skin like a pool of milk on his olive body, and writhing together, their touches will become gropes as they lick and suck and fuck through the fading hours of the night.

'Are we still playing?' she asks, rapping her knuckles on the booths table.

He remains quiet but there's a quiver on the surface that says, 'Maybe.'

Under the screen, the barman sneezes again and wipes his hand on the back of his jeans.

'Well, I'm not,' she cuts into the silence. 'You probably are.'

'Untouched or playing the game?'

She sips her wine.

'You're a journalist,' there's acid in his voice as he makes the accusation. By the unmoving shape of her features, you wouldn't know she's been taken off guard. In fact, there's a twinkle of amusement in the way she sets her glass down that urges him to go on. 'Ava O'Dwyer. Writer at ChatterFive. A voice for young women who want to care about the world and look good while doing it. My solicitor would not be too happy if he knew we were here together.'

'You know more about me than I do about you.' Ava is relieved more than anything. She won't need to twist his arm to make him talk.

'I doubt that.'

'You shouldn't be so suspicious. Maybe I'd like to write a nice article on you. Something that will make everyone see what an upstanding member of society you are.'

'It'd be a lot easier to write a damning one.'

'Alistair,' she says. If James was a lump of clay, this name feels like a finished sculpture in her hands. She moves her fingers along it's edges. 'Alistair, Alistair, Alistair. How does it feel being UPD?'

'You tell me,' he stretches in the seat, challenging her, but lets out an amused sigh when she doesn't answer him and cracks an ice-cube between his teeth. 'They say it doesn't feel like anything. That's where the name comes from isn't it? The UPD live in a world not connected to anyone. Sounds terribly lonely. Me, I just know what I want, when I want it and how to get it. If other people want to make all of that more complicated for themselves then that's their problem.'

'They seem to be making it a problem for the UPD of late. It isn't so different to any other trend, really, is it? One minute they're in, the next minute they're out.'

'The law,' Alistair sneers. 'Social Agents. Career bureaucrats who invented jobs for themselves to get a good pension. They're as bad as the taxi alliance. Men getting paid to sleep at computers that beep when something goes wrong.'

'I don't like it either,' Ava says this casually, but she's aware of the weight the admission might have. 'There's a social agent in our newsroom.'

'That's a tricky situation,' the doctor says, more concerned for himself than for her.

'He's an idiot. He wears a suit that looks like it was handed down to him from his brother and stutters through everything he has to say. If these are the kind of people we have running the country we might as well sink the whole thing now.'

'No class,' Alistair opens his hand in understanding. 'What will you do about him?'

'Do?' her skin crinkles. 'Why would I care if I get selected for processing?'

'We're untouched, remember?'

'I'm not untouched. And anyway, I've got him wrapped around my little finger. It's pathetic, really.'

Alistair hums, 'If you were untouched, and you didn't want to be processed, being seen with me could be very bad for the both of us.'

At first, she sees everything that's going to happen pulled away. Like a ghostly force has ripped her from beneath the sheets of their bed, she feels them slip over her naked skin as Alistair and the room shrink into nothingness. But it doesn't make sense. She knows that Alistair doesn't care about the social agent, that he's testing her again, moving away to make her come toward him. Her response is neither a step forward or a step back, but a simple cock of the head. He laughs at this and they consider each other for a time, a mirror looking into a mirror, deep and empty.

'If you did write anything bad about me, I could make a lot of trouble for you.'

'That's probably true,' she agrees. 'So, what are we going to do, Alistair?'

'Who knows?' he tilts his glass to watch the ice slide around. 'I suppose we'll get out of here.'

Standing, he watches as she fixes her dress, and she smiles back, enjoying the feel of his gaze. It's like she's being eaten. Once again he guides her with his hand at her back, but he's following as much as he is leading. He throws a note down on the bar and they hear a grunt of thanks and goodbye. Their footsteps are loud on the hard wood floor as they exit, the wood aching in relief when they're gone. As the door swings shut the note goes into the register and the barman returns to the screen. They might never have been there. In the taxi there's another sleeping driver. Quietly, Alistair's hand slides over Ava's. They could do anything. Say anything. As they arrive at her building the driver wakes with a shiver, and mumbles goodnight before the car drifts away with him at the wheel.

Paused by the door of her apartment, Ava dips into her handbag and comes up with keys. Alistair's hands are on her shoulders, unwrapping her scarf and letting it fall from her skin. The scent of it floods their senses as it moves. She opens the door and turns to lean against the wall, hands behind her back with her handbag dangling on a shoelace string. Inhaling the breeze as she allows him to enter, the room comes into view when the lights flick on.

Posing, he takes to his mark at the centre of the room.

Everything around him is square. A solid black coffee table gleams on thick posts on a smooth rectangular rug. Colourless sofa's made of slotted cubes sit into each other in front of an L-shaped kitchen unit. The counter, clean like everything else, has never had any food prepared on it. There's a steel lamp, here in the corner, and a series of vases on a shelf, three sizes in line from large to small, placed only because the apartment had come fitted with the ledge and needed something on it. No flowers, because they wilt when not cared for. No fake ones because what's the point. There's no art on the walls. The photos on display show shots of herself in crowds of beautiful people who she only calls friends when it suits her, and carefully chosen to be slightly less attractive than herself at that. He walks over to the long window and sees a dim reflection of himself in it placed among the furniture behind him, an ivory kendle armchair set, worth more for their name than for their comfort. Ava walks out of the doorway and into the image, linking her delicate fingers in his big bear paw, admiring the sight of him at her side.

Rubbing the length of his arm she finds a price tag on his sleeve and teases him playfully as it's tugged off with a smirk. He doesn't see what's so funny about it. As she pulls his jacket off his wide back, they appraise one another in the glass, assessments wet on the tip of their tongues.

'We're going to get caught,' Alistair says.

Walking away from him, she kicks her shoes off at the threshold of her bedroom, first one, then the other, unclasping her earrings as she goes. Constrained to follow her example, it's as if all the world has become a tunnel leading to the bedroom where she waits, and with loafers slipped off, the doctor walks into the dark, where everything that was going to happen, happens.

6

So much of Francis Mullen's work entails the investigation of that feeling one gets when entering a room and realising that the conversation by those present has hushed to an awkward silence. Not knowing what happens behind closed doors, getting to the bottom of what was said, in one way or another, his life is spent prying into these places he's not wanted. Reactivity, the observer effect, applies in both directions.

Francis finds his attention passing to the newsroom outside the cramped office he has managed to claim. Set to frosted, he can see the staff on the other side of the window but all they can see of him is a blur. Ava is lingering by the conference room, an errant lock of black hair falling across her face as she rummages through her purse. He had told her his name and didn't even notice. He'd blamed the hangover, but he hasn't had a drink since and doesn't feel any more confident in his ability to handle her. It was as if, along with his name, she had stolen a part of him and was now keeping it for ransom in that purse. If only he could snatch it back off her. More likely, he is going to have to pay for it. And still, he can't bring himself to hate her. As it happens, he has broken his rule of maintaining midweek abstinence. Last night, drunk with desire, he masturbated to the thought of her. In the sober interlude afterward, forehead dotted with twittering beads of sweat, he listlessly wiped them away and asked aloud if she was really something to be concerned about. He couldn't convince himself of an answer either way.

This in itself worried him, but soon enough he was swollen with longing again, throbbing all the more now as he spies on her from behind the one-way screen. An intern breaks the spell as she crosses his sight. The short red-headed girl chirps hello to Ava, but Ava, a butterfly alight, blanks the girl. Francis notes the happening somewhere in the swirling pool of hormones his brain has become, hoping he remembers to follow up on it, and cops himself on once more – This is his job, for fuck's sake, and he's good at it.

There are prescribed methods on how to maintain a detached attitude, but so much experience teaches a social agent that sometimes you just have to play it by ear. Like a chicken picker who can tell the sex of a new born at a cursory glance, a talented agent knows the UPD by the hollowness in their words. Several steps up the evolutionary ladder from chickens, people don't like their fates being decided by a stranger's instinct, separate as it is perceived from the whim of the universe. That's where the personality tests come in. Over the past few days he has been taking the staff in small groups to supervise the UPDSRP, a self report form. The circles they ticked were accounted for and a list of potential candidates assembled by the computer. Hardly a reliable device, the computer, the untouched are adept liars after all, and everyone else not always the most mindful bunch. So, regardless of their results, each member of staff is being taken to interview for Francis to compare their self-reporting with his own observations. On a tablet in his possession is a list of questions carefully designed to help him judge the behaviour of those he examines. The questions mostly act as a rough guide, something to fall back on when probing a given direction reveals nothing. Eye movements, hand gestures, vocal tone, language patterns, he will combine all these features to create a portrait of the subjects he interviews, but if you were to ask a standard social agent how they were so good at picking an untouched personality, you would be asked in return how you can tell the difference between a deep lake and a shallow pond. Francis Mullen calls it a knack. Surely a pretty face can't put the talent out of service.

As a knock is heard, he runs a hand over his clean shaven face, feeling soft and pudgy, and holds his tablet with questionnaire at heart level. Aware of the trial ahead of him, he opens the office door for his first candidate. Joanne, she's the number one suspect on the computer's list.

'Am I allowed smoke during this?'

She stomps past, allowing him a view of the familiar grid of cubicles. The heads are ever curious today as they glimpse his direction, and turning the other way, they move like grass in the wind as his eyes sweep over them. Shutting the door, Francis turns around to see the editor has taken his seat and is obstinately chewing on the plastic cigarette wedged between her lips. He tries a smile as he asks her to change places, then waits patiently for it to sink in – that in this room, he's the boss.

'How are you today?'

'Terrible,' she replies, hoarse, before rethinking her answer. 'Fine. I'm fine.'

Francis gathers a silence. Settled into his role as interviewer, he knows that the gaps between sentences can be as powerful as any question on his list.

As though she's figured out the answer to a riddle, Joanne asks, 'How are you, Agent Mullen?'

Her frayed golden hair, so neatly bunched at the beginning of the week, has become a nest of sorts to which she doesn't pay mind. Her make-up too, though Francis doesn't notice, is not what it was. The lipstick she wears has been smeared across her mouth by a jittery hand and her false nails, in dire need of replacement, have been bitten to nubs in the short intervals between cigarettes.

'I'm also fine, thank you.' He takes a long look at this body sat in the hot seat. With its tensely folded arms, one leg crossed over the other and twitching, it would seem a circuit in its motherboard has been fried. Smoke streams out of her nostrils to confirm it. He goes on. 'I'm just trying to get the lay of the land. I'll be asking about your relationships with people in the office and your observations of them, how they act around you and with one another. There are strings attaching everyone. I want to make a map of them and, more importantly, how you see them. Perhaps you've noticed somebody wandering around, unattached, so to speak, and not have comprehended what it was that made them feel so untouchable. I won't start another lecture about why we're doing this, but please keep in mind that your assistance is important in the process of keeping the psychic environment clean. In the same way that bad life experiences can build to make a UPD's symptoms worse, habits can form in a workplace, polluting it on a deep level in a surprising amount of ways.

It's what it means when somebody describes an entire corporation as untouched.'

Guardedly hugging herself, Joanne remains unimpressed.

'Let's get started then.' Francis scrolls down his screen and picks a light question to begin with. 'Who among the staff members do you get along with best?'

'They're employees. I don't make friends.'

'Just subordinates?'

'If they do their job, I'm happy.'

'Yes, I'm sure.' He bites his cheek as the next thought comes to mind. 'You seem to have a soft spot for Ava,' and his voices goes down a pitch as he says the name in an attempt to prevent it going up one. His struggle to disguise the growing infatuation is flustered at best, and yet nobody in the office has yet to detect it. Worried for themselves as they are, all they see in him is a suit that holds a checklist. Hidden behind the questionnaire his obvious interest is consistently unnoticed.

'Do I?' the editor challenges him.

'Do you?' he meets her.

Joanne opens her mouth with a loud smack, then closes it. 'I found her in the community. She was a college drop out. She didn't even apply for a job here. She was my little project. A soft spot? I have an interest in making her as good as she can be. You can't get comfortable at the top, as a company or an editor. We stay the best by retaining quality and aiming for more. You're asking about personal relationships in an environment where personal relationships are all business. Ava's a good writer and has a keen understanding of how to work under public scrutiny. She's valuable to me that way.'

'A protégé.'

Dodging the suggestion, Joanne takes a puff of her e-smoke.

'What attracted you to her writing?'

'It had balls,' she says in a rumbling baritone. 'You can't write a story today without putting a disclaimer on the end of it. She didn't do that. She doesn't hide the truth, our Ava. She just has a way of putting it in a nice Armani dress. And she's not afraid to say what she's thinking. Counter opinions are important. Between her and Barry, we're kept on our toes. If one of them didn't speak up, who would? Of course, it helped she had a large following in the community that came over to us when she made the move.'

'I see,' and switching direction abruptly, Francis asks, 'You've been divorced, twice, is it?'

'Excuse me?' Joanne balks. 'I thought you said you wanted to understand the newsroom. My personal life is off limits.'

'Well, I'd eh, like to understand you too,' Francis stutters, busying himself on the screen so her surprise doesn't engage him. 'I'll be asking the other staff members about you. The personalities at work here are what make the office what it is and you're at the top. We can rely on other people's opinions of you, or you can help me get a clear image...'

'Of my marriages,' Joanne bites the end of his sentence.

'Why do you think there were two?'

A bitter laugh erupts from a dark pit inside her. 'The hangover wasn't so bad from the first one, I didn't think a second could hurt,' and she swallows, taking time to arrange her thoughts into a civil manner. 'It was the same man both times. We were children the first go round. Years later. Well. You think you grow up but so much of that is just house keys and cars and paying bills. Shock twist. It turned out we were still the same people.'

'That's a sad lesson to learn,' Francis nods, satisfied that she was provoked into saying something so honest. 'And eloquently put.'

Not replying, she clenches her teeth and waits for him to go on, apparently having surprised herself with the confession and not wanting to be drawn by his attempt at intimacy. Focused on the wall behind him, her attention is pulled to one of the posters he had hung. 'Remember the Children.' Her startled eyes water in thrall of it.

'Does it mean something to you, Joanne?'

'Hm?'

'The poster...'

'What poster?' she asks, staring at the picture in question.

Sensing the woman's off guard, the agent takes a deep breath and tries for a push.

'Would you say that you've had a lot of sexual partners, Joanne?'

'Oh, you have some nerve!' she snaps back to reality, exasperated.

'I'll be asking everyone in the office the same questions. Believe it or not, everything we discuss is relevant to my task at hand.'

'How many would you say is a lot, Agent Mullen? Only looking at your rosy choirboy face I think you'd be offended if I've had more than one.'

Francis blushes in spite of himself, the set of questions on his screen wavering downwards as the flush of embarrassment goes through him. 'It's not about what I find offensive,' he says timorously, then, finding that the silence has turned against him, he offers with a shy smirk, 'You could just write the number down on a piece of paper if you like.'

•

Watching them is Ava. Sat at the duck blind that is her desk, she's eying the frosted glass of the room Joanne and Francis reside in. It's a boring hour, but after a while the blurs move apart, the door opens, and she makes a beeline to meet Joanne in her office. Noting the mood on her editor's face and letting it reflect on her own, she briskly closes the door and launches into a round of questions with, 'What a load of pish-posh. Really, just pish-posh, isn't it? What kind of things was he asking about?'

'You, for one,' Joanne says offhand. 'I mean, you and me. If we're anything more than boss and employee. His words. My marriages, my sexual history, my pets.' She picks at her thumbnail as she talks. 'I don't have any pets. What's that supposed to say about me? He must be some kind of pervert. Do you think we can get this thing called off on sexual harassment grounds?'

Ava gives this due consideration before shaking her head. She's scrutinizing the grid of desks beyond Joanne's door. Despite the undercurrent of paranoia, the newsroom is the usual buzz of activity, a wasp nest that shakes itself up every day to pump the noise onto the ChatterFive network. Joanne's office is set to soundproofed. None of it reaches her if she doesn't want it to.

'What's going on out there?'

The editor half suspects a team of investigators are sifting through all the computers in search of some despicable crime to pin on her. Ava has never seen the woman so unnerved. She throws her the painkillers she keeps on hand and catches them as they're lobbed back, unopened and unused.

'This is too stressful for you. Go on holiday. I could use your office for a while. I wouldn't have to listen to Barry take calls anymore.'

Joanne ignores the idea. 'Who's he talking to next?'

Peering across the cubicles to the room Francis has claimed, Ava sees the door is ajar. The information she gathers is filtered through the window, and then, filtered through her eyes and out of her mouth to Joanne's ears. 'He's just sitting there, lost in his notes or something – I don't think he's entirely right in the head, Joanne.'

Putting her own spin on it, Joanne says, 'Probably looking at my online history. I knew I shouldn't have been looking up that stuff about buying anthrax.'

The social agent stands abruptly and calls to that funny haired girl as she passes by. Jumping to catch up with her, she beams in response and they walk into his office together. With the door closed behind them, they're just soft shapes on the glass now, hues Ava can't understand.

'She's a trouble maker,' Ava mumbles. 'That intern. The one with the awful hair. She keeps pushing that silly doctor gossip.'

'I don't blame her,' Joanne laments. 'I wish we could use it. That riot story went nowhere. The Gards were calling about that bloody lost girl you centred the piece on, by the way. You need to get back to them.'

'We helped enough, getting her story out there, maybe they can do something for her now, you must realise that. And you'd have had it buried just to get some smutty medical scandal on the front. That doctor story would have had this place bombarded with lawsuits.'

Joanne doesn't hear this, 'How can they not know what happened to her?'

'Who?'

'The girl you took that photo of. The one you said we helped, Ava. They want our assistance tracking her down!'

'Translation – please solve the case for us.'

'It's not a case. It's damage control. They don't want to look bad.'

'Yeah right, next they'll be asking us to give their uniforms a make-over. Well, it's not for us to find out. We've done our part.'

'Says the woman who started the story!'

'Anyway if she hasn't been reported missing she must be fine. Her parents probably don't want any publicity and haven't come forward to announce they were there. Honestly, you'd think we could respect the last good people in the world that don't want to milk attention out of a disaster.'

Frowning, Joanne finds her e-smoke battery has run down. 'Tell that to the Gards. And do you think they're going to find anything? This is just going to fizzle out to nothing. One more riot that caught our attention for a minute. Just a clap of thunder. I'm tired of the snacks you people keep bringing me. I want a story with meat. Type something up to kill it. Say the cops have several leads and are pursuing them in earnest. Hopefully something terrible will happen in the world tomorrow and we can move on from it all.'

'Alright, fine, and what are you going to do about Susan?'

'What?' Joanne asks, frustrated. 'Who the bloody hell is Susan?'

'The intern who keeps causing trouble!'

'Jesus, Ava, I don't know. She hasn't done anything that bad has she?'

'Pretty sure she's the one who's been stealing food from the fridge.'

'She could stand to lose a pound or two,' Joanne finds herself agreeing and with it, a stone drops into a well. Business is a mercenary affair where I'll scratch your back if you scratch mine is the definition of friendship. Ava wants the girl gone and Joanne wants Ava to remain a pillar of support in this turbulent time. The reasoning for it, whatever the girl did to offend Ava, is the last thing Joanne wants to discover. She has survived this long in the media world because she has learned the hard way that, counter intuitive to her profession, sometimes it's more important to not know what is happening. To remain ignorant is to remain innocent. This credo exists like a poison in her veins. So, as she realises that somewhere in the course of their griping she has struck a deal with Ava, she stops herself from wondering what motivations might be at work and tucks in her chin to sheepishly mutter, 'I need a drink.'

Ava walks over to a filing cabinet and finds the sparkling wine Joanne keeps hidden at the back. Seeing the bottle, Joanne excitedly takes two mugs from her drawer and lets Ava serve double measures.

'I'll tell the newsdesk you said to give the girl her notice. They'll email it on to her in the morning.'

'Can she sue us?' Joanne takes a swig to resign herself.

'She's just an intern.' Ava brings the mug to her mouth but doesn't swallow any of the liquid. Licking her lips, she sees Susan leave the social agent's office as he calls for another candidate.

'Look who's up next.'

7

Bobblehead Barry! A knobby hand slams onto the desk, placing a bobble-headed figurine in front of the social agent. Following the hand to the arm and the arm to its conclusion, Francis finds a matching face for the toy in Barry Danger. Skin tight on the man's skull, his lips are stretched into a severe grin.

'You can keep that. I've a drawer full of 'em.'

'Thanks,' Francis delicately examines the thing, afraid perhaps that the head might fall off, bobbling about as much as it is while it laughs at a joke he's not let in on.

'I had an advice column running for a while and we were going to send those out to people who wrote in. Well, turns out nobody wanted my advice. There's a warehouse in Naas storing crates of the things.'

'It's even got the same funny suit as you.'

Barry grips the collar of his outfit, a brown gridded jacket, slacks mismatched with a shiny purple vest, and puffing his chest out proudly, he peacocks the style while the sweat stained cuffs of the shirt stretch a finger's length out of his jacket sleeves. The ensemble seems to have been pieced together in a number of different charity shops but, in his own assured way, it's become a brand. The matching icon confirms it.

'Or do I have the same suit as it?' Barry waggles a finger.

'Excuse me?' Francis asks.

'It's a mystery. One of life's little oddities, isn't it?'

'Funny gimmick though.' Placing the bobblehead on the desktop, Francis adjusts it so that he doesn't have to look at the thing. 'You could give them out to top commenters and such?'

'Then I wouldn't have any to give to my good friends, Doctor Mullen,' Barry winks at the social agent, who takes it as a warning that this interview won't be any easier than Joanne's.

Francis had scrutinized her as gingerly as he could, searching for safe spots among the mass of sensitive nerves, but he might as well have tied her down and screamed the questions. Though she'd tested high in the UPDSRT, she was falling below average on the comparative report. By the end of the interview she was defensive to the point of going mute and he had to make do with the behaviour he'd observed up to that stage. It wasn't like a boss to decline an opportunity to talk. Coming off the back of that, and facing a journalist who could more aptly be described as a professional troll, he has chosen a less invasive tact, though his tablet is still held between them.

'I'm not a doctor.'

'Counsellor?'

'You know I'm not a counsellor, Barry. Just a social agent.'

'That's right, but-see, I'm not really sure how a bloke becomes a social agent. I would've guessed there were psychology classes involved somewhere along the line.'

'An arts degree helps,' Francis exhales tiredly. 'Generally you get into a branch of the civil service and work your way up. Social welfare's a good entry. It helps to know the right people. Not that I ever did. After that it's like any other job. Do what you're told, don't be late, and learn to fill in the right forms.'

'Another civil servant trained to check the right boxes,' Barry nods to the tablet.

'Circles, actually.' The screen is clogged with them. 'And we should get started filling them in. Are there any old rivalries in the office?'

The question is met with a chuckle.

'Are you good at this job, mate?'

'I suppose we'll find out.'

A humble response. Before he can parry, he's questioned again.

'What other places have you investigated? Just curious. I'll answer your question if you do mine.'

'This isn't a negotiation,' Francis says. 'It's up to you how you act in here.'

'You've never been in a newsroom before.'

The tablet lowers slightly.

'Come on, Mullen,' Barry chides.

'You're aware this is the first media outlet to be processed.'

'Yeah. Where else have you worked though? Social Welfare?'

'Over the past year I've been processing the County Councils of Leinster.'

'Different to here.'

Considering this, Francis reluctantly jokes, 'There may have been a noticeable difference in IQ levels. It did tend to make contesting parties easier to spot.'

Barry Danger, with a stiff rigor mortis grin, signals that they've arrived at his point. 'Let me tell you something then, mate. You're going to need a new questionnaire to figure this place out. Rivalries?' he scoffs. 'I took a donut from the fridge last week without asking whose it was and within an hour someone in the office had started a community group against me saying my articles are full of hyperbole and egomania, that I've got a small Johnson and am probably taking all my frustration out on the world because of it. Who started it? Bloody hell, pick a head, they're all suss.'

'You didn't try to find out whose donut it was? Apologise and appease the situation?'

'No, I took another one the next day though. When you have a group like that onto you you'd better make it worth their while, right?'

'How would you feel if you were chosen for the scan?' This is Francis going for a jab.

'Inconvenienced,' Barry yawns.

'That's all?'

Leaning forward to return the jab, Barry places his fingers on the tablet the social agent holds, and lowers it, gently, so that it's level on the desk and there's no wall between the men. 'I've got one for you. Humour me a minute, you might find this interesting.' The change in Barry's demeanour is so drastic as he takes a turn for the serious that Francis assumes he's leading up to a joke. 'I'm walking down O'Connell street one day and I see a lady get her leg clipped by a bus, do a three-sixty in the air, and hit the road, hard, landing on her shoulder.

The driver of the bus, he mustn't notice, taking a nap or something, because it keeps going, right? Why else wouldn't he stop? And nobody else on the street seems to notice either. They're all sleepwalking too, dreaming about a brand of toothpaste that'll keep their smiles pearly white, and me, Mister Brown Teeth, I'm the only one who's awake. That's a nightmare in itself, isn't it? It must be true though because none of them see the woman on the middle of the road crawling off at a turtles pace for fear of being run over by another bus that doesn't bother to stop.'

Francis waits quietly for Barry to reach a conclusion, hands poised to lift the tablet.

'So, I jog to help her.'

'Of course you did,' he says, relieved. 'Anybody would.'

'Nah mate, I didn't run. I jogged.'

'It's a shock, seeing something like that...'

'No, I just didn't want to be late for meeting a friend.'

'What do you mean?'

'Well, I jogged, like I said, steady pace, hoping a bloke across the way would get to her before I did and I wouldn't be delayed. Lucky for me he did, and lucky for the woman on the ground, he knew first aid. I stroll up to them and he tells me to call an ambulance. Part of me wants to tell him to use his own bloody phone but I'm hating myself enough as it is. Really, new heights of self-loathing. I'm on the outside of it all, floating above the three of us, shocked to find I've got a bald patch now and thinking what a prat I am in general. I see myself down there, ringing nine-nine-nine, passing instructions on how to position the poor woman and reporting back to the emergency line on how she's doing. I see myself doing this. I see me watching the man who's helping her and I say, Alright, you've got this, I'm going to jog on – and the man – he looked at me, calmly, like you're looking at me now, except with all the spite a person can have for the world and see it embodied in another human being. Nah, don't worry about it, he says. Just fuck off.'

The insect tapping of journalists typing dominates the room, muffled as it is through the door. Barry, apparently, has ended his story and as explanation for it only offers a broad shrug of his shoulders. Francis opens his mouth to comment. Instead his chair strains a squeak and he screws up the features of his face.

'You regret this?'

'Not really.'

'That's what bothers you. You think you should feel bad about not acting more responsibly.'

'It should bother you too, Mullen. Think about it. If I get scanned, and I'm not UPD, what does that mean?'

'I couldn't say...'

'You couldn't say,' Barry hoots. 'And that bloke who helped her, you wouldn't be surprised if he tested positive, would you? He could be off the scale, pure malevolent psychopath and it wouldn't make you bat an eyelash.'

'No,' the reply is curt and the tablet is once again picked up to indicate that they are going to go back into interview mode. Barry roars with laughter at this, like Francis has just hit the punch line of the joke he had set up, so the social agent finds himself raising his voice to speak over the assault. 'The processing exists for exactly these reasons. You can't measure a person's condition by their actions alone. For all you know he was helping so he could steal her purse. That's an extreme example, but if he was untouched there are any number of reasons he might have gotten involved. It's more likely he just wanted a bit of excitement, or if he was particularly narcissistic, a story to tell of what a gentleman and saviour he is.'

'Jesus, Mary and Joseph, that's some way you have of seeing the world. I won't be doing any good deeds around you.'

Bewildered as he feels entrapped, Francis insists, 'I just meant if we're assuming he was UPD, those could be the motivations at work.'

'And you're happy to do this job, to mark people up in your rows of numbers on a scale of how healthy they are for a given group.'

'You're being glib and you know it,' Francis tries full-stopping the exchange.

'I'll tell you what I think,' Barry says, determined. 'Some people are untouched, and the rest of us are just arseholes.'

'There are those who would say more people are arseholes in an environment that rewards untouched behaviour, that you can hardly expect a crowd of people to engage the world with a moral sense if example isn't shown from the top down.'

'There's a danger society gets warped when you let the wrong people get to the top?'

'Exactly.'

'Or that the wrong people get to the top because the world is already warped?'

At this, Francis once again realises he's been led down a path he doesn't want to go, and huffs with a shake of his head to try and deny it, but Barry, plucking the bobblehead off the desk in front of him, twists it around to face Francis, it's manic skull wobbling side to side with a mocking grin. The English journalist matches it's expression.

'That's the game, isn't it? Did bobblehead have the suit first or did I get the suit to match the bobblehead? Which of us wears it best, do either of us really like it and should I be suss if I don't? Not even a counsellor, you said? Bloody hell. Aren't you worried you're working with very small pieces in a very large puzzle? UPD on a media site. So what? What could they do that the rest of us approved personalities don't already? You think I'm a journalist. That I have a say in what goes online. You've got it wrong. Data processing, that's what the news is here. Our criteria for a story is keep 'em cheap and keep 'em safe. Nothing that might provoke repercussions. I get the news from the community, or the wire, branches of government, PR departments of whoever can afford them. All I do is reword the things. Joanne can't even give me the time to leave my desk and check if any of it's true. And most importantly, you must remember, give the people what they want. They're not watching the news for complicated stories, mate. They need sound bites to latch onto so they can join in the banter down the pub and their hunger for 'em is relentless. The system is there so the system must be fed. You want to know something? I'm amazed my job even exists. Surely Joanne can just get some software that grabs the day's press releases and rearranges them for any given publication. Set it to liberal or conservative, have it tailor stories for your customer's taste. A computer offended on your behalf. Wouldn't that be something? I'd still need to sit at my desk and watch it work though. Couldn't have it spouting gibberish. We'd need to have it read comments on articles and speak to what the audience wants, exaggerate attitudes they show and have it spout it all back at them, or better yet, say something that gets their hairs up, rankle them and stir it up some more,' Barry stops abruptly and lets a burst of surprise illuminate his face. 'Sheppard and flock both. That's what we are.'

The social agent across the desk gulps audibly.

'Well I'm going a bit off topic.' Sounding genuine for the first time in the interview, Barry appears to have discovered a thought he hadn't planned in advance. 'All I mean to say is, we don't have as much influence as you think we do.'

'You'd have us frozen in inaction because the world is absurd?'

'No, Mullen, I don't suppose I would,' Barry says weakly. 'I guess I'm just resigned to being a spectator. You're a player though. I'm watching you with no small amount of interest, make no mistake about that. I think you're like me. You've got doubts, Mullen, and you're in a job where the people you're up against haven't an ounce of them. I don't envy you.'

Though Francis absorbs the statement, he manages to raise his tablet to hold between them once more.

'And what will you do if it turns out you are UPD?'

The notion delighting him, a twinkle returns to Barry Danger

'Then I'd move back to London, where I'd be appreciated.'

Francis Mullen's head is left spinning. Next up is Ava. He should probably make a quick visit to the bathroom to relieve himself of some confusion before she arrives, only, he is so very short on time.

8

He's wearing his good suit today, but thinking about the brash pinstripes now, it feels more appropriate for a first communion. As Francis is sifting through Ava's article history, starting at her days within the community and moving up to the present, he's learning just how badly dressed he is. Even if it were for a first communion, he'd feel like he'd rented a bin liner for the occasion. Not to mention his shoes aren't polished. He assures himself that it doesn't matter. He's here to do a job, not to impress the candidates. There is no room for doubt in the work of a social agent, the sound bite echoes in Barry Danger's voice. Agent Mullen has doubt, formed in his mind like a stalagmite in a cave, drip by drip it grew over the years. Now it stands, an impassable pillar.

'You look tired, Francis.' Ava hands him a cup of coffee. It's the solution to a problem he didn't know he had. 'Up all night I imagine, scouring the archives, putting together your little list. Barry's at the top of it, I should hope.'

'Miss O'Dwyer,' he beams involuntarily.

Jerking out of his chair to greet her, the tip of his tie lands in the coffee with a vulgar splat. Withdrawing the thing, it droops sadly in his hand and drips onto the desk as he looks about timidly for something to clean the mess, horrified that of all the people it could have happened in front of, it was her. What little nerve he had built to face the woman has been spilled onto the table.

'Ava,' she corrects him, conjuring a tissue and watching as he dabs at his tie. 'You're inside my mind, Francis, we might as well go by first names.' She sees the articles on his tablet. 'You can't find that prattle very compelling'

'I've learned my shirt doesn't go with this jacket, anyway.'

Sympathetic, Ava hums, 'You look good.'

Disconcerted, he tries to find something to say, but to his mounting concern realises he can't. The complement hangs in the air until Ava decides to break the spell.

'This is a very small desk. I thought you were going to have the conference room to work in.'

'Ah, Joanne,' he says in explanation. 'She likes to have it available in case she needs to put her head down. Says she gets claustrophobic. It doesn't matter, I don't need much space.' There's a long pause again as they look at one another. Unable to bare it he gives her a thumbs up and says, 'Thanks for the coffee,' immediately feeling like an idiot for doing so. Taking a deep breath, he forces himself into the role of interviewer. 'Ava, take a seat. I'd like to talk about your work. Barry had some, eh, interesting thoughts on modern journalism. It made me curious about what kind of writing you people get up to exactly.'

'Oh dear, you shouldn't listen to anything he says.'

'You've got different ideas to him?'

'I'd be surprised if you could pin down any idea of his. He has a habit of playing devil's advocate. What were you talking about?'

'I think he was trying to say that he's more of a construction line worker than a journalist.'

'Mm,' she purrs knowingly, 'he must be having a bad day.'

'Oh?'

'We all feel like that sometimes don't we? No matter what job you're in, it's about taking something in and putting something else out, right? I think ChatterFive does well, all things considered, especially compared to other media outlets.'

'Go on,' Francis says.

'It's thanks to the likes of Joanne, if I'm being completely honest. I know she can seem like a bit of a crank, but she really is committed to providing a valuable service. The way the business is going, media sites like ours are a rarity, an actual staff journalists on the payroll and working in a room together.

Other places, they're just glorified message boards, uncontrollable climates where the mob rules, everybody following their own interests and only coming together on inflammatory issues. Well, we kept our main page, right? When you log on with us there are preselected issues that are important to the world which the customer is exposed to. If they could customise the site to only see what interests them then you'd have to really go out of your way to find important information. That's why you're here, right? Because what our outlet does is so influential, because the person at the top of it all has to make the right decisions if we're to do a good job. And she does. The place wouldn't be what it is without Joanne. I can't tell you how much admiration I have.'

It's a moving speech that also manages to shift the blame for anything that happens in ChatterFive entirely onto its editor's shoulders. Francis hasn't noticed. Hypnotised as he is by the monologue, he's only moved by her optimism and passion for the job. She had complimented the work he does too. Given him a saccharine view of the world, so much easier to swallow than the bemused pragmatism Barry had offered. If there wasn't a system to follow, he'd be standing up now, hand outreached to thank her, ready for the next candidate to take to the chair. But the questions and her article history remain on screen. He's obliged to follow through and, pinching himself, gets on with the task.

'I went back as far as I could in your article archive. All the way to the stuff you did in the community.'

'Oh please, don't, they're like old school photographs.'

Glossing over the comment, his voice lowers to a confidential level. 'I was reading your pieces from around the time of the first untouched scandal, when the ministers were on trial for, eh, neglect of basic humanity?'

Certain references have a way of ushering a mood into being that demands respect. When tragedy strikes a family for example, names and places attached to the deceased gain an unmanageable weight. In the case of the first untouched scandal, and with the aid of the information campaign built around it, the leaflets and posters and educational lectures, it has gained more mass with each year gone by. Mentioning the specifics of the first incidents can't fail to create a morbid sense of loss, and with it, the behavioural expectations on those present.

Ava nods in understanding of this.

'It was a crazy time.'

'That demagogue, Minister Whelan,' Francis breaths carefully, 'she was a monster. What happened to all those children under her watch...' he lets the unfinished sentence describe the horror, ready to gauge the woman's reaction to it.

Ava though, she sits, eyes like pennies as she waits for more input.

'Neglect is a nice way of putting it...' he continues.

She blinks once, not trusting where she's being led, 'I don't like to think about it.'

And he waits for her to go on but she has nothing else to say. Bewildered, he gives her another while to realise that she should say something, a token line of grief that any UPD would surely know to repeat, but she continues to just sit, waiting for the next topic like it's only one item in a clothing line she has to consider.

'No. Nor do I. Not many people do,' he stutters in agreement. 'It's important that we do though. Like you said, that's why people like me have jobs like this.'

'Plus you're so good at it. I could never do what you do.'

'Yes,' he says, more to something he's thinking than to Ava's compliment. 'You started out as a fashion writer. You covered Minister Whelan's trial from that perspective. It's an odd lens to look at the world through, but valid,' his voice fades, and grows again to confirm it. 'More than valid.'

'Thank you,' Ava doesn't hide her confusion. 'It's nice to know I'm valid...'

'You said in the article. You said, if Minister Whelan had worn a little more eyeliner and a little less blush she might have gotten off.'

'Oh,' Ava lets out the long vowel sound, relieved at last to know what it is the social agent has been building up to. 'Oh, that's all you're getting at. It's a cold thing to say isn't it?'

'It'd freeze an Eskimo,' Francis says, also relieved.

'There's a give and take when you're writing for an audience. You have to be able to read the mood. Taking it out of context years later,' Ava explains, 'you can't have a sense for that.'

He hears Barry's concern underscoring her words.

'That article got me this job. I must have read the mood right. Like you said, she was a monster. A lot of distance is needed for you to sell the attitude that even monsters deserve mercy.'

'I think I understand,' Francis lets the conspirator tone dissipate. As his awareness expands to the other details around them, he notices that for the first time since he'd arrived in ChatterFive, the office on the other side of the door is peculiarly still. The journalists have muted their alerts, they're typing softly, and there's a smell in the air, like the damp hush before a storm. Those outside are trying to measure how Ava's interview is going. The hairs on the back of his neck stand when it dawns on him that as he tries to peer inside her, all he can see is static. 'I'm not used to working in the media. It seems to be everyone's job to read the public mood and go with it, condemning one day and sympathising the next, working everything up into frenzy and reacting to it like you didn't start the craze... It would make a good article.'

'I'm afraid that might be a bit too introspective for ChatterFive's readers,' Ava smiles.

Disappointed, he addresses his screen, seeking another prescription to assist him in his work. He wants to keep her talking about the nature of her job but she doesn't seem to be taking the bait, and now, interrupting them, her phone chimes. She offers Francis an apology and checks the message on its display. Much to her satisfaction, it's from the doctor:

I'm outside. Meet me at the smokeing area.

Confusion crumples Ava's paper white skin, but when she remembers that Francis is waiting for her, she smoothes out the creases and surprises him by returning to their discussion. 'You're thinking that the news should be an informative lecture that gives you the history of every speck of dust that moves and it's nothing like that at all. It would be impossible. It's more like, a beat by beat story that we help unfold, revealing whatever sections make the narrative work. That riot I was in? We didn't know what it was about, not specifically, we just published that it happened. It created an interest that put pressure on the police to find out what the source of it was, but really, nobody cares.

They just want to know what happens next in the story, that it gets taken care of. It's a chaotic world and we put it in some kind of moral order. All they want is for ChatterFive to paint an ugly portrait of it and have the cops stop them, then they can sleep well at night.'

'I see.'

'You can understand why it's important, can't you Francis?'

'I wouldn't be as experienced as you in these matters,' he's happy to have gotten her talking freely, but it's nipped in the bud when her phone chimes again.

Pausing their discussion, she checks it, this time masking her reaction to the message. It's the doctor again:

If your not coming outside I'll go up there.

The phone feels like a stick of dynamite in her hand. Regardless, she manages to type back a furtive response, correcting the doctor's spelling and instructing him to stay put.

'Are we almost done here? There's something brewing I need to check on.'

'Breaking news?'

'Something like that. I should go check on it.'

'Um, let me see,' Francis ignores her attempt to leave, and returns to the tablet which has been flat on the desk up to this juncture. He hasn't got to most of the suggested questions and in a flurry, feels her need for haste infecting him. 'Are there any old rivalries in the office you're aware of? Someone who puts them-self before the team? A few of the others gave me the impression that this might be a redundant question.'

'Francis,' she says in answer, addressing him like a child as she straightens her blouse and prepares to stand.

'We're not finished yet,' Francis insists, the tablet firm in his fingers.

Her head titled beneath short straight hair, Ava freezes to test how serious the social agent is. He responds in kind and it isn't until she's sat again that she realises he was holding his breath. He's nervous, she thinks to herself. Roused, she forgets about the messages on her phone altogether.

'It's a dynamic job, I understand, but you should think of this interview as a part of it, just for another few minutes.'

'Of course,' she puts her hands in her lap. 'What's next?'

Going over the list of questions on his screen, Francis lets out an exhausted sigh, guessing her answers to them, the body language, the assumptions, all the ducking and weaving that will count for naught in the end, because he's already made up his mind. Deciding if she's untouched or not isn't the problem. 'Alright, one more thing,' Francis brings up an image on his screen and turns it around for Ava to see. He's skipped to the final section of the interview. It's a black triangle set on a white background and the question that goes with it is, 'What do you think of this?'

Ava knits her brow.

'It's a triangle.'

'Yes,' Francis agrees, his tone implying that whatever she says it's going to be the wrong answer, 'but what do you think of it?'

'What do you want me to say?' Ava tries to win him over with the warmest smile in her stock, but the triangle seems to deflect her attempt.

'Whatever you think is right,' he says.

'Can't you give me a clue?'

Francis stares back at her resolute and in reaction to the stance, he sees a fork of lightning appear over the horizon in her eyes.

'I don't like games, Francis.' Though she recovers quickly from the display of irritation, the clap of thunder is left rumbling over the social agent when she holds up her phone. 'I really need to take care of something.'

'Alright, I think we're done.' Laying the tablet down, he stands to watch her exit the room. 'Thanks again for the coffee.'

Ava stops in her tracks when she hears him grasping at straws like this.

'Let's say you owe me a drink. I like wine, Francis. A cabernet. Something Chilean.'

When she's gone, he falls back into his chair, devastated by the suggestion and its implications. A drink, he swallows the thought. She likes wine. Chilean wine. Do they sell that in Tesco? From his seat he sees an Ava shaped cloud dissipate as she races past her confounded editor and right on out of the office. Waves are left in the woman's wake. The journalists jostle in them, some amused, some afraid, each assuming that whatever happened inside that office has fazed the unshakeable Ava O'Dwyer, and soon will happen to them.

There are five-hundred and twenty-three dots on the ceiling. At least, that's the number Francis manages to count up to. A mysterious gravy stain covers a panel in the corner. He's trying to keep from thinking, angry for letting her get to him – And how? What has she done to get under his skin? He notices the smell of perfume hung in the air. Inhaling it deeply, her face shimmers in his mind, balanced and soft, plump lips set on startling white. No, he assures himself, it's the newsroom that's getting to me. Whatever she is, she's only doing what everybody else in the office is. His finger is a ticking clock on the desk. Is she the one setting the tone for the room though? One person? In his interview guide there are circles that need to be filled. There's no fields for comments or questions beside them, and this troubles him all the more, because with no release valve, his comments and questions are swelling inside. Doubt, the sound bite plays, doubt is a dirty word in Agent Mullen's profession.

'If she'd worn a little more eyeliner and a little less blush my job mightn't exist.'

The coffee has gone cold. He wanted her to save herself so he wouldn't have to face questions he doesn't have the answers to. Is she really any worse than the rest just for being untouched? He opens a file on his screen to type his thoughts into some kind of order, but finds he only has one thing to write. Jotting it down purposefully, he underlines the short remark before reading it out loud – But she set off the fire alarm.

It couldn't have been anyone else.

There's a circle that should be filled. Francis finds he's just sat looking at it, caught in the pull of its centre. It's as though he's been called on stage by someone in full magician garb, and everyone is waiting for him to pick a card, but he's stuck, a dumbstruck fool staring into the spotlight.

9

Drumming the elevator button and watching the numbers pause on every floor, Ava grows frustrated and makes a dash for the winding stairs instead. Spiralling downward, when she's met by the guard's smile at the front desk, her own freezes tersely, each corner stuck to a cheek by pins as the thought flares – Maybe he was going up in the elevator as I was running down. One heel follows the next as she spurs herself forward. If he is up there, his arrival in the newsroom would be, for all its effect, a bomb blast. The concern turns out to be unfounded. As she pushes through the door to let the light of day blind her, she squints to see the doctor standing in the smoking area. Propped against the rail, Alistair has one leg hitched over the other and a bunch of roses held haphazardly in the hand hanging at his side.

'What are you doing here?' Ava shoves him away from the car park. 'Are you trying to get me fired?!'

'I was bored,' he says, then quickly adjusts to a syrupy inflection. 'I brought flowers. You work hard, I thought you'd like a nice surprise.'

Ava snatches the flowers from him. A stream of petals spill into the air as she dumps them into a dustbin they fly past.

'Alright, so you don't like roses,' he says. 'Tulip's next time? They're a bit cheap aren't they?'

'There won't be a next time,' she snaps and glances over her shoulder to the building that looms behind them. 'My editor has been pushing for a story on you and so has everyone under her.

That's not even taking the social agent into account. That's the social agent who knows your face, is searching for UPD candidates and–'

'And what?'

'And seeing you here, giving me flowers. It might give him the wrong impression. Do you think that you can show up and they won't notice? That they won't connect it to me? I don't want them thinking I'm burying your story to benefit my own personal life. That we're cohorts in some dramatic conspiracy.'

'What do you care?' he asks.

'What?!'

'I said what do you care, you're not untouched, right?'

'You know I'm not.' Ava stops in her tracks and wraps her coat tightly around herself.

'So relax,' he pulls her close.

'I don't need the hassle, Alistair. Group self report sessions? Personality reviews? I'm here to put other people under inspection, not submit myself to it. That damn electric scanning machine he's lining us up to suffer. What's it even for?'

The building's panel of glass is grey. Impenetrable from her angle, the Dublin coloured sky is spread across its surface. Inside is the social agent, armed with a set of questions designed to tie a noose around her neck. Outside, here in the windy parking lot with Alistair, she can breathe again.

'Let's go somewhere,' he chooses the boyish smile for his face, knowing she's back on side. 'I'm horribly bored. They won't let me do anything practical in the labs. I'm just sat around an office all day choosing who I want to call up. You should be happy it's you.'

'I'm honoured, really. Top on the list of bimbos you count as entertainment.'

Ignoring the sarcasm, he takes her comment as agreement, 'Alright then, let's go.'

'I have work to do,' Ava protests.

Exasperated by her dragging feet, he insists, 'You can do it from anywhere. Why do you people even have an office?'

Stumped by the question, Ava is forced to accept his argument and with a link of their hands, they're away.

'Where are we going?'

'You're the one who got me out of work!'

It's Alistair's turn to pout now. In the short time they've known one another this is the pattern they've formed, swapping positions as it suits them, alternating who is to withhold affection, making each other work for the other's company. Though it's a constant wrestling match, there are precious occasions when the pair manage to sync their good moods. It's possible that someday both of them could play the cold shoulder and really, just give up altogether, but in this instance, Ava sees an opportunity and decides to reach out. She has her mind set on fine tuning his style and directs him to take her into town.

Since she found Alistair, Ava has done little research into the crimes he was accused of, and even in close observation of his behaviour, hasn't been looking for slips of the tongue that would reveal his seedy past, the body count he had supposedly racked up, and the list of women offended to the point of legal action. All that mattered to her was getting him under thumb. No easy task and one to be handled delicately, but, however difficult, the investment seemed worthwhile – Oh, the places they could go and the things they could do... Yes, she would train him, inch by inch if that's what it would take. When they arrive at the shopping centre, Alistair is demonstrating the rare ability he has to appear and disappear in plain sight of those around him. Charm fully under his command, he can sink into the background one minute, and like a spotlight has revealed him at the click of his fingers, he has the attention of anybody he wants the next. With this ability, his own interests are pursued at whim. Intently fascinated by a given person, he might bore of them in a heartbeat and move on, patiently searching for another form to hold his attention. The nutrition facts on a packet of crisps have no less potential to do this than the man who sells them. Chomping down half a packet, he might drop them lightly as they leave his mind and somehow conveniently land the rubbish on a serving tray they pass in the food court. A bad habit he has, which irks Ava to no end, is stopping at windows and staring past himself as he fixes his hair, forgetting altogether their surroundings and the woman he's with. At first, this aloofness seemed to Ava the doctor's own method for seizing power in their relationship, a juvenile strategy to remain free and do as he pleased, but as their time together collected from hours into days, she supposed more and more that it was just who he was, and something she would need to take into account when whittling him down to a less unwieldy shape.

Regardless, she was staunch in her struggle to get him where she wanted, and once they entered the shopping centre, put up with all of his delays in her stride. It isn't until they arrive at the counter of the jewellers and he announces, 'I don't want a new watch, I like the one I have,' that her patience finally snaps and she pinches his arm between two long fingernails.

She knows his watch already. In fact, it disgusts her. Having taken her time with Alistair to judge his closet by the outfits at each meeting, she has approved of his wardrobe. Tailored suits, slacks hanging just right over an ever changing selection of shoes and designer shirts, always ironed to the same standard, no matter the day, he could have been a runway model. She realises Alistair doesn't understand or care why his suits are so good, that he just knows that they are by the price tag. Normally a safe rule, she was happy enough with the man she reeled in until she noticed there was one glaring problem with the catch – an ugly thing he wore on his wrist, the gaudy black and gold Rolex with chunky chain links and large roman numerals set into the face. It looks like something a wealthy deep sea diver would wear.

'My old man gave it to me,' Alistair pines.

'And when was the last time you saw him?' Ava asks, unconvinced. 'It's lovely for the right occasion, Alistair. A school reunion, a wedding, a funeral, that kind of thing. But you need something a bit more subdued for your profession.'

From here, Alistair might as well just be a hand Ava has taken along. Everything else happens between her and the sales clerk until they're in another taxi with a tote bag dangling unnoticed in Alistair's fingers.

'I hate these sleeping drivers,' Ava complains, despising the bald, speckled skull of the man at the wheel.

'They never have anything interesting to say when they're awake,' Alistair says. 'You want to hear about his kids? His gambling? I get enough of that from my subjects.'

Ava sits quietly, considering if she wants to accept the point, then, turning away from him to look at the stumpy buildings of Dublin swish by, she asks, 'Why should they get paid to sleep? It's health and safety gone mad. Like he'd wake up in time to do anything helpful if there were an accident.'

The doctor barks. 'You've got a social agent in your office, picking people's heads apart, and you're saying the taxi drivers are a health and safety issue gone mad.'

'They are. Anyway, they're just as bad,' Ava cuts through his laughter. As an afterthought, she says, 'It's a world of nanny states. Whoever got your medical license suspended is a part of it. You could be changing people's lives right now and they won't let you near the sick. And I bet you're the best doctor in the city.'

Alistair sours in agreement with her assessment. Sinking into his jacket, it's like he's fallen into a bog, and sapped of energy, his suit shoulders push up to his neck. In a dearth of emotion, he seems to be peering out from something inanimate. It's that same expression he gets when he studies his reflection, only there's some foreboding movement in the black pools of his eyes. Ava doesn't notice.

'For crying out loud,' she mumbles. 'He's snoring.'

'I hear that,' Alistair says, a warning in his voice.

'He's getting paid for it too. We're giving him money for this.'

The doctor does not deign to reply.

Arriving at her apartment, the engine murmurs tensely. Ava leans forward to insert her card, but stops when she's interrupted. Alistair is lightly tapping the glass that separates them from the man in the driver's seat. He calls to him and the man snores louder again, choking on some phlegm that gurgles in his throat.

'Hey!' Alistair shouts.

Ava jumps. 'Oh, leave it. What do you want from him?'

'You don't like sleeping drivers,' his tone, coated in sugar, matches the one he used to deliver her a bouquet of flowers, 'I'm waking him for you.'

'We're already home, Alistair, I don't care anymore.'

Tightly linked to her on the back seat, he shows her a blank smile, their faces so close she can see the cogs grinding to dislodge a trapped thought, and as the moment passes, he turns back to the window in front of them and sinks lower into the seat, pulling his overcoat up to give his legs room to manoeuvre. Ava is about to ask what he's doing when his foot springs up and out, smashing the heel of his loafer against the glass to make a crack that grows a leg.

'Alistair! You're going to get glass all over us!'

His foot smashes the window, which shatters into jagged marbles, and his heel clips the driver's ear as it breaks through. Dazed, the driver groans and searches for a wound with a shaking hand. Having flung the door open, Ava pulls Alistair with her as she shimmies out of the car, makes sure to hide her face from the dashboard camera, and brushes pebbles of glass off her skirt as she stands on the path. Alistair is shouting abuse at the car as they walk away, taunting the driver whose hand trembles all the more as he finds blood on it. When they're around the corner, Ava is seething.

'You are just trying to get us caught, aren't you?'

'What?' he asks, confused. 'You think he wants to catch up with us?'

'I don't need our faces seen together on the six o'clock news.'

'So don't write a story about it,' he laughs.

'You're on his camera,' she says, exasperated.

'Oh please. He won't report us. He was sleeping on the job. He doesn't want them checking the footage.'

Ava replies with silence, appeased but refusing to show it. Alistair watches his feet as they walk, at a loss as to why she would be so angry with him. The puzzle pieces are all laid out in front of him, but they don't seem to fit together. Sensing his confusion, almost feeling sorry for him, Ava pushes her anger down into the pit of her stomach and grabs his hand. It's a grip that says he's forgiven. Later, the incident is all but forgotten.

•

Lying in bed, knotted in a post coital embrace and tranquilised by the serotonin released on orgasm, the lovers remain a thousand miles from one another. Alistair is perplexed by his new watch. It's side by side his old one on the bed stand. They sit like clock towers among the scattered artefacts of his pocket. His wallet, his keys, a bottle of medicine.

'It doesn't look like it cost as much as it did.'

'You just don't know how to look at it,' Ava purrs.

Propping his head higher on the pillow, he adjusts his position in an attempt to see them from another angle. The Rolex and the simple piece Ava selected.

One looks like it could be traded for a Ferrari and the other, maybe it could buy a pair of shoes or a dinner, but not a comfortable pair and certainly not a four course meal.

'I feel like I've paid money to show off something that doesn't look like how much I paid for it.'

'That's the point,' Ava tickles him. 'People with class will know it's a good watch. People you want to know. If they don't have any style, what worth are they themselves?'

'Everybody I know likes big gold watches,' he rolls her over and pins her with an accusing glare. 'Everybody, except you.'

'I'm not a bad person to know, Doctor Evans. You don't think the nice article I might provide is more than that? One thing leads to another and before you know it you're a media star. We'll make you an institution all in yourself, brick by brick.'

'Under your supervision.'

'It's not a terrible deal, is it?' Her hip pushed into his, the trimmed tuft of pubic hair scratches his skin. 'It's your choice. Personally I think there's a good way to go and a bad way. Why don't we think of your new watch as a first step the right direction?'

He grins knowingly, eyelids drooped, and says, 'I love you,' by way of agreement.

'I love you too,' she replies.

It's a handshake between them that seals the deal.

As Ava sits up to hug her knees, her gaze goes beyond the watches to a bottle of pills erect on the stand. She thought she left her painkillers in the pocket of her purse. Unsettled for some inexplicable reason, she begins to realise that they must belong to Alistair.

'What do you have those for?' she asks.

'In case you get a headache,' Alistair smirks.

Once again, it's her turn to withhold affection. Ignoring the doctor's hand running down her back, she fixates on the bed stand coldly. Alistair reaches over her and makes a show of putting on both watches. Displayed together on his wrist, he holds the arm level with her face.

'I could wear the two of them. I'd be able to trade for a Ferrari and a pair of shoes.'

Ava has no idea what he's talking about.

'I don't think you keep those pills for yourself or for me, Doctor Evans.'

'Mm?' he sounds suggestively.

'I don't,' she confirms.

'Maybe they're not painkillers.'

'Oh, shut up.' She's already tired of this nonsense, but when another minute passes the comment has made her itchy enough to ask. 'What are they then? They look just like the bottle I carry in my purse.'

'Maybe they're poison and I like to keep them on me for the thrill of it. Death in a bottle. It's a funny feeling, you know. Like having a loaded gun. Strangling people is so messy. I did it once. Spit everywhere. Piss too. Poison is much more elegant. Like the watch you got me, isn't it?'

Ava puts a tick in her negative column of Alistair facts. He'd exhausted her with his untouched game when they met and now he's at it again. The doctor showing up at her work unannounced and his incident with the taxi driver are both noticeably absent from her checklist. The uncomfortable feeling she gets is more from the idea that the games he plays amuse him exactly because they aren't that. He's displaying morbid facts as red herrings and relishing that he can do so without consequence. She knows because it's exactly what she'd do. Everyone's entitled to their perversions, so far as Ava's concerned, just don't rub them in her face. She pushes his floating arm away from her.

'I think I like wearing two watches. What do you reckon?'

'I'll throw that gold one out the window next chance I get.'

Alistair barks his laugh, 'And I'll throw you out along with it.'

Palm pressed over the man's lips, she feels him giggle madly against her fingers. When he stops, his hands tighten around her and she runs hers downwards, drawing white lines as she claws lightly on the flesh of his neck. In response, he leans forward and pins her to the mattress again. Now her eyes are an animals, lit up in the dark. All's to be forgotten until there's a knock on the apartment door.

Ava jumps at the sound, but Alistair leans heavier on her, pushing her legs apart with his knees. Frozen, like they're caught in a searchlight, Ava's first thought is of the taxi driver, standing in the corridor with a Gard at either shoulder prepared to arrest them for vandalism and assault. She's already inventing ways to excuse herself from the matter and growing angrier at the driver for bringing it to this.

What a petty man, she thinks, getting the police involved in something already finished. Her second thought is of the Agent Mullen, ready to have her scanned. But he wouldn't arrive here, at this time, would he?

'Awfully late,' Alistair says. 'Another man in your life?'

The knock is followed by a torrent of pounding. Feeling her wrists squeezed, Ava says, 'Alistair, you're hurting me.'

'Tell me who it is.'

'How should I know?' Irritated, she tries distracting him with a question in the hopes that he'll let go. 'What time is it?'

His mouth peels open to reveal two rows of gleaming white teeth. 'Three o'clock and three o'clock.'

With her chest heaving in the effort to get out from under him, he remains poised, passively observing her writhe.

Wary, she asks, 'Are you going to let me answer it?'

Ava is powerless against the man. A struggle would only make him feel stronger. Riled now, she realises – Oh, here it is. In his possession she is a bag of organs, wrapped in a sweaty bundle on the operating table their bed has become. Beneath the nippled skin of her breasts, blood pulses through veins, stretching across a rib cage that expands and contracts at the inflation of the paired wet sacks that are her lungs. His eyes are a knife, running along her body, testing where best to take a slice. The light from outside is caught on Alistair's lips and, as a bulge grows, Ava feels herself growing wet against him. Heedless of the razor edge she's being dissected with, she's ready to surrender to the arousal, but when the door pounds again, she's reminded that they're at a crossroads in their relationship and how she handles the situation will mark them for a long time after. In recognition of the critical impasse, she makes the decision to come out on top. He's lying to himself if he believes his physical advantage can keep her in check. Calming herself, she invokes the words needed to remind the doctor that she's more than the jabbering slab of teeth filled meat he's considered spoiling on a whim.

'Your hairline is receding.'

The sentence, spoken flatly, prompts a blink, and as the doctor attempts to grasp the comment, he's brought back to the world of the living. When Ava feels his grip loosen she risks a command, 'Let me answer the door, Alistair.' It's a steady voice that tells him she has more to give than he can take by force in a pitiful power trip.

To begin with, he shows no comprehension of how their relationship is to be, but like a switch is flicked in his head, a lethargic grunt sounds from his throat and he rolls over and falls to land on his back. Bare skin painted with a silk robe, Ava glides around the bed, finding slippers, a bracelet, a hairpin, and like the night has been leading up to a practiced trick, from the knock on the door to her circuit round the room, her hand snaps up the pills to palm into her robe, ready for use in a later scene.

10

Night, the dull blanket draped over Ava's apartment, mutes the room, it's bare white walls now an ethereal blue. Ahead of her is god knows what. Behind, Alistair looms in the bedroom, ready to pounce. A strip of light splits the room's curtain and scans her body as she skips by. Toward the pounding door she goes, meeting it's pinhole of light with her own contracted pupil. A mass of straw hair is bunched atop a teetering head on the other side. Warped in the funnel of glass the face it sits over is lost. Ava knows who the unexpected visitor is by the time the latch is off the hook. As she swings the door open to confirm it, an obliterated version of her editor is revealed. The woman is absolutely hammered. Streaks of mascara tears stain her cheeks. She's dressed in a crimson bandage dress, nude leopard heels, sparkly clutch, and a wide leather belt that's strangling her waist and pushing her cleavage up to her chin. In college Ava and her friends had a name for this kind of woman: a clawless cougar. Too drunk and too old to even know what she's doing. She's sorry to see her like this, really, disappointed. Joanne Victoria, though tawdry on a quiet day, has been a giant that demands respect. Now here she is, just another withered divorcee out on the town desperate for a good ride. What has she been up to since that drink in the office? It's clear this isn't the first stop she's made on her drunken odyssey and, given the wobble in her walk, it's likely the last.

'How did I get here?' she stumbles past Ava.

'Joanne,' Ava greets her loudly so that Alistair will hear. 'It's late. We have work tomorrow. You can't run a newsroom with a hangover.'

'Ava, it's all gone wrong, oh, we're in big trouble.' She jumps in fright as the lamp flicks on, then looks at it accusingly. 'Don't scare me like that.'

Falling from one wall to another, Joanne is on a course for the bedroom, no doubt hoping to find an empty bed where she can hibernate. Ava skips behind her and lightly directs her away from it, trying to find a place among the carefully selected furniture to set the bumbling editor. Choosing the two-seater couch she watches the woman collapse. With her face planted into the cushions, Joanne mumbles, 'I don't know what's going to happen.'

'Joanne, it's three in the morning.' Pulling the cushion away from her, Ava checks it for make-up stains. 'Do you even know what day it is?'

'Judgement day,' she cries a laugh.

Taking pause, Ava glides into the kitchen in search of something to sober her guest. The cabinets and fridge are bare. The best she can cobble together is a glass of juice. 'You should be sleeping this off at home.'

'Do you want to know something Ava? Everything that's happening is because of that dribble of a man, Timothy Walsh. Him and his grubby hand on my waist. All of these bloody UPD reforms that are strangling us came about because I can't stand a sleazebag. County councillors aren't worth reporting on, my editor said. There's not enough money for them to embezzle, is there? Go for the big fish.'

'If you're only here to reminisce…'

'It's much more than that,' Joanne begs Ava. Something in her soul is hungry for compassion. 'I can't keep these things to myself. They're rotting inside me. I just, I need you to listen.'

Ava nods, resigned to the fact that she doesn't have any choice, except that her editor's drunken attention has already shifted, 'Where is the vase I made you?'

'Joanne…'

The woman is fixated on a slot in the windowsill once occupied by a carefully crafted piece of pottery she created in her short but passionate affair with homemade gifts. She'd presented it to Ava as a house warming present shortly after her promotion to assistant editor.

At the time, Ava had gushed over it and placed it in the cubby where it became a centre piece for the room. But when she noticed that Joanne had never returned for a visit, it made its way to a table in the hall, and shortly after that, suffered an accident in the swing of her handbag. That had solved that problem. Now Joanne has found the empty shelf. To avoid the question, Ava insists, 'Get on with the story.'

'Yes, the story,' Joanne slurs. 'I'd had this tip. This little tip. Walsh takes the envelope in the bar of the West County Hotel once a month from a local TD, a building contractor of some kind. They skim on materials and split the profits. An even split. Bribing him to look the other way. Is taking money to look away better than doing it yourself?' She's confusing herself, jumping to thoughts that are meant for later in the story. Finding her footing again she goes on, 'Just like that anyway, he takes the envelope, they knock back a Guinness each and off they go like they'd never met.'

'Who?'

'I could feel the grease on his hands through my blouse, that smarmy bogger, and the stink of Major's. I can't stand the smell of them, you know that. And listen to what he said to me – Even if you caught my hand in the church basket, they wouldn't have the guts to let you type it up.'

'What are you talking about? You have to be more clear.'

'Timothy, I told you. Timothy Walsh!'

'Why Timothy Walsh? The first UPD? Why are you talking about that?'

'I'm talking about how all of this,' she waves her hands about the room and Ava follows their journey, expecting to gain some understanding from the gesture. 'How all of this started.'

'You're agitated and confused. Drink this, calm down, and start again.'

Joanne takes the glass automatically and, not realising that she's holding it now, forgets Ava's advice altogether. The filter between her thoughts and mouth has been knocked completely out of order.

'If you didn't like the vase you could just say so,' she mumbles from the corner of her lips. 'I know I'm no artist. It gave the place some colour though.'

Ignoring her, Ava moans, 'Why are you telling me about Timothy Walsh?'

'Well, my editor was right you know. Even with a photo of the two circle jerking the newsdesk wasn't going to let me anywhere near him. Too popular. On the high end of a seesaw and not ready to be knocked off. Timing is everything. Like that freak doctor. We have to know when to hit him. You said that, didn't you?'

There's a faint noise from the bedroom. Alistair has giggled. Neither of them notice. Joanne's rant is at full steam. Ava, watching the glass in her hand, wrings the cushion in her fingers, half expecting the juice to topple and ruin the rug beneath them. As she reaches out to take it back, Joanne brings it to her lips and slurps at it greedily before making a baffled face. The woman was expecting alcohol.

'He whispered it in my ear though, Ava. I couldn't let it go.'

'Where have you come from? You don't normally drink on your own. Why are you all dressed up…?'

'I don't know where I came from,' she hiccups. 'I don't know anything anymore. I don't even know why I did it.'

'Did what?' Ava's voice drops dramatically, aware now that something bad has happened. 'What did you do, Joanne?'

Her editor's mind though, is compelled to the distant past.

'I wrote about it anyway. I got the newsdesk passwords, you don't want to know how, and I changed them and I put it online. That's where it all started. People don't say it enough, but I know, I know when history looks back on it all that's what they're going to say. That article, that one line in it, that's what changed the game. A single comment about him being sexually intimidating, a bully and a misogynist. If only I'd known. Trashy comments like that change the world. They're worse than a badly worded press release,' Joanne stops abruptly. Her finger, which had been swishing through the air is stuck in it now, her expression lifeless. Ava is inclined to check the woman for a pulse. Just as she's about to say something, the editor jolts back to form with another hiccup. 'Control the conversation, Ava, that's why you're one of my best, you know that. Don't answer questions that lead to a talk you don't want to have. Do you see what I'm saying? I couldn't have known, could I?'

The juice jumps upward and splashes back down. Ava's eyes dart to the rug, watchful for orphan drips. Annoyed, she tries reaching out for the glass again, but it's away, up and around as Joanne uses it to draw her story.

'Nobody cared about it, the article, it would have disappeared only for his bloody team wanted to nip it in the bud, discredit it in case it picked up any momentum. So they steered the conversation their way thinking that they were going into smooth waters. Ha! How could he let them do it? They made a point of attacking the sexual bully comment – Timothy Walsh is one of the most recognised family men in the county and will not let allegations like this affect the view his wife and daughters have of him – gave a long list of donations to charities for children and community work. Oh yeah, a real saint. They were right anyway, nobody cared about the bribes when sex got dragged into it. But they really should have asked what he gets up to in his spare time if they were going to fight for him. They started the conversation and all of a sudden these people, these victims, started speaking out, saying he abused them. Children he was supposed to have been helping. A sixteen year old girl, fourteen, younger. My god he was a monster and people had voted him in to fix the lousy roads. Like even a good man could do that. And it all went back to my article. To his grubby hand on me in the bar! Remember The Children, Remember The Children! How could I forget the bloody children! Everything, Ava, these shoes,' Joanne flings her heels off in disgust and one lands hard on the coffee table, making Ava cringe at the thought of a scratch. 'These shoes and this necklace. I'm wearing the profits of all the misery.'

Joanne is infected with contagious hysteria. Ava though, seems unaffected.

'We don't just get to report good news Joanne. That's the nature of the job. We all profit from it. What's important is those people wouldn't have gotten justice if it wasn't for you.'

'Oh yes, I know,' Joanne concurs, but clearly takes the words in another way than they were meant. 'One family speaks out and another and then that weasel Walsh is throwing allegations at other people, other councillors, TD's, Gards, civil servants, a whole ring working inside every sector of our government. Paedophiles. It was like the church all over again. The rats escaped one sinking ship and infested the next. People didn't want to believe it. If it was true then they were guilty for being blind to it, do you see that Ava?'

'Oh shush,' Ava hides a tired expression behind her slender fingers.

She's sure she hears a thump, but can't imagine why Alistair would be moving about. She's beyond caring though. She just wants the night to end. 'You must be giving yourself a headache. Do you need a pill?'

'I want to know where the damned vase I made you is gone.'

'Oh my god!' Incensed, Ava grabs her editor by the arm and tries pulling her out of the chair, 'It's in the bedroom Joanne. I moved it and I didn't want to hurt your feelings. Do you want to see the damn thing? Come on.'

'Oh never mind,' the editor cries, 'you have to let me say this.'

'No, I don't,' she digs into the arm, but Joanne refuses to budge. 'Let's go see the vase. It's right by my bed.'

'Do you know dead people never shut up, sweetie?'

Letting go of the arm, Ava falls back into her seat. Elbows propped on knees, her face falls into the palms of her hands. Of all the reactions to a statement like this – confusion, shock, curiosity – Ava's is something altogether different. She's angry. Joanne has been assaulting her with a barrage of information so inconsequential it could best be labelled as white noise, and now she's capping it off with something even more disgusting – the absurd. Her editor is trying to impart ideas that she doesn't need. Like the ugly vase that had no place in her home, Ava's neatly arranged world doesn't have room for any of it.

'They're a storm,' Joanne insists, trying to make her young colleague understand that the words are a revelation. 'Every child that was ever molested and killed joined a black cloud on the horizon that couldn't be ignored any longer. They were thunder,' Joanne brings her elocution lessons to the fore, intoning dramatically, 'A country's dead and how they died are it's identity. Our murdered rebels were getting outnumbered by molested children and these kids, they were demanding justice. We were guilty and they were the witnesses. People were rattled awake now, oh you can believe that, and once they got their head around what was happening they had to shift the blame.'

Ava is a statue now, vapid and abject, Joanne invisible to her as she waits for something relatable.

'Untouched, Ava, the people who knew what was happening and did nothing. UPD, the lot of them. That was the name we came up with. Ignorance wasn't the crime once that term came in to play, was it?

You could imprison the rapists but what about the people who turned a blind eye? A few politicians tried standing up to it but they were shouted down: Sure if you protest, then you must have something to hide, and besides, what rights should an untouched have if they don't allow us any? Once a decade we're galvanised into action and this had done it. Women – my god – women were letting children be abused. Mothers. What was it that minister said at her trial?'

'Whelan,' Ava remembers. Her make-up was terrible.

'She said she could do more good if she stayed in power, and she wasn't sure that she could retain it if she rocked the boat. The bitch was in charge of the hospitals and covering up rape scandals in the children's wards, for god's sake. Cops were in there. Doctors. Half of them molesting patients, the other half looking away. If that boat doesn't need to be rocked, what does? For Christ sake when the charges were put against them all they tried turning it into an argument over which political party had molested the most!' Joanne's head falls to a side, too heavy for her limp neck to hold. 'This damn electric scan, all because of a grubby hand on my waist, Ava.'

'I don't see why you're so upset. It's a good law. It keeps types like her out of power. People can get on with their lives knowing they're voting for officials with a conscience. Not being tricked by some masked animals.'

'Oh, really, Ava, you don't believe that.' Joanne spits, dead set on finishing her rant. 'Everything I have is because of those children and it's all coming down on me now. Don't you see? If I can live like this, the way I do, if I can go on happy, it only means one thing doesn't it?'

Ava, drowsy, blinks once.

'And when I'm taken for that god damn scan it's going to say it. I'm untouched.'

Words can tire a mind. They build into sentences that go around in circles, running on top of each other in such a fugue that, unless they can be flushed out through the mouth, drive a person to madness. Joanne had come here to vent, and now, emptied of the story, she's reaching out for reassurance. Ava senses this and is relieved to know her obligation in the matter, to pat her editor on the back and tell her everything will be alright, has finally arrived. She lifts herself up with a deep breath, sure she can summon the warmth to do so, but before she can, Joanne has sunk to the ground and the glass that her hand had coddled drops from her fingers to roll in an arc on the rug.

Ava is about to scream, only now that the thing is empty it doesn't really matter. She picks up the glass and puts it on a coaster. Joanne is on her knees, retching on an attempt at a guttural cry and clawing at Ava's night gown, who, looking down on her, bites her lip to keep from calling the woman repugnant. She can't be untouched, Ava decides. She's too pathetic.

11

'Nice dreams?' Alistair asks, sardonic. He's never had a dream.
'I don't remember,' Ava sniffs. She rarely has them herself.
'I thought I heard you laughing in your sleep.'

•

It's a brand new day, wrapped in gift paper for the couple like a thoughtful Christmas present. Through a sleepy haze Ava spots a blemish on Alistair's back, the swollen mark ugly on his olive skin. She rolls over to find a better view. Rising, he lets the sheets fall from him. Ava hears him open the curtains and stretching in front of the window, naked, until his back makes a series of pops and he prowls about the room, cracking other bones along the way. He slips into his underwear when he happens to see them and stalks about searching for the other pieces of his costume, a shirt and a tie, slacks. His coat is balled up in the corner. 'Socks,' he says, whistles, and says again, 'Socks.' As he checks under the bed, he changes the statement to a question.

'Sitting room,' Ava mumbles into her pillow.

Her memories of last night have yet to rouse her. When they do, it's in a rush, as shocking as a bucket of ice water thrown over her bed. Oh no, she remembers, the days aren't separate. Events from one bleed into the happenings of the next. It can be a terrible inconvenience.

She jumps after a beat, shook by the image of Joanne on her couch, probably still asleep – if she's lucky. Alistair's hand is reaching for the doorknob when she bolts up and warns him to stop, but he opens it anyway and stands looking at the putrid woman. She's wheezing, a cushion is over her head to block out the harsh morning light, and splayed like a starfish, her skirt is knotted up to her waist, one leg hanging over the side so that her foot is planted on the ground in a practiced method to keep her head from spinning. Ava, quietly angry, puts her hand over Alistair's to pull the door closed. His arm goes stiff as oak to keep it open.

'Alistair.'

'She doesn't seem so important.'

'Well she is,' Ava hisses, 'she could destroy you if she wanted, so if you don't mind, let's save the introductions for another time.'

Joanne rolls over, the cushion falls to the ground, and her elbow pushes a groan out of her mouth as it leans into her side. Hand on forehead, she howls in pain. Ava, expecting the mummy to rise, pushes Alistair and fights him for control of the doorknob before he gives up. Interest already lost, he falls back onto the bed.

'I need to be out of here in half an hour,' he announces.

Hushing him, Ava is incredulous, 'Are you actually being this stupid right now?'

'If you don't get my socks and wallet out of there I'm going to have to get them myself.' He explains the matter to her like it's a simple mathematical problem, a situation where it's silly to get emotional about the only solution, 'Half an hour is plenty of time.'

Experienced as she is in devastating looks, Ava tries to cut him down with a narrowing of her eyes. 'She's hung over. She won't leave till noon.'

'Thirty minutes.'

At that, Ava turns about, teeth gritted as she opens the bedroom door, and slides through a crack to close it behind her. Stood over the woman, the reek of alcohol, stale cigarette smoke and perfumed sweat forms a cloud that floats up to meet her gagging face.

'Good morning,' Ava claps her hands.

Clung to the couch in surprise, Joanne is afraid she's about to be tipped over and pushed off into a never ending fall. As she squints, it's apparent she doesn't know where she is.

'It's me,' Ava says. 'You must have had a fun night.'

Joanne opens her mouth to talk but her throat is clogged with gravel. 'Sleep well?'

Cringing under Ava's accusing look, she mutters, 'I'm in your apartment,' and examines the room to confirm it. 'I came here last night, to talk about…' she's hoping Ava will finish the sentence for her, but finds she has to piece together the events herself. 'The riot?' she asks, not without a hint of hope in her voice.

'You'd make an awful poker player. You don't remember do you?'

'I have a headache,' Joanne stammers. 'My throat is dry, Ava, darling…'

A thud comes from the bedroom. Alistair's after hitting the closet door and both their heads swing around at the sound of it. Feeling the pills in the pocket of her robe, Ava rolls them around in her hand, considering the light bottle between her fingers. They do feel different than the painkillers she normally keeps, though she can't exactly say why.

'What was that?' Joanne demands, frightened.

Ava cocks the lid on the bottle open.

'Is someone in there?'

And ignoring the question, cocks the lid closed. 'I don't have any painkillers Joanne, we'll have to go down the shop.'

Confused and sleepy, Joanne turns back to Ava. 'Yes, the shop, just, I need some water darling, and maybe lay down a little longer, rest a few more minutes.'

Another thud sounds from the bedroom and this time Joanne jumps at it, while Ava, prepared, is a model of composure as she pretends nothing has happened. Concentrating on Joanne's queer behaviour instead, she's acting as if the woman has imagined something that isn't there.

'You must hear that?' Joanne pleads.

'Joanne, you're falling to pieces,' Ava reaches out and brushes a strand of hair behind the editor's ear. 'You're too stressed. Take a few days off, the place won't fall apart without you. You've had all your interviews with the social agent, right? You just have to wait and see if you're called up for the electric scan.'

'And how would dodging him in the meantime look? I swear, I don't think I could handle it if I get called up. Of all things, why electric shocks?'

In the kitchen, Ava gets some water for Joanne while she keeps an eye out for Alistair's things. She sighs inwardly when she sees the wallet beside Joanne's purse. Joanne, following Ava's gaze, looks behind herself, paranoid, and flicks her knotted hair to the side.

'Go on, drink this.'

The editor guzzles down the water and feels like a new woman for all of thirty seconds, then sinks back into the chair, instantly ready to fall asleep again. Ava uses the distraction to reach out and snap up the wallet, sliding it into the pocket of her robe with a dab hand.

'If I wasn't talking about your story, why am I here?'

'You tell me,' Ava wanders about, pretending to tidy the sterile room as she searches for Alistair's missing socks.

'You weren't at that riot.'

Joanne's voice has taken a deep plunge and sounds up to Ava from the bottom of a well. By the echo of it, Ava understands how deep it goes.

'What do you mean?'

'I think,' Joanne, knowing she has Ava's attention now, acts perturbed, rubbing the temples of her forehead in vexation. 'I think that's what set me off, but, where was I before I got here?'

'What set you off Joanne?'

'The riot. Your story. It isn't true, is it?'

'It happened,' Ava says, offended that anybody would say otherwise. 'Are you saying I made the whole thing up?'

'I was just saying you weren't there, but I suppose you could have made up the riot too,' Joanne, spiteful. 'Why stop at one lie?'

'What exactly are you accusing me off?'

'I think it's very clear what I'm saying.'

'That I'm a liar.'

'If the shoe fits...'

Ava, stunned by the bluntness, winces. 'You don't sound worried about it.'

'Either do you,' the editor responds with a knowing curl of her lip.

'Don't think I couldn't fire you, Ava.'

The threat is an empty one. Ava is sure that her job is safe, so, ignoring the warning she says, 'I don't see why this would have triggered your private meltdown.'

'God, I hope it was private. Did I say anything I shouldn't have?'

Rolling the question around, Ava decides to bite her tongue on the matter. 'Nothing of consequence. Most of what you said made no sense whatsoever.'

'That must have been fun. Wish I could remember it. I need a good laugh.'

'Where did you hear this nonsense about my story anyway? User complaints? Just ignore them, nobody reads those things. Just a bunch of internet cranks.'

'It's a bit more delicate than that. The Gards are involved too, remember? We're looking for this phantom child of yours. We are, in fact, tethered to the police in our commitment to a reality that doesn't exist. Just another day at ChatterFive.'

Ava brushes off the accusations, 'Do they know?'

It's the closest thing to an admission she'll ever utter.

'The Gards found out shortly after I did, probably from the same tipster and frankly, are more embarrassed about it than I am. Do you know how much work they've been saying they've been doing? The leads they said they had? It's all nothing. No, they want it buried too, no public embarrassment for anyone, not even you. It'll be our filthy secret.' The words are tart on Joanne's tongue. 'Another body in the rose patch.'

'Who told you about it?'

'An anonymous source,' she mouths, and to assure Ava she has no idea who it could be, she says, 'The email came from a disposable account. The photo of the girl you used is remarkably similar to one in our Belfast archive. I suppose that means the tipster is someone in our office, so either they hate me, they hate you, or they hate their job.'

'Nobody hates me.' Not giving Joanne a chance to brood on it, Ava clenches her jaw, and glosses over the clue. 'Anonymous though. That doesn't say much about the reliability of the source. Can you show me the stock photo? I'm sure it's different to mine. This will all come to nothing.'

'Will it?' Joanne asks the room. 'Do you know how vulnerable this leaves us? We don't know if he's a nut job or some mastermind who's willing to blackmail us – or worse, a nutjob who realises he can blackmail us. This is going to be hanging over us for a long time Ava. You, me, the government. If another media outlet cops onto it – I don't want to even think about that.'

'Nothing is hanging over me,' Ava, indignant now. 'A riot that's been confirmed and a girl that's clearly real, and you're trying to pin a crime on my article.'

'But the girl was at a completely different riot...'

'I gave you a story. It happened, Joanne. Other outlets covered it the night previous. If you want to believe some crazy person's problem with the details I added then that's your issue, but don't try weasel some admission of guilt out of me. Setting me up as an accomplice in case things go wrong for you? That's sly Joanne, real sly.'

'I don't need to drag you into anything. It was your lie, Ava!' For all the bewilderment on her face, you'd think Ava had just slapped her. 'Anyway, I just, I can't bare another secret to carry on my own.' At this, her scattered thoughts begin to come into some order. Her actions last night, her drunken rant to Ava – nothing understandable she said – are just about in her grasp. 'Another secret,' she repeats, using the words to see through the billowing fog. With a sober look, she lets Ava know that she remembers what she told her, everything about the untouched scandal and how it weighs her down. And Ava was going to pretend it never happened, for what? To save face? Joanne picks at a thumbnail, wondering maybe for the first time who exactly is Ava O'Dwyer? The body she talks to doesn't reveal a thing.

A phone rings in the bedroom. Ava goes back to cleaning the place, apparently deaf to the incoming tone.

'Aren't you going to get that?'

But Alistair already has. He's picked it up and a muffled burst of laughter sounds from him through the bedroom door.

Quick to comment on it, Ava snarls, 'So now you know Joanne. I met a guy and we had sex. Are you going to make it homepage news?'

'I didn't say anything,' her editor reacts defensively.

'No, you just got drunk and showed up at my apartment in the middle of the night.' Finally, Ava see's the socks, whips them off the ground, and opens the door of her bedroom slightly to slide in without giving Joanne a view.

Alistair is dressed, sat on the corner of the bed when she throws the socks at him. His phone is tucked between shoulder and ear as he chats with a woman. The inane female voice can only be described as that of a chipmunk, squeaky and irritating. Ava goes to clip him on the ear when she recognises that it's the girl he abandoned that night at the auction.

'What?!' Alistair rubs his head.

'I know who that is,' Ava whispers.

Then, snorting, he simply replies, 'She has her uses.'

Rushing through her closet and drawers, assembling an outfit for a walk to the coffee shop with Joanne, Ava ignores the remark. She's about to leave when Alistair calls her back, index finger held up to attract her attention.

'Five minutes,' he says.

Ava slams the door behind her.

'Who is it?' Joanne teases.

'Just some idiot I wish wasn't here.'

'Ha!' he replies through the door.

'Here,' Ava hands Joanne her handbag, 'let's get you some coffee.'

'Either that's somebody spectacular you don't want to share, or someone very ugly you're ashamed of.'

It's a narrow escape. On the street, the anxious editor rummages through her bag, desperate for her glasses to give the world a recognisable shape again. She's trying to explain this to Ava as a motorbike rumbles by.

'I didn't do anything wrong,' Ava says.

Joanne, curiosity screwing up her features, searches for some guilt in the statement but finds none. It irritates her. She's being told she's in this on her own. 'Oh, you're completely innocent Ava. So was I,' she says, sarcastic. 'It's in hiding the mistake we're becoming guilty of something. That's your choice, isn't it? Hide it or let the world know. We're in it together now.' She's confident that Ava is happy to obscure the origins of their story, though Ava doesn't acknowledge that she heard what Joanne said at all. There's nothing there to read, but there are gears turning underneath, and as they leave each other outside the coffee shop, Ava turns to reassure her.

'I'll see you Monday.'

It won't be until later that night, as Joanne opens a bottle of sparkling wine with a pop, she'll realise there was nothing reassuring about those words at all, and come to think of it, it sounded vaguely like intimidation.

When Ava returns to her apartment, it's empty, the bedroom door ajar and the bare kitchen cabinets left open. At least he kept the fridge closed, only when she opens it she discovers he drank the last of the milk. Stepping out of her shoes she walks to the makeup stand in her room. Now, listen to this. In the time it's taken Alistair and Ava to agree that they're in love, he has shown up at her work, threatened her, played with her like a cat plays with a mouse, physically intimidated her, attacked a taxi driver and almost introduced himself to Joanne – but all of that is forgivable. Seeing the gold watch absent from the bed stand though, and the black-silver one conspicuously left behind, is a line drawn in the sand that she can't abide. When she sees it sat there in a hoop, she stops in her tracks, incensed, and stomps over to the bed stand to grab the thing. Though she knows he's long gone, she goes to the window in search of the man on the road below. And when she can't find him, she screams, the jagged knife edge in her voice cutting like the empty howl of a banshee. Then, the sound stops as suddenly as it starts. She has other errands to pursue, and a snitch to meet. Nobody in the newsroom hates her, but there is one man who would see her strung out to dry nonetheless. He's not in work today. She learns that much from calling ahead. She does, however, know exactly where to find him.

12

When Barry first moved to Dublin he'd gotten to know the city by walking it. A car, so far as he was concerned, a bus, earphones, even a bicycle, were all incubators that would keep him from inhaling the town's life and in turn, breathing his own into it. So he walked. From the morbid stillness of Dundrum on the south side to the stark grey of Santry on the north, he'd pick a pub on the map, memorise the route, and march. The walk was important of course. It allowed him to learn the feel of these postcodes he would be writing about. But his primary objective was to choose a spot to settle in, and the pubs, they were to be the decider. Stumbling into drinking holes, he'd judge the establishments by the friendliness of their bar staff. He likes to be chatted with, Barry Danger, not handled. Quiet days were important, busy evenings a must. The clientele should be despicable. When he found the pub he liked, a square trad bar on the edge of Harolds Cross where the terror of Crumlin all of a sudden goes flat, he moved from the hostel he'd been living out of and rented a room near his chosen tavern. In time he'd gotten his name in enough bylines that the pub garnered a quiet reputation for being his local. The decisive test though, one which he'd neglected to take into account, was how the staff would deal with customers who didn't like his articles.

'Barry, y'English prick, this guy wants to know what you've got against the taxi union.' Stood beside a slouched drunk with a pulsing red head, the barman asks, 'You don't let drivers nap on the job in London?'

But then, nowhere could be perfect.

Barry, hunched over a browned paperback and an empty pint glass, replies, 'If I was working in London I'd be bitching that they don't get enough sleep.'

The barman chuckles and returns to his place by the register.

'Mercenary.'

Barry holds up his wallet and nods for another drink, 'What does that make you?'

Chin buried in neck, the barman pulls a pint of Guinness and stops halfway to let it settle.

'You ever heard of Johnny Carson?' Barry takes a much needed break from his book and waits for a shake of the barman's head. 'Johnny Carson was a chat show host in the states way back when you only had a choice of two sources of information, channel-A or channel-B. Simpler times right?'

'I'm a channel-B man meself.'

'Well, one night, during his little comedy routine, Carson thought it'd be funny to make a joke that the city was running out of toilet paper and that the shops only had left what was on the shelves. It got a bit of a giggle but there wasn't any punch line. Not until the next day anyway. Half the city was running down the shop to stock up on toilet paper. Fighting over it at the counters, pure mayhem. So what does Carson do? He apologises for causing the chaos the following night, says he was just joking, that there wasn't a toilet paper shortage and that it wasn't meant to be taken seriously. He gives it a beat for comic timing,' Barry smacks his lips, 'and he goes on to say, In other news, there is now a toilet paper shortage in the city.'

The Englishman's eyes go two directions as he rattles off a wild laugh. Snatching the money he extends, the barman suppresses a grin.

'You should have been a chat show host.'

Then, Ava is standing at the door, coiled like a snake and ready to spring.

'Oh it's fun enough where I am.'

If Barry wears the bar like a pair of well worn shoes, Ava examines it like a rag she's been handed. The stale smell of the previous nights session ferments in the musky interior. Smoke, spilled drinks, the bleach used to clean them, and the vague scent of urinal cakes, all stir together in a noxious odour for her to consider.

Taking careful steps into the sweaty room, she watches as the barman tops off Barry's pint before diplomatically walking away.

'What do you think you're doing?' she demands.

'Having a pint. If that's alright with you.'

'You're supposed to be in the newsroom. You could answer my calls couldn't you?'

'Sure I could,' Barry closes his book, 'but then I wouldn't have got you out for a drink, would I? It's nice having you here, down on the proles level.'

'Don't pretend it wasn't you.' Taking the provocateur's stance, Ava is refusing to acknowledge that he might have something over her. Answers she wants and answers she will get. 'Tell me why you did it.'

'I have no idea what you're talking about.' Barry does his best to keep a straight face, but cracks under Ava's intense gaze. Breaking into peals of laughter, he tries to catch his breath between bursts, palm firm against his chest. 'I'm sorry. Really, I was going play dumb for a while, but you should see the look on your face.'

'You want my job.'

Barry places a bony hand over hers, 'That's the last thing I want, sweetheart.'

Grinning over his shoulder, he leads Ava to a booth tucked away at the back of the pub. Dressed in shadow, it's been prepared to host their confrontation.

'You must want something,' she says. 'Get to it.'

'Nah, me? I just like seeing you flounder.'

Ava stands, set on the exit, and Barry raises his hands in surrender, bowing for her to sit down. Nostrils flared, she waits for a reason to stay.

'I can understand why you didn't check your facts. The riot happened on Westmoreland street, not Grafton, a fifty metre difference, who really cares? But materialising a girl to push the story? Why were you so desperate to get it on our homepage in the first place? What was in it for you?'

Ava perches on the stool, engaged with him but ready to leap. 'Does there have to be something in it for me?'

'With you? Yes. No question about it. You benefited from it somehow, O'Dwyer, I don't doubt that,' he considers his pint as he says this.

'I kind of admire you for it actually. Pure selfishness. It's something to behold, seeing a person go for what they want with all the certainty of a heat seeking missile.'

'And all I get to see is you wallowing in the mud. You're going to let this fact checking thing blow over if I tell you why I pushed the story? Is that it?'

'I suppose it depends on how interesting your answer is.'

'You think I'm untouched,' she sets the accusation on the table, sure that he'll claim it. 'That's why you think it's alright to mess around like this. You wouldn't turn the screws on any other journalist, scrutinise every miniscule detail of their stories. It's alright to do it to me though. Give somebody a label and you can toy with them however you want. They're not human, right?'

'No-no,' he lectures with a wiggling finger. 'Less of the victim act, please. Let's get something straight here, UPD or not, you're guilty. That's what this is about.'

Ava ignores the distinction. 'You're the untouched one, thinking like that. Relishing every minute of this. You're a vampire, feeding off other people's misery.'

Barry's face folds in on itself, embarrassed for her. 'You're accusing me of that as if I'd be bothered by it. You think I'm afraid of getting scanned because that's what you're afraid of.'

'I'm not afraid of anything.'

'That's hardly an appropriate defence,' he taunts. 'You don't like being cornered, do you? Walls are closing in and you're running from one to the next, scrambling for a way out. What are you going to do when there's no more room? When you're about to be squished? Oh, I just want to see it,' bouncing up and down on his stool, he inhales excitedly. 'I just need to see what happens when you're caught in the trap. You don't think you're untouched. I don't think I am either. And the number one rule about anybody who thinks they're not untouched is – DING DING DING – they're untouched. What a world, eh.'

'If you spread anymore rumours about my story–'

'You'll what? I'm the one with the leverage here sweetheart.'

'And what are you going to use it for?'

'Entertainment,' Barry says dourly. 'I'm going to tell our friend, Agent Mullen.'

'Mullen? What does it have do with him?' she spits.

'I think our social agent is a little constipated by a clog of ideas. He could do with some assistance in getting the mental bowel movements back on track. I reckon a fabricated and published story might do the trick. Never mind the cover-up. It's been a lark watching you and Joanne slink around the place trying to dodge him, and I'd hate to see the show end so soon, but, one must take chances when they're there for the taking. I want to see you scanned.'

'That's all,' Ava almost sounds relieved.

Barry, wiggling his eyebrows, takes a long sup of his pint. A thick moustache of cream is left to dribble down his chin.

Repulsed, Ava stands again. 'If I knew that's all you were up to I wouldn't have bothered coming down here.' There's not much for her to worry about. So long as it doesn't occur to him to release the accusation publicly, start a campaign against her within the community, true or not, something like that might knock her career out of its upward trajectory. Francis though, Francis she can handle.

'I'll give him a call then.'

'Do whatever you want,' Ava walks by, and swinging her handbag onto her shoulder, narrowly misses the side of his head. 'Don't be absent another day or I'll have the newsdesk give you a warning. You probably don't think that's much of a concern, but keep this in mind Barry: Joanne is going to be retired someday, and you're not exactly a prospective candidate set to replace her. The things you do now will be remembered. However far down the road it is, there will be consequences. Try to think more than two steps ahead for once, you might last another while.'

When she's gone Barry wipes the sloppy moustache off with the sleeve of his shirt and wanders over to the bar, taking the stool where he'd left his book. The nosey barman manages to count to thirty before he saunters over, steps echoing on the hardwood floor as he cleans imaginary stains along the way. 'So are you going to call him? The social agent?'

'Hm?' Perplexed, Barry leaves his glass down and watches the foam billow into a head. He'd never shown an interest in landing Joanne's job. Never demonstrated a desire to improve his career prospects on any but the most concessionary levels.

Ava had insinuated that she could take it all away from him, years from now, if he didn't play it smart. The threat was preposterous and she seemed equally bemused by the suggestion that he inform Mullen of her antics. The interaction was so disjointed, it's as if he'd been talking to the woman from another plane – they'd taken swipes at each other only for their balled fists to pass through thin air. A smile grown, he wonders if there was something more to her comment that he hasn't perceived, and contented to be left with the curiosity, takes another long sup of his pint, because besides all that, he laughs, 'I called him an hour ago.'

Laughing all the harder as the barman walks away, Barry's head wobbles so much it almost snaps off. Balancing once more, he manages to grab the bar just in time and saves himself from the fall.

13

The scoffing bobblehead had followed Francis home, Barry's gift to him in the days previous, it now takes pride in being a part of the social agent's life. He had meant to bin it. Or to shove it in a dark drawer somewhere in the office. Now it's in his room, making a place for itself among the collection of rubbish that has become his life – magic trick books and heist movies, old musty records and piles of dirty laundry, all falling atop another in his cramped bedsit. It needs to be put out of sight so that it can't probe him with its constantly amused expression. Pleased in its new position, the inanimate object is already acting like it owns the place.

    The lights are off. Split shadows from a decrepit tree break across his room and the lines, so black, crisscross the social agent's clammy face. He doesn't know what to do. He doesn't even know what to feel. Betrayed? No, loyalty was never offered. Stupid? That sounds about right. Relaxing into his armchair and dropping his pants down to his ankles, Francis had set about relieving his stress at the end of another long day in the newsroom. He let an image of Ava, splayed naked on a bed, come to the forefront of his mind. Wanting to savour whatever expiring bliss he could squeeze out, he made sure to take his time and rouse the brisk feel that her eyes had left on him in their first meeting. Thigh gripped with free hand, he observed the woman's sinuous convulsions through a crack in the closet door he had imagined himself hidden, watching unknown as she pleasured herself. Before him, she groaned on the white sheets, a dark patch sprouting through her fingers as he had her whisper his name in panting breaths.

She begged for Francis to come to her. It was useless though. Grasping for inspiration, he multiplied the sight of her, two Ava's, three, bent before him, caressing each other in uncanny ecstasy, and in a blink the three became one again. She was always so far away, unreal and out of reach. As soon as she spread her legs to invite him in, he'd gotten a fright. There was nothing there. No comfort to be found, only a gaping mouth opened to swallow him whole. Before he could consider the strange thought, he'd remembered what was beside him, observing, impossible to ignore. He shifted the blame for his change in mood onto it. That damned figurine. As usual he had hemmed and hawed over what to do with it until it ended up in his pocket, and now, there it stands, triumphant on his closed laptop, challenging him to do something – anything. Instead, Francis started a staring contest with it, his bare legs dotted with goose bumps as he held it's gaze. He was about to knock it over when its doppelganger had phoned. He couldn't help but feel the real Barry was gloating when he'd informed him of the subterfuge in ChatterFive, but then, everything the man said sounded that way.

Her story's got more holes than a colander, mate. Francis could hear him grinning down the phone, satisfied with a greedy gulp of his drink.

What business was it of Barry's? Why did he care enough to inform a social agent of Ava O'Dwyer's activities? Barry Danger, worried about the state of journalism? He was dancing on its grave in their interview. Barry Danger, reporting a possible UPD like any good citizen would? No. What difference would a UPD make at ChatterFive? He'd asked as much himself. The man was playing with Francis, winding him up to see where he'd walk, maybe even let him go so far as to waddle off the side of the table. And besides, how could Francis tell if the stock photo being claimed as the original wasn't the fake? Barry should be the one selected for scanning, the social agent's stomach knots. Barry's the one who's suspicious.

Headlights spin the shadow branches around his wall. A truck is rumbling by, rattling the room so that the bobblehead waggles in smug protest.

And if he's not UPD, that's a scanning slot which could be filled by a more likely candidate. Francis is allowed take only so many people for the final test. An opening would be gone, simply because he didn't like the man's attitude.

So Barry thinks his job is a joke. That the world and the intersecting lives in it are just fodder for a comic routine. It would be suspect if only for how clearly the melancholy notes in his voice were heard. It wasn't a happy laugh he used when he provoked Francis with his ideas. What about Ava though? She loves her work, doesn't she? She believes in the power to make change for the better. She'd said so. It had been exactly what he wanted to hear. Like a pick up artist, she knew all the right things to say to generate chemistry, but didn't feel a drop of it herself. They were just words. Once, he was suspicious of that, now, his questionnaire left in the office, he's full to the brim with desire, latching onto the positive again as a sign of her devotion, a quality which he'd be happy to reward if not for his impotence under the glare of that scoffing bobblehead.

So what if she is untouched? Francis defiant, he looks at his bedsit as if for the first time. The cosy nest he's made for himself now more a lonely hole dug into the ground. This is what I've gotten, he thinks. This is what my good work has gotten me all these years. Every decision he's ever made has been second guessed and turned over in his head, examined from every angle. Each act in his short time on the Earth has been dully considered so as not to hurt another. He moved through existence stepping to avoid snails on the path, never hurting a fly, never breaking someone's heart. Well, he's tired of it. He wants something now. Why shouldn't he grab for it? All he has to do is let her pass. Carefully move her from one line to another. Don't take her for processing. Once she gets to that stage it's the end for her. Just let her slide by. Simple enough. Fill in the questionnaire so she's safe.

After that? He laughs at himself. Ask her out on a date. He owes her a glass of wine. She'd said so!

The bobblehead quietly shakes it's skull, grinning.

Oh just say what you've got to say! Francis jerks his trousers up, buckles his belt, and, furious as he paces back and forth across the room, steps over an empty mug and snaps up the deck of cards his landlord gave him. He hasn't practiced since that night, a thousand years ago. Considering a visit to the old man, he wonders if it would make him feel any better and quickly decides that it would not. Whatever decision he makes, he comes out the loser. Why not choose the one with some amount of pleasure in it?

The toy, not buying into his reasoning, is wobbling in the corner of his vision. Stomping over, he slaps it across the room. Dead on its back, it can shake no more, and still it wins. Francis can't look at the thing.

In the kitchen, he searches frantically through the cabinets. Stocked full of spices and snacks and cans of food, there's little room for anything else. Meat in the fridge, packets of pasta, a box full of wilted vegetables. All he needs is one or two more ingredients for the perfect meal. Easily amended. The main thing he's missing is the bottle of cabernet. Swinging around, he grabs a long coat to throw his arms through and lets the door close behind him as he charges into the night. The room, lacking it's occupant, is quiet now. Only the bare tree is heard. Pleading, it taps on the window pane.

•

Alistair is examining a bag of black beans, meditating on each seed for all Ava can tell. Floating through the supermarket, they're forever drifting into the paths of oncoming trolleys. They'd have crashed by now if only for the other shoppers steering to the side, aware that they are the ones who shouldn't be in frame of the catalogue couple's scene. Alistair, as usual, is a dog, sniffing at the shelves for something that catches his fancy, one moment fixated on a product, the next on a passerby. He has an imitation smile that he flashes compulsively, two rows of sharp teeth to beam at people who smile in return. The man just can't help but being liked.

When he arrived at Ava's apartment unannounced, as is his habit, it was with the promise of something amazing. Without really thinking about it, or of how annoyed she was earlier in the day, she'd flung herself into her Burberry coat and let the lights turn off behind her. Terribly bored now, her arm is hooked into the doctor's. They're shackled together and oblivious to it until the chain goes taut.

'I don't like black beans,' she informs him. 'And anyway you have to steep them for hours. You said you'd have this spectacular dinner cooked tonight.'

'I will,' he frowns. 'I'm the best cook in the world.'

'Can you at least tell me what you're making? None of the things you've picked go together.' She doesn't try to hide the irritation in her voice as she does a stock check of his basket – the bunch of bananas, a lime, pepper, chicken cutlets and bag of mixed nuts with raisins.

'We've been here almost forty minutes.'

Alistair checks the time to confirm this, which Ava takes as a slight on her.

'You're still wearing that piece of rubbish.'

Bag of rice in hand, Alistair seems to consider both her comment and the package in one short chuckle, then dumps the bag into their basket. Happy that she's taken a jab at him and amused she's even bothered, he asks, 'Is that why you have the hump? I thought you were still annoyed about that ignorant taxi driver.'

'You could have taken the new one with you. You could have brought it home.'

'So sensitive. Maybe I left it on your bedstand to make myself a new home. I'm nesting.'

'You left it there to get at me. You wanted to annoy me for being locked up when I dealt with Joanne. Don't deny it. You're so petty. A big man-child.'

At this, he shakes and pretends to be scared. Ava squints into the middle distance, choosing to concentrate on something else instead. Around a bend, people shuffle to feed the self-service checkouts which beep monotonously in return.

'I told you, it's my old man's. Do you know what he said when he gave it to me? Finally, somebody in the family will have places to go where they can wear this. He was a salesman and he said he never wore it because it made him look like a con artist. Don't ask me what the difference is,' Alistair lifts his arms, confused by the thought. 'It has personal value, alright? My Dad said he felt like he'd won the lottery when I graduated.'

'Your Dad was a prick,' she reminds him. 'You've said so yourself. He just liked you doing so well so he'd have something to brag about. I'm the one who's here. I'm the one who supports you. Where's he?'

'How should I know?'

'Exactly.'

'I can be sentimental, can't I?'

'I didn't say you couldn't be,' Ava allows. 'I didn't tell you to throw the thing out. But you don't have to wear it everywhere, do you? Every day? You wouldn't eat the same dinner every night, look at the same news story, listen to the same song, wear the same tie.

How do you not get sick of it? It's good to change things up.'

Alistair has already stopped listening. His hand lifts a scarf that rests on the back of a woman stood in front of them and lets the light material fall from his fingers. Ava grimaces, disgusted. She could give up on the matter, but it would mean giving up on him altogether. That wouldn't be so bad. She could walk away right now and grab a taxi home, order Indian food and put her feet up. It would certainly save the remainder of the evening. Then she feels Alistair hold her hand tighter and with the squeeze of it she knows that he's reciprocating what she's been trying to get – devotion. He doesn't apologise, but the grip is all she needs. With a little more wheedling the black-silver watch will be on his wrist a couple days a week, and shortly thereafter, weekends and special occasions if she so desires. It will get boring and outdated too, but by that stage she'll already have got him accustomed to change and it will be together with the gold watch in a dusty drawer, or better yet, on the jewellery section of ebay. She tweaks her expression from vacant to happy, a simple matter that requires less than a second. 'Let's just cook a stir fry.' Stepping around him, she stands on tippy toes to press her lips against his. 'I feel like something spicy.'

Seeing himself in her gaze, Alistair replies, 'Good idea.'

But as he tries to twist her around, she's stuck to the spot, feet glued to the floor and her eyes gone intent as a shark's.

Down the long aisle and into the next, a wormy man is weighed down on one side by a bag of groceries. The man's terrified face contorts grotesquely, forced into a shape it's never had to pull, and his mouth split open is a festering wound. Alistair turns back to Ava, who appears to be the source of the man's anxiety. She looks down at their joint hands and pulls away, breaking their grip, as if his hand is an iron hot enough to burn.

'Get away from me,' she says.

The man at the end of the aisle has dropped his groceries. They're scattered on the floor among a smashed jar of pasta sauce. He's bent over to pick them up, but as he sees the shattered pieces he regards it all helplessly. Frustrated by the mess he's made, the man gets the bloody pool of pasta sauce all over his chest and hands. All in a hurry, he glances timidly at Ava and the doctor, grabs a bottle of wine which survived the fall, and makes a break for the sliding doors, clearly desperate to escape the pair.

Alistair, seeing the man sprint away in fright, feels a deep rooted instinct to give chase, like he's spotted some game on the run. Managing to suppress the impulse and remain still, he watches curiously as the hapless fool disappears. Ava though, she's tipping forward to follow him out, running as fast as her high heels allow.

'What's going on? Who's that?'

'I said back off Alistair. Just go home!'

Already halfway down the aisle, she's given in completely to the instinct which the doctor managed to ignore. Ava is away on the chase.

14

In a growing flurry, the beat of her heels accelerate the further she goes. Caught in perpetual motion, she can't stop until she gets what she wants. Arriving at the end of the aisle she hears Alistair shout again.

'Who the hell is that?!'

The languid shoppers that mill about turn their heads to look at him, dimly confused, and though Ava doesn't stop to do the same, she feels him burning a hole into the back of her head. Kicking her way through the groceries that Francis left piled on the tiled floor, she sidesteps the shattered jar of sauce into the parking lot where the social agent turns a corner onto an unknown street. Breaking into a sprint, she ignores the sound of a car horn, dodges a van and trolleys along the way, and ignores the cry of the doctor again.

'Francis!' she calls.

Arriving at a shuttered charity shop on the bend she spots the social agent at the end of the road, a speedy figure on the winding city street, one hand pocketed, the other holding something, ticking it back and forth as a metronome for his stride. Hesitating to shout after him again, a cautioning voice tells her that it might be a bad idea to draw attention from the strangers with her cry.

'Francis!' she shouts anyway.

The shout seems to ricochet around the narrow road, hit the back of the social agent's head and knocks the rhythm out of his walk.

He falters on regardless. Ava is at full trot, a hair's length from the man when the sound of her steps plummet down on him.

'Francis,' she says breathless, a tincture of amusement in her voice. 'You're going to make me think you don't like me.'

'We shouldn't be talking outside of the office,' he warns, stern.

His steps are long but hers are small and fast. She's trying to outpace him, to get an angle on his face and capture him with a look, but he's doing his best to keep his head forward, not letting her get a lock.

'We talked outside the office before,' she objects. 'In the car park.'

Francis replies with a vicious snicker. It's the kind of noise that could turn into a fit of hysterics, depending on which wires get crossed.

'Why are you acting this way?' she reaches out for his arm.

He flinches away. 'The car park at work is different.'

He regrets the comment as soon as it's out of his mouth. Aware that he's opened himself up for a conversation that he doesn't want to have, the man resolves to keep his lips shut. Do not engage, he tells himself. Freeze her out.

'Why?' she asks. 'What's changed?'

Not answering, only cold clouds of breath pass between the two. Shops at either side become decayed and vacant, faded for-sale signs decorate them and empty allotments are covered with billboards. Soon they're on a pedestrian road. Redbrick townhouses to the left and right are guarded by wrought iron fences, streetlights buzz overhead, and a tree passes them every ten paces. Branches and power lines swipe their faces while odd numbered lampposts are counting down as they go. In the distance, the aircraft light of the spire in Dublin's city centre blinks as they march toward it. The smell of rain is in the air and a dot of water flicks the pavement, hesitantly followed by another. Ava continuously talks at him, trying to find a soft spot. Francis feels the figures about them, other pedestrians hunched over for their walks home. Their presence help him keep his resolve to be silent but the deeper they go into the tree lined neighbourhood, the less of them there are and soon they disappear, one by one, emptying the street to avoid a coming downpour. Behind her, Ava can feel the doctor abandoned at the shop. Apprehensive, she checks down the way to assure herself he's not out there, hiding and listening behind a tree, a rubbish bin, a car.

'Is this because you saw me with that guy? Because you like me?' she ventures shyly. 'I like you too.'

It's the worst thing she can say, because it makes Francis realise what a fool he was to ever think she could have. Didn't a part of him know that already though? And wasn't he thinking about taking a chance with her anyway? All the more reason to keep his stupid mouth buttoned shut. When Francis doesn't respond she trips, emits a meek yelp, and falls into a limp.

'These damn heels,' she whimpers capriciously, tearing as she tries to keep up.

It's a lie of course. Another fabrication ready to flick off the tip of her tongue. She probably didn't even think about it, just initiated the act in a flash of inspiration. Francis knows that much, and still, it's not enough. There are certain sounds in nature, so universal, so painful, the cry of a baby or squeal of an animal, that even in a man who knows a fake, a shiver is sent down the spine. 'Francis, slow down,' she cries, the shrillness of her voice triggering Francis in this way so that all at once there's a lump in his throat.

He stops and faces her.

'I knew you were untouched. You don't need a government cert to see that much,' he laments. 'But I didn't think you could get involved with something this seedy. This loathsome.'

'What do you mean?'

'That man. That doctor. You think I wouldn't know who he is? That's not a face you can forget. He's a murderer.'

'He's a story,' she says, emphatic. A story. The suggestion hangs in the air, waiting to be taken. Everything it could mean. All of this a misunderstanding. A chance for her to redeem herself. To prove her innocence. She's a picture of virtue as she pushes the idea on him. 'Just a story.'

Francis screws up his lips, expecting her to go on, but she lets him take what he can from the defence without adding any more to it. The soft sell. It isn't until he tries to walk away from her again that she pipes up.

'I want to know everything about the scumbag before we take a shot at him. I don't know what you think is going on, but that's all it is.

We don't have any solid paperwork. No safe witnesses. Just a bunch of rumours and gossip. I'm trying to get a concrete lead. We need to take him down, Francis. ChatterFive can do it if only we had more to go on.'

'And I thought investigative journalism was dead.'

'I'm bringing it back,' she quips, trying to make light of his sarcasm.

'So if I rang Joanne Victoria, she'd know what you're up to?'

Francis is sure he's trapped the woman now. At last, he can move on without her.

'She wouldn't let me do something like this,' Ava, not missing a beat, balks at the idea. 'Spending weeks on a story she doesn't have the guts to publish? Risking an even bigger lawsuit? I'm out here on my own, doing what needs to be done. She'll be happy to use it when I find more dirt on him though, you can be sure of that. Let me do all the leg work and give ChatterFive all the glory.'

Francis quickens his pace, 'This is pathetic.'

He's admonishing himself as much as he is Ava's attempts to wriggle out of being caught. It gives him the strength to renew his walk.

'This isn't a joke, Francis,' her voice sharp as she catches up with him, her limp miraculously healed. 'You can't just go around judging people for doing their job, living their lives. I'm a human being.'

That's exactly what I do, Francis realises with a sinking feeling in his chest.

'I haven't done anything wrong,' she insists, rabid, her breath hard at the end of the sentence. 'Who are you to say I have? You're freaking out because I didn't follow some arbitrary journalistic code of conduct you've made up? It doesn't exist, Francis. The only code is don't lose the company money. I can do what needs to be done without that happening. And you can't even look at me. You've got some nerve.'

'He's a monster, Ava!' Francis shouts, desperate to see an honest reaction in her face.

Missing her cue, she simply replies, 'Well I'm not.'

And all he could say to that is she is. But he can't. He doesn't even know if he believes it. Incapable of convincing either she nor he of anything, Francis holds his arms up and lets them drop to his side.

'You don't put a murderers lover on trial, do you? And I didn't even sleep with him. All I did was try to get to know him better. Oh I forgot, this must mean I'm UPD, that I'd let the world burn to get a kick out of it,' she says, cynical.

'Yes!' he screams, struck by the feeling that they're talking in different languages. 'That's the general idea. You don't give a damn about any of us. About me!'

'You don't believe that,' she says, hurt.

His head shakes weakly in response. It's a feeble reaction but he can't think of a rebuttal, when really, all he has to say is, 'I do.' He doesn't even have to believe it. The statement is not one to be considered. It's a deflection designed to give him space until he can think about it privately. They're stood in the empty street, considering each other tiredly. He falters again under her determination by breaking eye contact.

'You don't,' she spots the chink in his armour. It's as much of a revelation to her as it is to him. 'You don't think I should be punished but you're going to anyway.'

'It's not punishment,' he says, holding up the fact like a shield. 'It's the law.'

'The law,' she repeats, swiping the shield away.

Lost in the street he clearly knows, Francis can't get his baring. Blindfolded and spun around, he's being pushed left and right. Taking the cover off now, he notices a post box, and disoriented, he spots the door to his building, the paint peeled off in chips. If only he could get inside and lock her out. All he has to do is stomp up the steps and go in. She wouldn't follow him, surely? It might as well be on the other side of Ireland for all the distance he sees between him and his flat. If only the landlord would come out and swat the woman away. Francis could shout up to him, ask to be rescued. Instead, he fingers the keys in his pocket. They jingle as he considers a run for it. He can slip in and slam it before she knows what's happening. So why does he feel trapped? What is it in the woman that has a hold on him? Ava reads his mind.

'This is where you live.' She points to the bottle he holds. 'Is that the drink you owe me? Chilean, just like I said.'

Discovering the bottle in his hand, it's as if he's only just found it. Francis backtracks to figure out where it had come from. Remembering that he'd left the flat to do some shopping, he wonders where all the groceries he bought have gone to, and then, oh yes, he sees them scattered on the floor of the supermarket. At a loss for what to do, he looks right into what he's been trying to escape.

'It's cold out here, and I heard there might be a flash riot tonight,' Ava says. 'Let's sit down with a drink inside, where it's safe. It doesn't have to be like it's been, this silly argument. We can chat about it till the trouble passes, alone together, can't we?'

Dizzy, he's trying to see something he can't quite make out, something under that iridescent skin she wears. It's frightful as a ghost but he's drawn to its purity nonetheless. Leaning forward to get a better view, he almost falls, but manages to catch himself. She tries to make him focus on her but as he answers her, he continues to speak from faraway.

'There's nothing to talk about.'

She steps closer. 'It's my life.'

'Nobody's taking that from you.'

Another step. 'They are if I can't work where I want.'

'There are other jobs,' he says quietly.

Her hand goes up to his arm. Hypnotised, he doesn't think to wrench her off.

'This is my career and you are going to take it away from me. You're going to convict me for being good at my work. For a law you know isn't right. You think it isn't something that can just be forgotten. You're all wrapped up in it, bowing down to some imaginary concept. But you can make a difference. You can let me pass. Things can change.'

'This isn't how things get changed though.'

'When the law goes this wrong it's just a shared delusion. They've taken people and turned them into numbers, you can see that, surely. Oh no, damn the consequences, just do your job and protest against this turgid mess the slow way, meanwhile my life's been devastated. Everything I've built is swept away because you don't think my motivations worthy. Well damn you, Francis, you're a coward. Hiding behind a title and a piece of paper.'

He doesn't hear her, petrified as he is.

Seeing as much, Ava takes her chance, the final stab at Francis Mullen. He lets her hand move him toward the door of his building. His key goes into the lock, setting the springs and traps open. He forces himself to try and find what it is behind those eyes one more time. Is it loneliness that's sparking desperately in her synapses? Believing that would be a foolish projection of emotions based on the only model he really knows – himself.

No, it's not loneliness that's in her. If it can't be cured, if the love offered can't be understood and returned in kind then it is something altogether different. All he could give her is matter to be devoured and forgotten. Francis has a secret. He became a social agent because all of his life he's been afraid. Something out there was so powerful that it's pull on him was impossible to escape. Behind the title of his job he has had some protection from it, a constant reminder of the dangers it represented. In his work he has been granted the power of logic and reason, but with no tablet to hold between them now, he's robbed of the certainty it lent, and pulled into the black of her eyes, he's left with nothing but her grip to bolster him. Veering forward, he's on the edge when he realises what it is he's really feared all this time. With her hand guiding him, supported by the strength of a thousand, he's forced to step off, and falls all the way into its infinite depths.

15

The sound of rain, drumming lightly on the window in a chorus of pudgy toddler fingers, had pitter-pattered in his dreams throughout the night. As morning approached, the drizzle became a storm and announced itself with bursts of wind which intermittently pounded against the glass, half waking the two who dozed snugly in bed. In their drowsy state, they'd wrapped round each other all the more tightly. Feeling the woman's finger nail writing suggestive notes on his chest now, the man's mind is tempted closer to the surface, but it's a shrill ringing sound that jolts him awake. Detective Dylan Wong's eyes spring open like two traps set to trigger in unison and his wife, also snapped into reality, withdraws from him. The panicked seconds between recognising the disturbance and silencing it are an eternity for Dylan. It's familiar and alien at the same time, that ringing set to a tune. He thinks he knows it but doesn't remember hearing it in a long time. Laying motionless in bed, the light shade comes into focus, and steadily, he becomes aware of the room around him as he vaguely wonders if there's a fire. No, it's only his phone. His hand slaps about the nightstand until it lands on the device and he picks it up, thumbing aimlessly in the hopes that he can stop the inane ringtone. Succeeding, the chirpy tune is replaced by an equally irritating voice. Caustic, it greets him.

'Good morning, Dylan.'

Dylan attempts a greeting which comes out as an incomprehensible slur.

'What?' the voice asks.

He swallows the bitter taste of morning and at once a picture of the world comes back together for him. His wife and he had been snuggling but she remembered they were fighting and turned to the wall. He'd been lucky to even have a place in the bed . The ringtone that had been playing was a children's rhyme. The Teddy Bear's picnic. He hadn't set the phone to play it on receiving calls, but he has a good idea who might have.

'I said,' Dylan rolls over to plant his feet on the ground and speaks in halts to rid his mouth of marbles. 'I said it's my day off.'

Shrunk into himself, he wonders if he was drinking, but remembers that they were in bed by eleven. Behind him, his wife has thrown on her robe and leaves a chill as she slides out of the room. Taking this call has not helped Dylan's position.

'You do it to yourself, Dylan,' the voice needles.

There's a knot there, in the floorboard, stuck in the grain, unable to move. He knows what he's going to hear. Half asleep, he imagines it coming from under the synthetic planks of wood.

'You took lead. You went over the flat. You found a perfectly natural dead man and decided maybe it wasn't perfectly natural. You got the autopsy results to show that, yes, he just had a bad heart. No-no, you insisted, look a little closer, I'll buy you a beer. How could I decline the offer? You know I'm always parched for a drink. You took advantage. The system doesn't allow for hunches you know. These tests cost money. If the bloods came back clear you'd have to have been pretty creative with your reasoning to justify it. But of course your luck won out. You're making us look bad. And now...'

'And now?' Dylan asks.

'And now you don't have a day off.'

Dylan lets out a good humoured groan. 'What was it?'

'Poison. I didn't recognise it. Ran a quick search and found it's connected to failed medical trials run by SimperP. They're some company. Very powerful. It's registered to them. Quite the innocuous little creation. It hides among white blood cells in the body and little by little congeals in the chest. It actually carries more oxygen than the standard white blood cell, but it clogs the arteries as it does it, unnoticed.

Antibodies don't have a chance to identify it until you're already dead, and good investigators like ourselves mistake it for a consequence of genes and bad lifestyle, overworked as we are.' The voices pauses. 'I would say you've found something very interesting.'

'Interesting,' Dylan repeats.

Still staring at the knot in the wood, the set glaze of his face gradually evaporates as he realises how deep a hole he's dug for himself. He's at the bottom of a pit with that dead body. Why couldn't it have been a nobody? Just another loner who died with no-one to care for them. Or better yet, the fool could still be alive. He considers what a world without murders would be like. I'd be out of a job, is the most creative thought that comes to mind.

'Interesting is not good,' Dylan mumbles.

'I eh, need to forward the results to the department chief,' The voice apologises. 'I figured I'd give you a heads up. Get some tea into you. You said this guy was an active agent in the UPD service? Where was he processing?' When Dylan doesn't say anything the voice goes on without him. 'Well, wherever it was, this is going to get messy. When the service gets wind that their guy was killed on the job, while investigating... Jesus. First murder by an uncovered UPD?' The voice whistles. 'This is a real hot potato buddy.'

'A real hot potato,' he parrots the phrase.

The voice tuts, aware it's not being listened to. 'Don't forget about that drink you owe me.'

Dylan is left with a long dial tone as he debates whether he should stay in bed.

First lies were invented, then politics was. It will be twenty minutes before Dylan's department chief gets the news. It will rocket up the chain to his desk, send him into a panic and have him ringing the UPD service offices. There'll be a ten minute talk, quick phrases of condolence, a self conscious back and forth about publicity trouble, political consequences, the committees that will be formed, people breathing down necks. The chief will assure the other end of the line that it's under control, say that his best men are on the case, hang up, check the file to see who's got lead, and curse himself when he see's it's Dylan Wong. Then Dylan's phone will ring. All in all, half an hour will have passed.

That's a thirty minute lie in until he has to deal with the world.

Shouting good morning, his son appears at the bedroom door, delighted, and springs at him, jumping onto the bed to crawl on top of his father and place tiny hands on stubbly lips. 'Breakfast time!'

Flinching at the scream, Dylan twists onto his belly and presses his face into the mattress as he feels his son crawl around him. With a few more shouts and some childish slaps to the back, Dylan is brought to life and shouts, 'Alright! Away we go!' Hoisting his son onto his back, he walks into the kitchen to sit the boy down on a chair, and taking one beside him, he's sat at the table in his underwear.

'Good sleep?' his wife, stood at the cooker, surprises him by talking.

'I feel like I've been unconscious for a decade,' Dylan replies. 'Was I having nightmares last night? Tossing and turning?'

'You were like a log. I tried pushing you away from me when your arm took over my side but there was no budging.'

Considering an apology, he decides it won't be worth much to her now. He rubs his hands over his face, trying to rid himself of the feeling of too much sleep as she places a mug of tea in front of him.

'Cheers.'

His wife is busying herself at the sink, shuffling dishes about into piles with no real aim to organise them. The fridge motor is humming quietly and stops. A dog barks a stone's throw away, in the neighbours garden. His son is sucking on the straw of a juice carton, contently ignorant, enjoying an altogether different kind of silence.

'Are you all set for today?' Dylan's wife asks him in a patronising tone which he understands is as much for the benefit of their child as it is a poke at him. She knows that he won't be following through on their plans, that the job has called, and so that, as he so often says, is that. She goes on anyway. 'I found your swimming trunks at the bottom of the wash basket so we won't need to buy a pair.'

Dylan gives her a long sigh. He's mulling over whether he should tell her now or wait until the chief rings, make a charade of it and pretend he's surprised – argue with him maybe, in front of her, that it's his day off. Put on a good show. The chief would like that. But she's already read the meaning of his sigh and turns her back on him. Strained now, she watches a puddle dance in their garden.

'Today was important,' she says, her voice unchanged, though the sound of the dishes she's moving in the sink get louder. 'It's not just a swim.'

'I know,' Dylan agrees meekly. 'The job. It is what it is.'

Their son has noticed the change between them. Like a dark cloud passing over a sunny day, he sees all their plans disappear. The shade stretches from one parent to the other, and though he knows they're not going swimming now, he thinks that maybe, if he finishes breakfast without a peep, things will work out in his favour.

'We said we'd make more of an effort. You said that.'

'I need to get out of homicide. We have to wait on the paperwork. They'll put me in an office somewhere. I'll push them to get a move on,' he says, attempting to sound enthusiastic. Aware that he hasn't actually put in the request form yet, his voice falters in the try. 'This is just paying up front. After that it's a desk, nine to five, and every weekend off till the pension comes in.'

No acknowledgement is given him. She has heard this line of reasoning many times in the past. Hugging her from behind, Dylan finds she becomes an icicle at his touch. Then the Teddy Bears Picnic plays again. It's the chief. His apologies are ignored and he walks away, into the sitting room to keep his family from overhearing the discussion.

'You get the good news?'

Finding a creek in his neck, Dylan arches his body.

'You're killing me with this, Wong,' the chief grumbles. He hears the sound of the man's big ape fingers trying to type something on a keyboard. The chief, a short portly man with a patchy goatee, reminds Dylan of his old school principal. A bureaucrat, more concerned with keeping up appearances than doing any real work. The older he gets, the less he can stand this type. Really, it's why he hates his job. 'What made you ask for those bloods? You don't have a reason on these forms, you just crossed out the question. This is a real middle finger to me. I should take it out of your pay. You're lucky that guy was actually murdered.'

'I guess that makes me the number one suspect.'

'Believe me, I wish you were.'

'Alright, dock my pay and we can go back to pretending he died of natural causes.'

'Don't give me that shite.'

'It's my day off, by the way.'

'Do you know how many people are going to be on us about this? You're going to pay for it, one way or another. You got our nose stuck into something bad this time.'

'I'm not the one who killed him,' Dylan says lazily.

'This is a real hot potato,' the chief says. 'My phone hasn't stopped ringing. I was supposed to have a game of golf this morning.'

'Well, just keep everyone out of my hair and I'll do the best I can.'

Dylan winces at the sound of laughter that assaults his ear.

'Out of your hair? We already had a team out by North Circular road canvassing for witnesses. Nothing, not a peep from anyone. Like they've all gone back into their holes and are just waiting for us to disappear.'

This is becoming a headache. 'Teams of cops will have that affect on people. You should have let me canvas alone. I'm going to have to go back anyway.'

'It's a tough life, eh? Some things are out of our control now. Sooner or later it's going to be news. Under the public gaze. What's that they say about observation changing the subject? We can't just investigate, we have to do it in style, and we have to do it quickly, and we have to work with every arsehat who thinks they know how to solve a case.'

'I know, I know.'

'And that means working with the UPD service,' the chief presses. 'I have a meeting with their department head in five minutes. He's waiting over the way as we speak.'

Stood by his curtains, Dylan watches the hanging sheet of rain. Across the road the Sullivan's are making runs to and from their car, packing it for a holiday. The worst thing any of them has to worry about is whether their puppy will be okay in the neighbour's care. Beyond them, the hive of families sprawl, each living in their cell, going about identical lives, having identical thoughts. Even this dull impression that Dylan feels isn't one anybody else hasn't had – the housing estate, buried away in a lifeless nook past Lucan, is a nursery for those who won the coin toss. If it wasn't for his job, Dylan would never see the city at all.

'If there weren't any murders,' plays like a song in his head.

'And you've got to hook up with their social agent. He's your partner on this.'

'What agent? A partner?'

'We're working with them so that means you are too.'

'What do you want me to do with him? I'm not a babysitter. When I need a personality test I can give them a call. Their guys aren't even cops.'

'They might as well be,' the chief says dryly. 'If there's any untouched in that office they're prime suspects for arrest. That's on the spot, Wong, in handcuffs. Jesus, I pray there's one in there. This case is going to be a mess if there isn't.'

'Guilty until proven innocent, right? The land of the untouched.'

'When a social agent is dead and everyone in the country has their watches set to time the case, yes, that's the way it bloody is. Just get it done.'

'Give me the agent's number. I want to drop by the crime scene first, snoop around the neighbourhood. I'll meet the guy after lunch.' Just as he speaks, Dylan realises he has no intention of doing so and will dodge the social agent as much as possible.

'He's already at ChatterFive!' the chief cries. 'You're slow today. I need you on your game. And please, do things by the book.'

'Bloody hell.'

'Get down there now, let him know you're in charge, and don't make us look bad.'

So, the social agent is there ahead of him, dashing every lead in the place. If there were finger prints and foot trails he can see the man now, rubbing them out of existence in a good natured attempt to clean up the place. It's all set in motion, the people and evidence, bouncing about like a crate of balls dropped on a flight of stairs. Right now, whoever murdered that man is in that building and an investigator who Dylan Wong doesn't know has probably tipped them off to the fact that they're on the case.

By way of wishing his detective goodbye and good luck, the chief warns, 'If anything goes wrong, you're the one that's going to get the blame.'

Left with the distinct impression that he'll be lucky to get a desk job when all of this is over, Dylan scratches his balls. That table, with its laptop and security, is fast disappearing over a distant horizon.

Waiting for him are his wife and son.

'I have to go.'

In the kitchen, through a framing arch he sees half her form, tactful as she expects him to leave. His son is looking to him concerned. Dylan gives the boy a smile and steps over a set of Lego bricks to reach his wife. Hugging her from behind, he doesn't let go until he feels her thaw a little in his arms.

'There's a clean jumper in the sitting room. It's not ironed but you can at least smell respectable.' It's meant as a playful jab, some begrudging sign of acceptance from her, but given the state of things it doesn't cut him any less.

'Sorry champ,' Dylan rubs his child's head. 'And stop messing with my phone. We're not all teddy bear picnic fans.'

When he's leaving the house his wife insists that he puts the car on automatic, contending that he's too tired to be driving.

'I will,' Dylan assures her.

But when he's around the corner of their model estate, he switches back to manual, feeling the cold steering wheel on his hands. 'Francis Mullen,' he says the name of the murdered social agent aloud. The day was taken from Dylan, by who or why he doesn't yet know. Francis Mullen's life was taken too. These things just happen. So much of existence is out of a person's control. This is the smallest thing Dylan can do, he thinks as he changes gears. Today, he feels like driving.

16

It's a tumultuous scene. Dylan has arrived at the newsroom halfway through the film, not knowing the characters or why they're screaming. At the end of the office a cinemascope window overlooking the conference room is playing the ongoing argument. The glass is unfrosted, the door open, and soundproofing set to unproven. In the picture, two women, a dark haired young lady and an older one, blonde, as well as two men, one a scarecrow and the other a handsome clean-cut type, are going at it. They're shouting over one another, their voices tumbling to come out on top in a competition of who will run out of breath first. Though the blonde woman's indignant howl effortlessly rises above them, the others manage to find gaps between her sentences where they can wedge their thoughts in. For what little fear they have of her, it would appear she doesn't have much sway in the office. If he had to guess, he would say that the dark haired girl is a manager of some kind and on further observation, the clean-cut man, who attempts now and again to the defuse the squabble, also seems to maintain some detached influence in the matter. The newsroom drones, who are hanging on every word, set back to work as the detective walks by, not knowing who he is but sensing his authority. Like a teacher who has returned to a classroom just as the children were about to launch into a nervous knife fight, a blade, quickly passed from hand to hand before being dropped to the floor, has been kicked into hiding. Everyone knows where it is, but nobody is going to say it and he's waiting for that first telltale tic to give it away. Dylan finds himself wading through the tension.

'Can I help you?' A girl whispers.

'I need to go in there,' Dylan informs her.

'I wouldn't if I were you.'

The blonde woman on the other side of the glass notices the two tentatively stood outside, and at the dark haired one's instigation, frosts the window and slams the door. Her voice returns to hollering among the others.

'I'm going in anyway,' he waves his badge. 'Is the social agent from UPD services around?'

Understanding who this man is, she forgets his question and comments instead, 'It's terrible what happened. Agent Mullen, he seemed so nice.'

Dylan Wong, policeman disposition firmly set, remains unmoved. When she blinks, he leaves her, opening the door to the conference room to face the barrage of voices head on. The clean-cut man is half smiling, holding his hands up to calm the other three. When he notices the new figure, he removes himself from the bustle to let them go at it, reaching out to Dylan in greeting.

'You must be the detective,' gripping his hand, 'I'm Agent Myers.'

'Dylan Wong,' he shakes back. 'What's going on?'

'A lot of finger pointing,' Agent Myers quips.

Not appreciating the humour, Dylan observes the contenders. The blonde woman has collapsed into a chair and is hiding behind a hand, and the lanky man with the English accent is laughing at the trim dark haired woman who is insisting that she's not the first journalist in the world to exaggerate something and that he is in fact doing just that right now.

'Ava O'Dwyer,' Agent Myers says, 'Barry Danger. The lady sitting down is the editor. They haven't been taking Agent Mullen's death very well.'

As Barry launches into a rebuttal against Ava, she peels away, having spotted Dylan.

'I suppose you want to arrest me,' she says, harsh.

'Oh yeah, ever the victim, aren't we, Ava?' Barry rolls his eyes.

'I don't know what this is about,' Dylan shouts to shut them up, then repeats quietly, 'I don't know what all of this is about. But I'm not here to arrest anybody,' yet, 'I need to talk to Agent Myers in private, so if you three don't mind waiting here, sit down and stay quiet. I don't want to hear a peep.

Keep the glass unfrosted and leave the door open.'

Just as he's about to step out with the social agent, he hears the editor ask him, 'What happens if we don't?'

His attention stalling on the woman, Dylan shakes his head and follows the agent into the office. He's not five steps away when the three are screaming again, their bickering voices jabbing at each other. Face to face with this agent, Myers, he feels the offices attention fall on them and takes a step closer to talk softly. The flat he'd been in days ago held a corpse, but this room, here and now, with its affected indifference, has the stench of a murder scene – a conspiracy of silence.

'What is wrong with these people?'

'A little professional competitiveness I suppose.'

'Did you tell them Mullen's death is being investigated as a murder?'

'I didn't even know about that until this morning,' Agent Myers dodges the question. 'And I've been in the office for days. When Mullen didn't show up for work I was here within the hour. Murder didn't enter my head until my boss called twenty minutes ago. Them, they've been paranoid about it since his body was found. This tiff they're having has been brewing a long time.'

'What are they fighting about?'

'Well,' Agent Myers scratches the back of his head, reluctant to say what he's about to. 'The pretty one, Ava, she'd written up a story about a riot experience she had, only, Barry is saying that she made it up. He says he told Mullen about it the night he died. He hasn't accused anyone of anything else but the implication is loud enough. The editor, she says she wasn't aware that the story was a lie, but Ava is accusing her of knowing full well that it isn't a lie at all, that it's one-hundred percent true.'

The information, a web of accusations and denials, is dexterously untangled by Dylan Wong. 'What about Mullen? Did that English guy really tell him all of this? Is it in any of his reports?'

'Mullen hadn't filed a report for days,' Agent Myers allows a gap in his explanation to highlight the matter's seriousness. 'That is beyond a breach of protocol, it's a suspendable offense. It puts him on the dark side of the moon when this happened. We have no idea what the circumstances leading up to his death were. Unless he was writing up reports and not sending them on.

There might be something in his apartment but your people aren't letting us in.'

Thank god we didn't, Dylan consoles himself, blood boiling at the thought of the mess this social agent has made by even being in the office.

'Was this guy your friend?'

Understanding that the detective is referring to Francis Mullen, the social agent sums up the relationship. 'I worked with him. He was well liked. I wouldn't say we were mates.'

'I get that your department has a personal stake in this, I get it, really. I mean, besides the shock of losing one of your people. I know there's going to be political consequences. But you need to understand you have already made my job more difficult than it needs to be. Can we agree that the best thing you can do to help me here is keep out of my way?'

Nodding imperceptibly, Agent Myers isn't quite sure what he's agreeing to.

'I'm no cop. I'm just with you to, eh, appease the big shots.'

Dylan groans at the not incorrect assumption. That they're in this together.

'So they know he was killed,' he thinks aloud.

'And that everyone in the newsroom will now be subjected to the electric scan.'

'Bollocks.' Only from the immediate stillness of those around the office does Dylan realise that he shouted. 'Why would you tell them that?'

The social agent seems to be much more aware of the audience they have than the detective. Covering his irritation at being chastised by a stranger, he says, 'It was going to happen even if it had turned out Mullen wasn't murdered. Maybe even if he hadn't died. He wasn't sending in reports. Something suss was up. UPD services have to be seen as harsh, especially in situations like this. A compromised social agent, we couldn't let that go by without repercussions.'

Dylan is automatically memorising the layout of the room. He is picturing Agent Mullen stood here, pursuing a potential criminal, an untouched personality, that with his death, has become a committed one.

Not for the first time does the detective wonder if there would have been a criminal here at all if nobody had been searching.

'Listen, you don't do anything without my say so. From here on out, you're just my shadow,' he says. 'How were they acting when they erupted like this?'

Struggling to find something useful to offer, Agent Myers only comes up with, 'The editor, Joanne Victoria, she's looked like death since I got here.'

'What about the other one? Ava?'

Agent Myers laughs, then, like it's an obscene thought he doesn't want to reveal, rubs the smile off his face. 'That's Ava O'Dwyer. She's the assistant editor, and fashion columnist, I believe. Your wife would know her.'

Correcting the assumption that she was the boss, the detective now glowers at the social agent until the man knows that any kind of personal talk is out of bounds – especially that to do with his wife and child – and tries to figure out what kind of person he's to be working with is. Myers guessed that he's married. Perhaps his wedding band had been spotted, but his fingers have been in his pockets since they moved outside. He must have registered it when they shook hands. Agent Myers, Dylan decides with some cautious satisfaction, is a man with a keen sense for detail. Hopefully it will come in useful.

As the men return to the conference room, the three journalists shut their mouths at their arrival. Agent Myers hangs behind Dylan, now an obedient servant. The detective's attention is compelled to Ava, his eyes unconsciously flicking up and down her pert body. She stands with hands on hips to grant him the privilege.

'I take it you all know why I'm here?'

'I can guarantee everyone on staff will be available for scanning,' Joanne blurts. 'We have nothing to hide. I certainly don't.'

Ava, at her side, places a hand on her shoulder.

'Right well, testing isn't my area,' Dylan says, mustering all the patience he can. 'I'll be investigating a murder. So far as I'm concerned the possibility of a UPD in the office is incidental. Do you understand that? Regular folk kill regular folk everyday and do just as good a job of it, believe me. I hope that my presence won't interfere with you or your staff's work.

Let them know I'll be floating about. I'll be pursuing leads elsewhere as well, but I'd appreciate full access to your employees along with a list of their work histories and contact details.'

Joanne is about to assure him that she'll do all she can to help, but finds that the words leave Ava's mouth first.

'I'm sure we can accommodate your needs.'

Glancing at Ava, and back at Joanne, Dylan taps the desk to make sure the editor is listening. 'We'll be as delicate as possible. I expect we can trust your staff not to leak any details to other media outlets. It's more efficient to operate these investigations under the radar. I can't order you to keep quiet, but your discretion is best for all involved.'

Joanne, Barry and Ava follow his sight to the muddled room of journalists.

'I want to talk with everybody separately, starting with you,' he nods at Barry Danger, who had seemed to be the more rational of the group in the short segment he'd witnessed.

'Him?' Ava asks, offended. 'Don't believe anything he says.'

'Ha!' Barry crows. 'Sorry pet, you can tell him what you need to from inside of a cell. Might as well call your lawyer now, save yourself some time.'

'Outside,' Dylan commands Barry.

'Wait,' Joanne stands abruptly.

At first, the detective gets the impression that she wants to leave with him. She seems afraid. Of what though? Something Barry will say? Something she wants to say herself? Ava is perched on the desk next to her, gently easing her back into the seat. Is that who she's afraid of? Dylan directs Agent Myers to stay with them, hoping this will appease her. In any event, she sits down to remain with the two and clams up altogether.

'She's gone off the deep end,' mumbles Barry.

'What about you? How are you taking all of this?'

'I was already off the deep end, mate.'

Outside the conference room, Dylan withdraws a pad from his pocket and opens a file to note what's being said. Seeing the device, Barry curses, 'Another one of those things.'

'I think it's best there's a record of what we talk about.'

'I'll try not to incriminate myself then.'

Another correction. The man's cool head seems to be more from a sneering detachment rather than a sense of order. He should have guessed from the tattered jacket, though the detective does try to keep people's choice in clothing from defining his view of them, he can't for example, arrest every kid in a hoody and trainers. If it were relevant to the case, Dylan's first note would be his adamant belief that this English journalist is a complete prick. As it is, he starts his questioning with, 'You said that Ava falsified a story. Does that happen a lot?'

'Yes and no,' Barry squints an eye, measuring the detective. 'Truth is more subjective than a newsroom can admit. Sometimes it gets so you can't see the people for the trees. Wong, is it? Was she at that riot? No. I can say that much.'

'How did you know?'

'I found a photo she used in our digital archives and I linked it to Mullen.'

'Can you forward it on to me?'

Barry whimpers a laugh, 'It's gone mate.'

'Gone?'

'Not in the archives. Deleted, completely irretrievable, replaced with zeroes.'

'So you might be making it all up.'

'That's right. But let's say I'm not. So Ava inserted herself into a riot across town. Is it a big deal? She obviously thinks it is. Joanne too. Agent Mullen? We'll never know how serious an offense he thought it was.'

'When did you tell you him?'

'That afternoon.'

'Email? A note? In person?'

Dylan is digging for evidence that the social agent actually received this report. Even a witness would do. Barry squelches his hopes.

'On the phone.'

'What time?'

'Four or five?'

'If I check I'll find a call from you at that time?' He's already submitting a request for access to the phone records, tapping at buttons as he converses with the man.

'It'll be from a pub in Crumlin.'

'Did anybody hear what you were saying?'

Barry chuckles, 'Jerry? He's the barman. I imagine he was privy to some interesting exchanges, but you won't have much luck getting him involved, especially not on my account.'

The pub and barman's name are jotted down anyway.

'Do you think Ava murdered that man?' Dylan asks, casual, like it's just a game of football they're mulling over.

'That's the million pound question, Wong. Ava? Why not? Joanne? Maybe. Me? I'm doing an alright job of setting them up, if I do say so myself. Well, there I go, not two minutes in and I've made myself a suspect.' Barry addresses the detective frankly, 'I don't envy you, buddy. I don't envy you at all. The last man I said that to is dead now.'

Raising an eyebrow to indicate that he's not amused, Dylan says, 'You think your editor is gone over the edge. She's not usually this jumpy I take it. Are her and Ava close?'

Through the window, Joanne is mute as Ava offers her advice. Barry taps the glass to get their attention. When they look, he gives them the middle finger. 'Close. Like snakes in a bag, my friend. Is there a murderer in the office? Yeah, I reckon so. I reckon every single one of us is the murderer.'

Dylan decides that that's enough time spent with the village idiot for the day and flicks his contact details from his pad to the man's phone.

The detective has never been in a newsroom. He isn't used to investigating office environments. Most murders he's dealt with were gang related, and the ones that weren't, family or lover squabbles. Thinking about it now, he'd never come across one that was professionally motivated. The crowds he has known, working class kids, minds addled by drugs and violence, in his experience, react to cops in one of two ways, either in a chorus of overlapping voices trying to shout over one another to give information, or as a united unspoken front. An over simplification perhaps, but on the whole he could divide them into those two categories. This newsroom, this office, this collection of people dressed in passively coloured shirts and ties and business skirts, fall on the quiet side of the line. Stolen glances and dour responses, all of these barely noticeable things add up to the sense that something bad has happened and nobody wants the blame.

In this climate, Dylan works his way through the series of interviews in the conference room, cross examining the employees in as efficient a manner as possible and suffering the social agent by his side all the while. Pressing Joanne about the possibility of publishing lies and what the consequences might be, agitated at the prospect, she describes it as career ending for whoever was involved.

'The only hope of surviving would be ignorance,' she remarks, languid.

On Ava's go around, he probes her feelings on being accused of falsifying a story but she's unruffled in assuring him of her innocence. When hoping to get her to point the finger at Barry, she doesn't jump at the chance, only noncommittally agrees that it could easily be an attempt on his part to sabotage her career, but that she doesn't know if he'd be capable of murder.

'I don't know who could do such a thing,' she comments at the end of the process. 'It's a scary thought. Thank god the Gards are here now. I wouldn't feel safe if it weren't for you.'

Dylan would be lying to himself if he said the attention of beautiful women wasn't a part of the job he enjoyed, too rare these days for not having the uniform to attract the interest of those who see security in it.

In the end, the picture he paints is a jumbled one, characters warped and showing sides that don't line up, the background they're set against all out of proportion. Good god, it's a post-modernist nightmare. More details are needed. On discovering them, ideally, they will all lead to one focal point. As of now, any of these people could have done it.

'I'll be leaving for a while and taking Agent Myers with me,' Dylan explains, pocketing his pad. 'You all have my number. If anything relevant comes to mind, use it.'

Agent Myers jumps to follow but they both turn around as they hear Ava call.

'Agent Myers. You dropped this,' she's holding up a pen for him.

'Ah,' he grins, arms folded. A couple of steps away she stops, forcing him to move forward. Taking the pen, his teeth shine back at her, 'Thank you, Ava.'

Playing witness to the exchange, Detective Dylan Wong finds a tinge of jealousy colouring his view of them, and now the two men watch Ava, her tight skirt hugging her legs close together as she walks away.

Joanne has moved to her office and Ava skips to join her. Over the fashion columnist's shoulder, Dylan catches a glimpse of the editor's state of mind. She looks up at the detective, sitting there like a hostage for all the anxiety she shows. In his line of work, sympathy is something often forgotten, but as he connects with her for a fleeting second, he feels it for the woman. Murderer or not, Joanne Victoria is in a lot of pain. Luckily, Ava takes a place beside the woman, to console her no doubt, and help her through these turbulent events.

17

'So how did you know he was murdered?' the social agent inquires.

Having followed the trail of breadcrumbs, they've arrived at the Phoenix Park end of North Circular Road. There's a line of tree stumps planted the length of the street. In the distance a crop of old trees remain, but there's a work crew felling and chipping them now. Soon they'll be back with a digger for the roots and not long after, another crew will arrive to plant saplings in their place. Dylan heard on the audio feed that one of the larger trees had collapsed onto a car and that this project to replace them was the result. At one time they were taller than the townhouses they guarded, bright green pom-poms in summer, stark broken branches in the winter. Now they're gone and the stumps are gravestones for what they were. Across the way a bearded drunk is soaked, his shelter from the rain gone. By the stunned appearance of his swollen face you'd think that the trees had been uprooted around him as he stood pissing on a trunk.

Leaning on the roof of his car, Dylan talks through the shower. 'There were two glasses on the coffee table.'

'Two glasses?'

'One was full,' he holds up a finger, 'the other was empty.'

'And that made you think he was murdered?'

'No,' Dylan twinkles sadly, 'it made me think it was worth looking into more closely. I've been wrong plenty of times. I shouldn't have requested the extra bloods.

When a hunch doesn't pay off it comes out of the department budget. But that's counter-productive thinking. Discovery, science, detective work, the law,' Dylan postulates, 'it's all trial and error isn't it? Process of elimination. I wouldn't let the chief hear me saying that-mind.'

'Don't take this the wrong way, but you don't seem dumb enough to be a cop.'

It's not that Dylan's colleagues are stupid, there are much better detectives in the world than him, in his department even, but their inquiring minds stop inquiring at why they do what they do. It's a trait that gives the police force its Alsatian image. The average detective can happily go about his or her work with commitment bias' and negative profiling they accumulate over years of experience, working from assumptions and stereotypes, questioning doggedly by compulsion without wondering where their gut instinct comes from and that much better at their job for it. Dylan isn't so lucky. There are occasions though, rare as they are, when his nose finds a trail that another's wouldn't have. It's small consolation for the times it leads him down a wrong path. Consulting the canvas report on his pad, he compiles a list of houses that weren't interviewed, whether because the occupants weren't at home or because they just didn't want to talk to the Gards. Today they'll be tackling those.

'So do you want to split up and do this? It'll go a lot quicker,' Agent Myers suggests.

'If I trusted someone else to do it we wouldn't be here at all. Let's start in Mullen's flat. I want to check it out again.'

Two rooms, not including the bathroom, though that was also an important one, made up Francis Mullen's life. He lived and died in the box that Dylan and Myers stand in now. Dreary at the best of times, it is now an utterly miserable pigsty that seems to be the only evidence he was once alive. Careful not to disrupt the clutter which before was just a mess and now stands as a monument to the man, Dylan rests his gaze on the armchair where the body had been found. He brings up the photo on his pad, cursing the angle the photographer chose. The corpse of Francis is reclined, his hands on the arms of the chair, his throat exposed like a lambs for the knife. Whatever killed the man did it from the inside. That poison. On the coffee table, the two glasses remain undisturbed.

Dylan snoops at the couch where the other drinker would have been sat and half expects to see a groove in the cushion. The ghost who killed the social agent, the phrase tiptoes through his mind.

'I wasn't expecting any more Gards. I was told I could clean up the place, go through his things,' the landlord speaks from the door.

'Have you?' Dylan asks, anxious at the thought of clues lost to the wind.

'I'm not a maid,' the landlord says.

Dylan and Agent Myers steal glances at one another, registering the petulant attitude.

'His family will get around to it when they're ready. I said they can take as much time as they need,' the old man's teeth jostle around his mouth as he makes the comment. 'Mind you, I should have given them a deadline, I'll be wanting a new tenant soon. Bills to pay. Always bills to pay.'

Agent Myers, one arm folded across his chest, does little to hide his contempt for the landlord. Dylan walks away from the pair to examine the shelves, piles of clothes by the bed, dishes left in the sink. There's a familiar pair of shoes, the same size as the detectives, except the sole of one is worn almost to nothing. Beside them, a Bobblehead Barry calls for the detective, suggesting with its silence that it knows something that it won't tell. Dylan doesn't think much of its presence. The English journalist tried pushing one on him earlier too. Some items have been moved since his initial inspection of the flat. Little things. He calls up the original scene photos to confirm it. He remembers a dish cloth being on the sink but now it's on the back of a chair and sure enough, the record matches up with his memory. A coaster that was on the floor has been picked up. The whole flat has the feeling of little elves having been there, rummaging about for tiny prizes. Besides that, he doesn't find anything he hasn't seen already, but hoping that something will leap out at him, he scans the room a second time. Nothing does. There are books laying in convenient places, easy to grab from wherever you sit. He liked magic, Francis, that's what Dylan has learned.

'Check his laptop,' Dylan instructs the social agent.

The air is stale from lack of cleaning. There's an assortment of pictures on the walls. Postcards and movie memorabilia. A young girl.

His niece? There's a gap in her teeth where a baby one has fallen out. It's not hung up, just leaning against the fridge. He wasn't planting any roots, that's for sure. These pieces of life only built up around him without his notice. Just another lonely person in the city. Dylan thinks of his own well run home – I can't end up like this. I'll sort out my marriage.

'He didn't get out much,' he says, expecting the landlord to confirm it.

'How should I know?'

Dylan cocks his head to elicit a conciliatory smirk.

'No, I don't suppose he did. Sometimes I thought I was his only friend. Sorry state of affairs when you can say that about a man.' The landlord has found an open box of chocolates and takes one, and another, greedily shoving them into his mouth. 'These were his favourite.'

'He was poisoned you know,' Agent Myers grins.

The old man stops chewing, but makes a point of swallowing the sweet anyway.

'You knew him well? Did he have any enemies? Old rivalries?'

The old man ignores the social agent and addresses Dylan. 'He was a good lad. I can't imagine anybody would have had anything against him. Nobody normal anyway. There's always those untouched people he was hunting, isn't there? They sound like a despicable bunch to me.'

'Was there anybody like that hanging around?' asks Agent Myers.

Again the old man ignores him, peculiarly intent on addressing Dylan. 'Are we done here? I don't like being around all of this,' the landlord gestures to nothing in particular, disgusted by the presence of death maybe, an insult to his ego.

Dylan tells the man to meet them outside and waits for him to leave.

'Find anything on the computer?' he asks Agent Myers.

'No reports,' he says in a hushed voice. 'That's no daily reports on what he was doing, no notes on the interview process, no forms filled in, nothing except a one line document he created in the ChatterFive folder.'

'Oh?' Dylan's curiosity is piqued.

'I don't know what it could mean. All it says is – But she set off the fire alarm.'

A car goes by the window, the sound of its wheels travelling the road like it's pushing up a river. When it's gone the pelting rain comes to the fore again.

'Who did? What alarm?'

'Your guess is as good as mine.'

Chewing his lip, Dylan asks, 'Was he not writing reports or were his reports deleted?'

'My pad didn't recover any deleted documents. The hard drive is pretty clogged with other files so any missing items would have been overwritten. Hard to say whether or not it was an intentional attempt to zero the drive, either way there's nothing to be retrieved.'

'What are the other files?'

Bewildered, the social agent informs Dylan, 'Quite a big stash of porn.'

Looking at the screen, the detective sees a towering list of movies.

'Jesus,' he says. 'Do him a favour and delete those. No point letting his family find them.'

Clicking them out of existence, Myers goes on, 'Anyway, unless he has another laptop we don't know about, my guess is he wasn't keeping any records.'

'You're not exactly helping us here,' Dylan says to the vacant armchair.

As they leave the room and close the door behind them, the landlord is waiting outside. 'Come upstairs with me,' he says to Dylan. 'Your friend can stay down here.'

'What?' the social agent balks.

'You heard the man.'

'I guess I'll wait in the car,' Myers says, exasperated.

'It's locked,' Dylan winks.

At the landlord's apartment, they stall for a minute as he goes through the latches, and opening the door a wedge, he reluctantly allows the detective entry ahead of himself. Inside, he hunches over the door once more and locks it three times.

'Lot of break-ins around here?'

'Can't be too careful,' the old man's lips wrinkle. He doesn't often let people in and doesn't appreciate smart comments from those he does.

Walking into the kitchen and pouring water into the kettle, he switches it on and leans against the counter as he measures Dylan up and down. Only when he's approved of the detective's demeanour does he decide to say what's on his mind. 'There was a woman at the apartment.'

'Oh?' With a vague sense of irritation in his voice, Dylan asks, 'You didn't mention this to the guys canvassing the street?'

Still, he's quite happy that he decided to come back himself. Vindication like this doesn't come often.

'Ah,' the old man sucks on his teeth, seemingly having difficulty telling Dylan what he has to say. 'I don't think she had anything to do with it. I hate having to get the cops involved in someone's life when there's no need. Once you're on a list, you know, you have to go through a grinder to get out the other side.'

'That may well be the case, but a man is dead and we're the ones looking for justice. Any information you have might lead to something useful,' Dylan feels a lecture coming on but cuts it off when the old man's creased forehead bends in contempt. 'You said it was a woman...'

'She showed up at his apartment door one night. Made a bit of racket. Didn't seem like the kind of person who can stand being ignored. I poked my head out you see, got a good view of her from the landing. She didn't notice me watching. Mad on getting Francis to listen. Only, he must have been out, because he couldn't have slept through the noise she was making. Banging so hard the whole road would have been shook awake. She was drunk, that's for sure. Slurring profanities. Crying one minute, angry the next. Some woman.'

All of Dylan's senses heighten at the hope of a lead. 'This is the night he died?'

'A day before.'

'Damn...'

'Mm,' the old man agrees. 'I was going to call the Gards, but around about the time I got fed up, she stumbled outside, found herself a taxi-cab to fall into and that was the last I saw of her.'

'Do you know what she wanted?'

'Haven't a notion.'

'What she was screaming about?'

'Gibberish.'

'Could you describe her?'

'Beautiful actually, a real looker for her age. I suppose she was in her fifties. Blonde. Big gold earrings. Posh accent. Dressed to the nines. High heels she could barely steady herself in. Walked like Bambi going out the door.'

The picture of the blonde woman forms all too easily. Dylan considers showing the old man a photo of Joanne Victoria, but decides against it, not yet wanting to alert him to the high profile status of the person he might have seen. Instead he says, 'You could pick her out in a line up.'

'I never forget a face...' The old man stops to tongue his upper gum. 'But I don't think she had anything to do with it.'

'Why?'

'Ah, how can I say it? You hear more in a person's voice if you can't see them. I was laying down on the couch when she'd started wailing. It was full of desperation.'

'Desperate people murder.'

'Maybe,' he concedes, 'but you're looking for someone untouched, and eh, they sound a lot more empty when they wail.'

'I'm looking for a killer,' Dylan corrects him. 'They're not the same thing.'

The landlord shrugs and makes a cup of tea. The spoon clangs against the side of the mug as it's stirred. Dylan thinks about leaving but remembers the locks and realises that he's the old man's captive audience.

'Let me ask you something, Detective Wong,' he says playfully. 'Do you think I've lied about anything since you got here?'

Dylan is taken aback, but at the old man's stone faced challenge he makes a visible effort to retrace his footsteps along the ground. After a cursory circle of the floor, he pictures his movements downstairs, then, placid, he says, 'Yes. You have. You said you didn't move anything in the apartment. That's the lie.'

The old man chuckles and puts his tea down on the dinner table and paces over to a cabinet by the couch. He's trying to find something that he wants the detective to see, all the glee of a child searching for a medal to show off. Opening a drawer, the sound of wood sliding on wood, he takes out a small rectangular packet. It's a deck of cards.

He hands them to the detective, who turns them around in his fingers.

'I gave these to Francis a few weeks ago. Fifty-two cards, as per standard. All there. I remember.'

'And now?'

'One of them is missing.'

'One of the cards,' Dylan says, dumbfounded.

'I snooped around his apartment for it. No sign. Just spirited away.'

Enamoured by the clue, Dylan feels a smile growing and asks the only question that comes to mind. 'Which card is it?'

'The queen of hearts.'

The smile takes over his face as he sees the landlord's joy in telling him this. Asking if he can keep the pack, he uses a tissue to put them into a zipper bag. The old man's finger prints are on them, his own too, Agent Mullen's, and if he's lucky, the killer's. A blonde woman's perhaps. He plays the note in his head a few times to see if he likes the sound of it, but can't decide either way. Something about Joanne being involved seems off.

'It's always in the last place you look,' the landlord winks.

Saying goodbye to the old codger, Dylan finds Agent Myers talking to a woman on the street. He'd forgotten about him and honestly, isn't overjoyed at the prospect of having to talk to the social agent again. The effort of chitchat is far too much for him today. The effort to be rude equally trying. Agent Myers has been braving the rain, asking passersby about the night of the murder, if they heard or seen anything. They canvas the neighbourhood for a while, catching people who hadn't been caught and learning nothing, until they agree to head back to the car, get some coffee, and plan what's to happen next. Sitting in traffic with his hands on the wheel, Dylan doesn't hear it when the social agent says something.

'I said you seem tired, why don't you put the drive on automatic?'

Ignoring the question, Dylan asks, 'What did you think of those two in the office. Joanne and Ava?'

He's trying to place Joanne at the scene, imagining Agent Mullen inviting her in – the killer was invited, that much is certain – and sitting down with him for a drink. Did she serve it? And slip the poison in? Take the card as a trophy? From his brief talk with her he's already having a hard time seeing her doing anything so subtle.

Joanne would be more inclined to bash her victim over the head and run away in frightened tears. Regardless, he can't rule her out. She is now the prime suspect.

Agent Myers' attention goes out the window for a minute, two, five minutes go by as they listen to the wipers swipe away the rain in loud streaks.

'Ms. Victoria has been a bit high strung. To be fair, you can't blame her for that. It's not exactly good publicity for their website is it? A potential murderer in their office? A social agent of UPD services killed for investigating them?'

'Any publicity is good though, isn't it? They have an exclusive on all this. It's in their interest to break the story before anybody else does. You don't think they're going to hype it up? Information sells for a lot of money, especially if there's sex and death involved.' Dylan shudders at the thought of his whole life turned upside down if the case isn't wrapped up quickly. His every move would be catalogued and examined. 'I don't want to be around when that happens,' he mumbles.

'I guess you're right.' Agent Myers drops his own idea of the woman and takes on board Dylan's. Like it was a hat that was passed to him and which seems to fit his head quite nicely, he remarks, 'She is difficult to talk to. She could barely look at me to be honest. Something in the eyes she doesn't want us to see. Maybe it's guilt?'

'You don't say?' Dylan begins to wonder who is leading who. 'What about Ava? Could she look you in the eye?'

'Ava O'Dwyer,' Agent Myers devours the name. 'Ava has a really nice arse.'

Cringing at the attempt of friendly male banter, Dylan says, 'I hadn't noticed.'

'Oh come on!'

'I'm a married man,' he reminds himself.

'Like that means anything. Your eyes practically popped out of your head when ye met in the conference room. Anyway, other than her posterior, I guess I didn't really think about her at all.'

'It's your job to find UPD in that newsroom and you didn't think about the goddamn assistant editor at all?'

'You seem pretty stressed by all of this.' Agent Myers snorts.

'What was my first impression of her? She's got a solid hold of herself. Some people have this kind of fake confidence, a bravado. Well, hers is real.'

Ignoring the observation of Ava, Dylan criticizes the social agent again. 'And you aren't stressed? This happened in your department. One of your guys is down. We don't know if it was terrorists or some lone mad man, but either way they could be targeting more social agents. Surely the first one they'll go for is the guy who replaced the one they killed. The one who's working with the cops to investigate the murder.'

Agent Myers swallows, 'I hadn't thought of that.'

'Well maybe you should start thinking,' Dylan says, the wheel gripped tightly in his hands. 'Forget what the bosses say, you're here at my discretion. Let's use those brains of yours for more help and less smartarse comments.'

'It's just,' Myers says, 'why should I be worried? We're going to be testing the whole office, right? Once we flush out the UPD, that's that.'

The unsettling fact of the matter is like a cold hand closing around Dylan's heart. If he can't find a viable suspect with more than circumstantial evidence, that, as Agent Myers said, will be that. Nonetheless, he defends the need to build a case.

'You really think it's that simple. What if they've got no connection to the crime?'

Agent Myers disagrees that there's an issue of concern. 'Who the hell else would want to kill this guy? You saw that apartment. His life was about as exciting as his wallpaper.'

Dylan doesn't have an answer for that. He thinks Agent Myers is right. Knows it even. He just doesn't like it. Not one bit. How many days does he have to figure it all out until it's taken from his hands and put into the social agent's? One? Less? Has there ever been a case built that fast? So, they drive in grudging silence, both of them feeling the clock ticking down, until one last thought comes to the detective's mind.

'Did that old guy have teeth when we were downstairs?'

'What?'

'He had teeth when we were in Mullen's flat. And he definitely had them at the door of his own, but, I don't know. Did he? It's like they just disappeared.'

With no explanation offered, all Dylan can do is wonder, and try to ignore the fact that his time on the case is running out.

He oversaw a set of medical trials that may or may not be connected with the deaths of some subjects, on top of which he has a sexual harassment suit pending. This would be where the red tape comes in. Any inquiries regarding his legal problems are to be directed to the companies solicitors and any new accusations tend to be met with pre-emptive lawsuits, slander, unfounded evidence, that kind of thing.' Dylan pinched the bridge of his nose and said forebodingly, 'And so on, and so forth…'

'We shouldn't be here…'

They were parked in the underground lot of the inner city building when they felt the weight of the corporation baring down on them.

'Our bosses certainly won't be happy. I have a back door into his office. I don't know how well it'll go down,' Dylan said. 'An unpaid parking ticket. Of all the suits against him, this one slipped through the net. Well, we can get up to his secretaries desk with it anyway. Maybe into his office if we're lucky.'

'He's not going to admit anything.'

'What time is it?' Dylan asked, irritated with the man's cynicism.

'Threeish.'

'I'm just covering all the bases,' he explained, unbuckling his seat belt. 'Is he involved with all of this? I don't know. Maybe he has a shady associate he'd like to direct us to. Maybe his secretary knows something about him. Maybe he's a mad man and is waiting for an excuse to admit he likes killing. People are people. They do all kinds of things for all kinds of reasons. Usually for the wrong ones. I just emit the pings and wait for them to bounce back. You can wait in the car if you like. I'll be back by three-thirty.'

There was no mistaking it, he was offering Agent Myers a chance to save his own skin, letting him know that this wouldn't be the best career move of his life. But Agent Myers, to Dylan's surprise, just smirked at the get out of jail free card he was being handed and threw it out the window.

'It sounds fun. I'd like to meet him.'

'Don't introduce yourself unless they ask. I'll do the talking. Hopefully you won't have to say your name.'

He gave Agent Myers another breath to reconsider the decision, and finally nodded, resigned to having the social agent in tow.

They would storm the castle together. Like battle hungry grunts, they emerged from the car and after an elevator ride, some confused directions through the labyrinthine building, constructed as if to keep only an elect few comfortable within its walls, they were sat outside Doctor Evans' office patiently waiting by the rude medical clerk to find out if they'd be let in. The fanfare they imagined accompanying their charge was all but gone. Half an hour went by and their attack on the keep seemed to be more a case of holding it under siege. They had nothing to say to each other, cautious as they were of the clerks ears. Agent Myers thumbed through the stack of medical magazines. The door to the doctor's office remained shut, and another forty minutes disappeared. Just as Dylan was about to ask how much longer they'd have to wait, the clerk's phone rang. It had been an hour and a half. She remained silent as she held the phone to her ear, choosing a spot just behind Dylan's head to focus on as she listened to a lengthy monologue. The detective squirmed to move out of her sight. Only then did she really notice him. Seizing a gap between the voice's sentences to inform it that the two policemen were still outside, in a piercing mousey squeak she explained specifically that they wanted to talk to him about an unpaid parking ticket. The laugh that came from the speaker was so loud the clerk had to hold the phone away from her ear. Dylan's teeth were about to crack. Noticing this, the clerk suppressed a smirk as she told them to head in. Agent Myers thanked her graciously, and Dylan grunted, happy to ignore her as he leered through the door.

 Doctor Evans was standing at his chair as they entered. 'Gentlemen,' his hand sprung forward to meet them as they reached his desk. 'Our lawyers won't be happy I let you in, for, what was it? A parking ticket. I couldn't help myself. I'm starved for entertainment.'

 Crisp in his reply, Dylan took a seat when it was offered. Agent Myers, following his lead, went one step further and reached to take a mint from the bowl on the desk. 'I thought doctors were supposed to have lollipops.'

 Dylan had wanted to elbow him.

 Ignoring the social agent now, he peers across the barren expanse and sends a humble message to the doctor. 'This is a little embarrassing. I shouldn't really be here, for a parking ticket of all things. But I saw your name and the company you work for, and I thought, well if anybody can help me out here, it'd be you.

'My young fella's working on a science project, you know,' he taps on his pad and flicks an image over to Doctor Evans' screen. It's the chemical make-up of the drug that killed Agent Mullen. 'And it got us really stumped. Maybe you could tell me what it is?'

Doctor Evans stares at the policeman, studying him like a cadaver. 'I'm not a chemist. My job mostly entails quantifying the side effects of drugs we test, making sure nobody gets hurt.'

'I'm sure you're very good at protecting the interests of your volunteers,' Dylan says, 'but maybe you've seen something like it? My young fella you know, he's real smart. We found this pill on the side of the street, near a playground actually, and it didn't look like a painkiller to me. I thought maybe it could be something bad, figured I'd bin it, but the lad, he's a real curious type and I'm always trying to find new ways to encourage him, so I tell him about our crime lab, how I could take him with me while we go get it tested. Well, you can imagine how stupid I felt when the lab guys couldn't tell us what it was. I mean, there goes my lad's interest in science. Not very impressive showing him how men in white coats are as dopey as we are. If I don't get some kind of an answer he's more than likely going to become a lawyer – touch wood...'

Amused, Doctor Evans says, 'I see.'

'So I was thinking maybe some smart guy who hasn't paid his parking tickets would be able to help me out here. Renew my young fella's faith in science. God knows I can't get him to mass.'

As the doctor's hand makes a fist, only a knuckle moves, rising and falling in place, a piston in the machine. He swipes the image off his screen. 'Like I said, I wouldn't know about these things. I'm just a low level supervisor, really.'

The chair's black leather squeaks to contradict his claim. The office is the size of a throne room. The furnishings around them are sparse in the echoing chamber, the assorted pieces of art that cover the walls have been chosen for their price rather than any aesthetic value, and the window, an indicator of prestige in and of itself, reveals the prime location SimperP occupies. Hazy and grey through the downpour, central bank isn't too far off.

'Assuming this,' Dylan ignores the doctor's claim to ignorance, 'Assuming it was a drug that came from here, it'd be mighty bad for it to just be found on the side of the street. I mean, someone would have had to have lost it.

People get fired for things like that. Or worse. I'd expect there'd be an internal investigation into the matter.'

And the doctor, visibly digesting the thought, salivates. Though Dylan wouldn't be surprised to learn that the doctor's mouth is actually watering, for all the surface movement it would seem he's just talking to an amiable wall. Letting a crack appear on his countenance, in a somewhat teasing, somewhat warning manner, the doctor comments, 'I'm sure there's worse places it could be found. You wouldn't want to find out that your son, for example, had swallowed it.'

Agent Myers, who has been sitting quietly up to now, shifts in his chair, stealing a sly look at Dylan. There isn't much of a reaction to see.

'So you're saying that it's dangerous?' Dylan asks, glossing over the vague threat in the hopes of entrapping the doctor.

And Agent Myers, barely twitching this time, shifts his attention back to the doctor, who grins at the attempt.

'It's unidentified, or so you tell me. I wouldn't want any unidentified pill making its way into the hands of a child.'

'Ah,' Dylan says, understanding displayed on his face. 'I see what you mean.'

'I'm sure that you'll be filing a report on its discovery soon enough. When you do you'll know if it's registered to us or not. Like you said, it's a serious matter. If you want you could let me keep this on file and I'll let our legal team know we might need to look into it soon.'

'Oh, I wouldn't trouble yourself,' Dylan says, rising to stand over the man, who somehow manages to cut an imposing presence from his seated position. 'I'm sure our lab people have already been in touch with your lab people.'

'But you decided to make a trip down here anyway,' Doctor Evans leads.

'The parking ticket. This is a second notification for the late fee,' Dylan flicks the warning from his pad onto the doctor's screen. 'I wouldn't put that one on the waiting pile. These kinds of things can add up, put a blight on your record. I'm sure you wouldn't want that.'

'Thank you, officer...'

'Wong. Detective Wong. It was my pleasure.'

'And the man who wanted a lollipop...?'

Taking a step away, Dylan tries to save the social agent from revealing himself, but finds that the effort is sabotaged.

'Agent Myers, UPD services. Your co-operation's appreciated.'

Ready to grab Myers by the ear and drag him out to the car, Dylan makes sure to keep his hands pocketed, hiding the tight fists they've become. To his amazement the man continues to talk, seemingly enjoying his exchange with the doctor.

'Nice watch,' the social agent comments as he grips the doctor's hand.

'Thank you,' Doctor Evans says. Surprised by the compliment, he admires the black-silver piece, confused as to how it got there. 'It was a gift.'

For the first time, Dylan notices how nicely dressed his colleague is. Though the doctor's suit is grey and the social agent's brown, the difference in quality is negligible. For his part, the detective is draped in a wrinkled outfit, like he's just rolled out of bed and wrapped himself in the bunched blankets. Above his lip an unshaved patch grows which his wife would say makes him look like a catfish.

'We'll let you get on with your day.'

Dylan's positioned himself to steal that glance at the workbook which the doctor was using when they arrived. It doesn't appear to hold anything of interest. It's only a patient file with a few words and sentences scribbled out. On closer inspection though, it isn't for the doctor's work that items have been censored. The rows of information are scratched out to create some kind of found poetry. Names and adjectives have been altered to look like vulgar outbursts such as – The B_Ear f__ucks Jane's____face – and – Shred_them all__and start again.

The sight of it has disturbed a dormant inkling in the detective. It's like he's seen the man naked. Behind the corporation's name, through its security, past the clerk's desk, resting among the trappings of success in this private chamber, under the title and inside the suit, is a man who makes ridiculous profanities of the people in his care. Is everything between that fact and Dylan just an illusion? This guy Alistair Evans seems to have just walked in off the street unnoticed, through the walls like they didn't exist, and into this position where nobody can question him. Could Dylan have done as much? The building feels real to him.

It's certainly giving him a fine view of the drenched city. If he tried walking through the office door without opening it he'd more than likely get a bump on the nose, and making his way back to the car he'll have to wander through the same labyrinth he came through. Nonplussed, he mumbles, 'You're not exactly dealing with a full deck, are you Doctor Evans?'

'Excuse me?' the doctor asks, not sure if he should be offended.

Dylan, taking a stab in the dark, is hoping to catch a tell, 'You're missing a card.'

But all the doctor reveals is puzzlement, followed by the understanding that he's just been tested somehow. It's left at that, until at the door of the office, he abruptly calls to the men as if he's only now remembered his manners.

'Detective Wong. It's raining cats and dogs. I could find you an umbrella.'

'We're in the car park,' Dylan says.

'Of course,' the doctor says. 'Don't get lost on your way out.'

•

'Untouched,' Dylan declares, happy to be back in the safety of his car. 'I don't know if he had anything to do with anything, but that guy is a billboard for the disorder. Jesus, a doctor. You think there's a lot of them working in the field?' Dylan pauses, then thinks to ask Agent Myers for confirmation rather than just assuming, 'He's untouched right?'

Agent Myers groans in thought, 'They're about as common as you'd imagine in the medical profession. I don't know the specifics. It's not an area we'll be processing.'

'You'd think they'd be first on the list.'

'Every section that is prescribed testing involve activities that directly affect public wellbeing. I was surprised the media got put so high on it. But well, doctors. There's certain jobs where it can't hurt to have a cool head. Do you want a surgeon who worries about every cut he's going to make or the one who doesn't doubt himself?'

'Oh I'm sure the UPD one is just fine when it suits him,' Dylan says pointedly. 'Who decides what professions get processed? I don't remember having a vote.'

Disinterested, Agent Myers says, 'UPD services have committees for that kind of thing.'

'And who decides who goes on the committees? Santa Claus?'

They're about done for the day when they get a call from Dylan's boss, angry at them for approaching Alistair. Word travels fast at the top.

'So maybe he had something to do with it?'

'Who knows. People can't afford implications and big money can pay them away.'

'Another wasted hour.'

Dylan doesn't agree. He's finding numbers for dots and hoping they match up. When it's drawn the numbers should make a circle around the dead body of Agent Mullen. In his head he has Doctor Evans as a one and Joanne as a two, but when he draws the line it's going at an odd angle, not a circle at all.

Distracted by a thought, Agent Myers backtracks and offers, 'You know where they're really common? Restaurants. If we had to test chefs you'd never want to eat out again.'

Troubled, Dylan tries to resist asking what he wants to. The words drip from his mouth like sizzling droplets of acid. 'What about cops?'

'Cops,' Agent Myers hisses. 'If we had to test the Gards we'd lose half the police force in Dublin.' The social agent directs the detective a pensive grimace. 'Come on man, it's no biggie. It's just a disability that isn't compatible with certain jobs. So there's a few asshole cops out there. You don't need a disorder classification to know that.'

'Right,' Dylan says, just wanting to end that line of thought. If he were to follow it to its conclusion it would lead to a nightmare. The gears in his head turn regardless. Fifteen years serving with the Garda and he'd seen enough seedy behaviour from his fellow officers to know as much. Even among them though, were lines that weren't to be crossed. He didn't like it, but there were people in cells who demanded thumps to the back of the head and plenty of men and women who were only too happy to deliver them. He'd known of suspects beaten unconscious. He might even have been privy to looking the other way. It was a part of the job. Anybody who volunteered to be a policeman was putting themselves on the line every night they went out. The risks they took, it meant you forgave the guy next to you for losing it sometimes.

You'd want him to do the same for you. Institutional cover up, he supposed the press would call it. It's what happens when a group with any kind of power have to protect themselves. But what of the UPD among them, invoking friendship that didn't really exist? Worse, he'd heard enough stories of officers who brought their work home with them to know that it was less than unusual. And he'd been close to it himself, bringing the work home. He sniffs, nauseated by the euphemism. He can feel his hand shaking on the wheel of the car, and when enough time has passed he rallies up the courage he needs to ask the social agent a question that's been troubling him all along.

'Do people ever volunteer for the UPD scan?'

'More than you'd think,' Agent Myers assures him. 'People worry about themselves too much. The country's drowning in guilt. Must be an Irish thing. They've got to go somewhere since the confession boxes went out of service. Why? Did you do something wrong?'

The detective slams his hand down on the horn, growing angry at an automatic taxi, which for no apparent reason, sails to cut him off.

'If I did,' he says, 'I certainly wouldn't tell you.'

19

The car comes to a reluctant stop under the uncompromising instruction of a traffic light. Dylan could have driven through it. The evening road is empty. Instead he sits. There's a message from his wife asking if she should get started on making dinner and he's holding his phone to type a response. Letting the engine rumble quietly, he watches a long exhalation from his mouth fog the damp glass. Droplets of condensation are finding staggered trails down the windscreen, catching pieces of red light as they go. It takes a conscious effort on his part to tell his wife that he'll be late getting home. How late? she asks. The windscreen wipers swipe across his vision twenty or thirty times until he replies with an apologetic – I'll let you know when I know – but the tone of his regret is lost in the message. Realising this, he quickly sends another – Love you – and holds his breath in anticipation of a response, dizzy before he understands that he won't be getting one.

In his rear view mirror he sees a Kinder Egg toy dropped among the crumbs of an empty Tayto packet, then, noticing the red droplets changed to green sometime ago, he pushes forward. I'll be home to put him to bed. Leaving the thought behind, he concentrates on the case once more, going over the steps in the process he has covered thus far.

During the office interviews, Agent Myers kept a tablet with him, supposedly to use the opportunity to examine the personality types, but he had spent the time fidgeting, bored within minutes. Dylan didn't need to ask why.

When the scans begin none of what they discovered will matter to the agent. The office too, for the most part, seemed to be comforted by the fact. After all, they won't need to get mixed up in anything distasteful if the killer is found by a simple test of the brain. Nobody feels the pressure of that eventuality but the detective. The scan isn't for finding killers and nobody seems to appreciate the matter but him. As he went through the list of employees, finding no information of note, he happened across one last avenue to explore. Susan, a bright redhead in her employee photo, had been fired when Agent Mullen was processing the office. On questioning the editor about this she could barely bring an image of the girl to mind. Nobody in the newsroom seemed to have more than the vaguest idea of who she was. This nobody, who barely merited a thought as far as her colleagues were concerned, was Dylan's last, best hope of finding a motive for the murder. With this weighing him down, he'd said goodbye to Agent Myers for the day and drove against the evening traffic to find her.

Having parked between a bin and bent lamp post, he hears the car beep-beep goodbye as he sprints across road, his shoulders hunched to keep the now lashing rain from running down his neck. Stalling under the shelter of a shop's awning, he sees the girl's apartment building, another run down town house on the edge of the city. As he makes a dash for the door, it opens and a woman wrestles a buggy and her child through.

'This is a storm,' she says, tightening a hood.

The floor is cold cement, as are the stairs. Looking up the winding case when he's at the bottom, Dylan stomps up the steps two at a time and finds himself staring down the spiral as he reaches the top. Out of breath, his knocks on the door of the flat bounce through the corridor. From the sound of them he guesses that nobody is home. He pounds harder, annoyed at the absent room for wasting his time. He has pissed off his wife to meet a girl who probably doesn't know anything and who doesn't even seem to be at home. His response to this is a miserable chuckle. Time goes by, nothing to mark it. He feels wetter for having nowhere to dry off and ruffles his cropped hair to keep the water from dripping down his forehead. By the time his breath is steady nobody has come to the door.

He should go home.

But for all intents and purposes his investigation will be inconsequential if a UPD is found. He needs to take advantage of the time he has. Groaning, he slides down the wall to sit on the stairs, a wet patch streaked on the plaster in his wake. Phone in hand, he considers messaging his wife, then decides to wait twenty minutes or so. Maybe it won't be long till the occupant's return, but twenty becomes thirty, thirty an hour, and an hour, well, it's too late to send her anything appeasing by that stage. He spends the protracted period playing games on his phone and remembers a packet of peanuts in his pocket. As he pats the last of them into his mouth and throws the empty pack over the banister, a muffled complaint sounds from downstairs and he notices the footsteps of two people sound out. Brushing himself off, he regains his composure just as the couple slow at seeing him stand.

'Susan?' he asks.

The couple don't respond, surprised by his presence.

The man speaks for them both, 'Who's asking?'

'I'm Merriam,' the woman says, an irritated tone directed at her friend.

'That's right,' Dylan says, remembering that Susan was a redhead in the employee file. 'I'm Detective Dylan Wong,' he flashes his ID. 'I'm looking for Susan Ward. I haven't been able to get through to her and I understand she lives here.'

'I guess she does,' the girl purses her lips. 'You would have had better luck a few days ago. I haven't seen her in about a week.'

'What's this about?' The man inquires, clearly annoyed at the girl for volunteering information so readily.

Dylan ignores him and talks to the girl. 'She's not in any trouble, but she might have some information pertaining to an investigation I'm involved with. How was she acting last time you saw her?'

'Acting?' the girl asks herself. 'She was annoyed about work. She always was though. Seems like a shite job to me. Nobody ever listened to her, she said. Except, ah, you know Ava O'Dwyer? She was starting to stick up for. Helping her get traction in the office. I guess it wasn't enough. She was talking about visiting her brother in the States. I kind of got the impression I'd need a new roommate lined up soon. She wasn't very happy.'

'Ava,' Dylan says, noting the friendship. 'Any specific idea of what might have got to her in the end? Something that would have given Susan the final push to leave the country?'

The girl shakes her head. 'They fired her by email. Maybe she thought she deserved better.'

'And you really think she'd just take off?'

'Wouldn't surprise me. She left some stuff in her room but her laptop and a bunch of clothes are gone. Her rent's paid up to the end of the month but there's only what? Three days left in it now? She won't get her deposit back that's for sure,' the girl says, almost gloating.

Dylan shifts on his feet. 'She'd leave you in a lurch like that? Having to find a roommate to make rent?'

The guy laughs and the girl elbows his side.

'We weren't exactly best friends.'

'And you?' Dylan asks the man.

'We, eh, dated briefly.'

The man's hand is holding the girls tightly. Dylan understands from it all the drama that might have led to Susan Ward abandoning her flat. 'Ah. Well, if she gets in touch, have her contact me. She could be very helpful,' he flicks his number to them. 'Thanks for your time.'

Jogging through the rain, his feet splash and scatter the orange streetlight a hundred different directions. The car beep-beeps to welcome him back and he jumps into the driver seat. Water is washing over the glass and he finds himself saying a word out loud.

'People.'

If that guy hadn't cheated on Susan he might have been talking to her now. More than that, maybe she could have told him something he needed to hear. He might have found out about her pushing the doctor's story in the office. About Ava's promise to champion her cause only to bury it. Lost in the dark he can only make guesses. It's because of this he'll be observing a computer test that tells him something he doesn't need to know, but which everyone else insists is imperative.

When he gets home, the lights are off in the house, and he wonders what time it is. It feels like midnight but it's probably later. He pushes his key in the lock and lets the door drift open, paces into the hall and shakes himself off. There's a towel draped on the stairs which he wipes his face with as he saunters into the kitchen where he finds a sandwich prepared.

Then, walking into the sitting room, he sees his bed for the night. His wife has made the couch up for him. The message couldn't be more clear – how nice for them life could be, and how bad things really are. Their future is in his hands.

Losing his appetite, he leaves the sandwich on the coffee table, peels his clothes off, the wet socks doing their best to cling to him, and slides under a blanket, yelping as he feels a sharp poke against his legs. It's the corner of a toy. Picking it up he's tempted to break it in his hand. Instead, a current of malaise pulls him under and he turns into the couch, curling up, trying to find relief that isn't there.

Fired over email, cheated on by a friend, and left the country without a goodbye. Some people, Dylan wonders at them all. The things they do.

•

As far from each other as the buildings they occupy, connected only by the length of fibre optic cable they're channelled through, a pair of disembodied voices speak. With no faces to accent their emotions, the language being sent over the line is just that, packets of thought to be registered, analysed, and responded to. The first distracted sounds are Ava's who, painting her toenails, is having to wedge the phone between her shoulder and ear. 'You've caught me at an awkward time.'

She's talking to Alistair. The man is spitting venom. 'Considering what happened to me today, you're lucky I've only caught you by phone.' After the detectives visit, he'd abandoned caution and sped to her apartment only to find that, besides not answering his calls, she wasn't at home. Spurred by the death of Francis Mullen, people throughout Dublin were locking themselves in and here he was scrambling from one end of the city to the next only to find a dead end. He'd contemplated kicking in the door and waiting for her in an armchair. Hands suspiciously covered by leather gloves, he would remove the things on her sighting of them. All he wanted was for her to understand how angry he was – not with the detective's prodding him, but at her ignoring it, essentially putting him into isolation until he was less of a contaminant. In the end, he'd stood there in her corridor, chagrined, aware that a broken door would hardly go unnoticed. Much to his regret, lock picking was not one of his clandestine talents. 'I should have made another visit to your office.'

That's a threat.

'You're not the brightest, are you Alistair?' Ava asks, sedate. 'We shouldn't even be talking. If I was in my right mind I'd hang up.'

'Well why don't you?' he challenges.

'Alright...'

'You clearly don't want to talk about it. No interest whatsoever as to why a homicide detective might have visited me, in work no less, under my secretary's nose.'

'I thought you'd be able to take a hint.'

There's a long pause in the dark as he struggles to understand what she might be suggesting. Her tone flat, it gives him little indication. 'What do you mean?'

'What I mean, Alistair, is I don't want to talk. I mean that I'm annoyed I have to spell it out for you. I don't want any links existing between us. The past is a thing best forgotten. I thought you knew that. Let's both of us just concentrate on our respective futures, uncertain as they are.'

The allusion to the investigation and what it could mean for them, though it's what he's wanted to talk about all day, and certainly has a huge baring over how the rest of his life will unfold, is of no interest to him now.

'You're dumping me?'

Impatient, she corrects him, 'Dumped, Doctor Evans! Past participle. It's already happened, you just haven't figured it out.'

'You can't dump me.'

'All evidence to the contrary?'

'What are you talking about?'

'Alistair, please,' she stops, expecting him to understand that he's embarrassing himself, but finds that she needs to spell it out. 'Haven't you noticed that the weather has changed? Let's say you were summer wear and now I'm on the lookout for something more current. I'm hardly an appropriate fit for you at the moment either. I don't know why you're making such a fuss about it. Is it the ChatterFive access you'll miss? I'll still do a write up on you in a few months if it means you'll leave me alone.'

Enjoying the banter, and having him squirm under foot, Ava is still hoping that he'll agree with her reasoning without putting up much of a struggle.

She bites her lip as she awaits his reply, concentrating on the wet brush that runs over her little toe. Satisfied, she examines the results.

'You think I don't know what happened?'

That's another threat.

Without allowing time for the implication to sink in, she replies, 'You don't know anything, Alistair, you weren't there. Don't let your imagination get to you. I'm sure you know better than to spout ignorance, which could put us both in a tight spot, over the phone. Why is it anytime I dump a guy they go crazy? Other people manage to have amicable breakups, don't they? Is it just me? How do I meet you loonies?'

'You're not dealing with a full deck,' he spits.

To the doctor's surprise she takes a hit from the comment. Even without a face to see, he can sense her attention leave her toenails and go to a point outside her window.

'Excuse me?'

Hesitant, he tries to push forward, but afraid of losing his advantage, he elaborates, 'You're missing a card.'

Ava is heard smiling, seemingly understanding where he might have picked up the phrase. 'That Wong guy really got to you. Is that all he was looking for? A card?'

Alistair doesn't know what to make of her response. His comment, meant to ridicule, was one picked up from the detective. There's nothing particularly revealing about it. Clearly, Ava has demonstrated otherwise. Somehow she managed to make the connection, and now, with his silence he's confirmed it for her. Glum, he gives up on imagining what it might mean and tries steering the conversation back into territory he can control. 'Among other things, Ava. Anyway, you're missing the point of all this.'

'Oh?'

'Your life is in my hands.'

Clicking her tongue, she goes back to painting her toenails. 'And yours in mine, Doctor Evans…'

Alistair's dumb response is taken as evidence that he doesn't know what she's implying.

'Listen, do you think I wanted it to end between us? Like this?

At the instigation of other people's problems? It frustrates me too. I've never been so angry. But it would be silly to pretend there's another option. All of this drama in the office is seriously becoming a chore, but I'm taking it in my stride. So, before you go and have one of your hissy fits, take my reaction as an example of appropriate behaviour and remember, if one of us goes down, so does the other. You can't hurt me without hurting yourself.'

'Mutually assured destruction,' he sneers.

'That's right.'

'You really are untouched.'

Stillness on her end of the line betrays her concern. It's the only thing he's said that worries her. 'You know I used to be so good at making people laugh, Alistair. You wouldn't believe it, would you? When I was a kid, that was me, the class clown. I'm not really into jokes, but people are just so easy to tickle…' Up to this point, everything Ava said was something for Alistair to compete with, now though, she sounds almost human to him, something to be granted empathy. If he was in the same room as the woman, Alistair might see her mind's eye go inward in search of answers about herself. Coming up with nothing though, she's provoked back to reality. 'Then I got older, and well, who needs to be funny when you're beautiful, right?'

'You're not all that special,' Alistair jabs at her childishly. 'Why are you telling me this sob story? If you've dumped me I shouldn't have to listen to this stuff.'

Not hearing him, she mumbles, 'The whole office is being scanned tomorrow.'

'The newsroom?'

'Yeah.'

'But if you get tested and they say you're UPD…'

'Mhmm,' she sing-songs. 'It will all connect back to you.'

Digesting the fact that his interests are on the line tomorrow, the first thing that occurs to him is to return to her apartment and cut off the head that might be scanned. The only thing he's unsure of in this plan is whether or not a severed brain can be analysed as UPD, though the concern is quickly dismissed as he decides that it can't be that hard to hide a head, after all, it's not like he'd have to get rid of the whole body.

A sports bag and a brick would be enough to sink it in the canal.

Reading his mind, Ava takes some pride in revealing that she predicted such a reaction, 'I'm not so stupid as to stay in my own place tonight, Alistair. I had a nice massage earlier and I'm about to order room service. You could ring around Dublin searching all the hotels, but it's not likely that I checked in under my own name. I suggest you just wait with the rest of us and see what happens. I don't like it anymore than you do, but this is where we're at.'

Taking this roundhouse punch, the doctor is left seeing stars.

'You can keep the watch Alistair, I'm sure you'll do well with it.'

Disconcerted, he falters backward. The future is out of his control, but surely the present is still within his grasp. 'You can't dump me!' he shouts, panicked, 'I decide when it's over! You think a message is enough to end it? We have a connection! It's special! If you don't think so, I'll make you! You know I can, you know what I can do! You've heard about the people I've killed. I've done more than that. And I can do a lot more. I know what happened! Don't think I can't make life hard for you, Ava, I can do very bad things when I'm angry, you'll be lucky if I don't cut your face off after this, run a knife into your spine, I can do it, and more, you have no idea–'

'Alistair,' Ava says, taking pause at the outburst. The words spilled from him with such ease it's as if he's been nourishing them from the start, that all this time she has merely been distracting him from the desire and that truly his secret joy would be to revel in slowly killing her. 'I've recorded everything you said. Leave me alone or I'll have it find its way into the open.'

'You little snitching cunt! That's not going to stop me doing whatever I fucking want! I'll rip your throat out of your neck, Ava, you bitch, I'll, I'll–' He goes on for a while longer, until after a time it's apparent that she hung up some while ago and that he's been attempting to terrorise a dial tone. Like a dog barking at the moon, nothing has been accomplished but his own ego reassured. She's frightened of me, he tells himself, that's why she's hiding. Well, to hell with her. Tomorrow everyone in her office will be scanned, and not a single soul, least of all Ava O'Dwyer, can escape it.

20

On arriving at work, the dishevelled journalists discovered that the office they knew, while unaltered from the day previous, was now an altogether different environment, one in which amnesty was in short supply. In sharp morning light, the fetid sentiment grew – the newsroom was no longer their own. Agent Myers had set up the hardware for UPD scanning in the conference room. A laptop, a hand sized pad, and box of disposable attachments made up his inventory. Nobody had seen anything that looked like electric shock equipment, but it was in there – somewhere – and none of them were thrilled with the idea. Agent Myers, seen now through the glass, is pacing, on call with somebody, snickering, then stoic as he arranges himself at the laptop, puts on a theatrical air. In other workplaces he had processed, the social agent could always depend on complete privacy in the hours leading up to a scan shift, to the point that even with an open door, nobody would poke their head in with transparent excuses such that they were looking for papers, lost pens of sentimental worth, or even a water cooler they knew very well was by the main entrance. But Agent Myers has never operated in a newsroom and in the time he has taken to prep, all of these things have happened, one after another, like children taking turns to peep into a haunted house, they tiptoed around him and legged it off in nervous excitement. The urgent reports they brought back were confirmations that they have been invaded, and all of their remarks, spread in a game of Chinese whispers, trickled their way to Joanne, who, a nervous wreck in her office, is in danger of dying of a nicotine overdose.

Clad in a black blazer, she's dressed for a funeral, expecting it's going to be herself toppled into the grave being dug.

'This must be a relief for you at least,' Ava warms up to Detective Wong.

'How do you mean?' he smiles in spite of himself.

'I'd expect it takes some of the pressure off.'

Just the opposite, he thinks. 'You seem more relaxed yourself.'

'It should sort out a few things, shouldn't it? I don't know why we couldn't have just skipped to the scan in the first place. It would have saved us all the bother.'

Tiredly deciding to indulge her, Dylan explains, 'Invasion of privacy. Probable cause is needed. The results of personality tests are generally the means of attaining it. Things having panned out the way they have, well–' he shrugs, jaded at calling to mind the death of Agent Mullen to justify all that is to happen. 'You wouldn't let somebody strut into your house without a warrant and sit by as they inspect your living arrangements. Why let them into your brain?' They stand for a time, watching the social agent, and pass no comment on the elaborate process in which he shows such flourish. When they lose interest in the act, Dylan remembers he had something to quiz Ava about. Scratching the spidery stubble under his nose, he asks, 'I don't suppose you thought Susan Ward had anything against Agent Mullen?'

'Who?' Ava pouts in an attempt to recollect.

'She was let go. I heard you two were close.'

'An intern, I suppose. You do a favour for one of these kids and they never forget it. I couldn't guess how many of them think I'm going to help them hit the big time,' Ava smirks, and brightened, she brushes the detective's arm. 'I've been so glad you're here during all of this. You've covered every detail, it's been a pleasure to watch. Everything was such a mess until your arrival. We should have a chat when it's all over. Get acquainted under more convivial circumstances.'

The invitation is hardly one he can miss, however understated her phrasing might be. Normally, Dylan would know to back away from such a suggestion, it's just that he has been spending a lot of time on the family couch of late, and her bed is probably a lot more comfortable… Silly thoughts. If nothing else though, he's grateful for the distraction.

'Maybe,' he says, putting off the decision for now.

'To be continued,' she says and strolls her editor's direction.

Titillated, Dylan can't help thinking what an unusual woman she is. Placidly observant, she seems set on registering the subdued nervousness simmering in the room. If he was to choose a word to describe her mood, he'd probably settle on exhilarated, but then everybody is on edge in one way or another. He doesn't have to go far in search of the reason. The obvious explanation is the imminent scanning process to which they'll be submitted. What seems to separate her from the rest though, is an awareness of the key change which has crystallised today. The detective who once dominated the investigation, is now sitting dejected in a chair by the break room as Agent Myers takes lead. Dylan is finished. The picture he'd managed to draw in the short time he was allotted featured a plethora of suspects but even more dead ends. Barry Danger's warning blooms freshly in the detective's memory: I wouldn't put it past anyone in here. Not a single person had been ruled out, and in a job where most of the work is eliminating possibilities, this left him with nothing but the unconfirmed sighting of Joanne at Agent Mullen's flat in the days before he died. If Dylan had a day or two more he would happily pull at that loose thread if only to cross her off his list. Such luxury is not allowed the modern policeman. The word had come down: Let Agent Myers do his work in peace. Dylan tossed and turned throughout the night, frantically putting together theories until, disgusted – it all stank of the conspiracy theory of a lunatic – he forced himself to close his eyes, and if not sleep, at least stop thinking. He is exhausted. Lost in the folds of the case, it is going to be down to a computer and the man who operates it to tell them who to put on trial. When the suggestion from his department chief arrived on his phone, that the ball was in the UPD services' court, he took it for the order it was. His presence in the office today is a joke, and he would have skipped it altogether if only for the insistence of his superior. The Garda are still in charge of this case, is the message Detective Wong is to send. Like a toothless old lion's roar, it seems more like a yawn.

In this spirit, Dylan has been accompanied by four low ranking police officers. Presently, two of them are escorting Barry to the conference room. The gawky English journalist is the first to be tested.

Agent Myers is standing at the door to offer a welcoming hand into the room. As he gets frisked for weapons, Barry is short on things to say for once, his face even becoming obscenely flushed as the office watches. To disguise his embarrassment, when the Garda nod that he's clean and Agent Myers allows him entry, he jerks around and shouts, 'My Dad always said I needed electro shock therapy. I'll get him to turn it up to eleven!'

Dylan finds himself giving the journalist an automatic smile as he's ushered away. He questions himself afterward why he did that, like Barry had pushed a button and triggered the gesture, but doesn't brood on it long. Instead, he becomes distracted by a confused group of firemen that peter through the door. At the head of the group, one man grips an axe, prepared for an emergency that doesn't yet exist. In a quiet lull, the office takes pause to note the addition to their already surreal day. Dumbfounded, they return to their work, effected only for the seconds it takes them to clock each other's reactions. Dylan is the lone person compelled to ask why the fire fighters have arrived. Sidling over, he shows them his ID.

'You guys a little lost?'

'You tell me,' the swarthy man, gripping his axe a little tighter, suspects he's the butt end of a prank. 'We got a call from your department saying we might be needed.'

'Needed for what?' Dylan asks the general gathering, and shakes his head in exasperation when he doesn't get an answer. He can imagine the panicked messages between his boss and other desk jockeys that ended with a call for the presence of firemen at a series of brain scans. Only in Dublin. The lead fireman, equally irritated, twitches a mouth just barely visible under his greying moustache as he awaits instruction. 'Make yourselves at home. We're doing some UPD processing.'

'Why are there so many of you guys? And what's with the paramedics outside?'

Preoccupied, the detective mutters, 'I guess they think there might be more than one person to arrest.'

The banter provides some respite from the tension, but it forms again in a minute as the firemen's heads all go to the impenetrable door Dylan gestured to, behind which Agent Myers is testing Barry, that sad laughing clown, and where they half expect the shrill screams of a tortured man to sound out.

Huddled together, small in their baggy overcoats and bulky helmets, the firemen look like children playing dress-up in daddy's work clothes. When nothing happens, they return their attention to the detective who sidles over to his seat. With a staff of suspect journalists pretending to work and a couple of bored street cops stood about, Dylan waits, his attention dully focused on the conference room from where fates are doled.

Set on the cubicle in front of him, a Bobblehead Barry peers down.

Joanne and Ava are stood outside her office, their backs against the wall. The editor is chain smoking and blinking at Ava's words, who in a business suit and minimal make up, is evidently taking things very seriously as they watch the room Barry entered. In there, Joanne sees a nightmare. In there, Ava sees just another box, holding another man.

'If he isn't untouched, I can't be either. What if I am though? That doesn't mean I did anything bad.'

'You're not untouched Joanne,' Ava assures her. 'Don't let the bigger case get to you. At the end of the day you're going to be walking back into your office to run ChatterFive.'

'Thanks darling.'

As Joanne rubs a smushed eyelash off her cheek, she locks eyes with Dylan and the detective salutes her, prompting her to jump like she's been caught with a gun in her hand, and dropping the imaginary weapon, she looks away. Ava gives the detective a good humoured purse of her lips and goes back to talking in her editor's ear. They're waiting for the lights to fade, a cry for help from Barry, anything to let them know something is happening in there. Dylan had read over the procedure last night and is only glad that it's not his job – though it might as well be at this stage. He feels like an obsolete cog in a very ugly machine. The pinch in his back makes it all the harder to bare. Arching in his seat, feeling a shooting pain go up his spine, he's sadly aware it's from his current sleeping arrangement. His home life bleeds into this work life like this, and his work life into his home. Today it's been for naught and, as if to highlight the matter, Barry returns.

Lost in thought, Dylan doesn't hear the door open. He notices the man's presence only when the rattled typing of the newsroom abruptly comes to a halt. The screen alerts fill the office with cautious anticipation and the Garda, startled by the Englishman, take wide stances at his appearance.

Barry raises his hands, mute in his surprise at being caught in the spotlight.

'I didn't do it.'

Agent Myers arrives behind him and nods to the officers.

'He's clear.'

There's a collective sigh of relief that's at once replaced by anxious mumbles – If he's clear what does that mean for us?

'That didn't take long,' Joanne grunts.

'Our man here is very efficient,' Barry pats Agent Myers on the shoulder. 'Gave me an STD test while we were at it.'

'Not so clear there,' Agent Myers chuckles.

As Barry wanders away from the door he looks at one of the young cops and lightly touches the fabric on his shirt. 'Zap!' he says. 'Full of beans after that,' and strolls away, ignoring the look of contempt on the Garda's face. Stopping at his desk, he notices the firemen and does a double take in the hopes that there's someone about who will share his amusement.

'Bloody hell,' he teases, 'you set the fire alarm off again, Ava?'

The joke flounders and Ava in particular ignores it.

Dylan though, almost puts his back out.

'Who wants to go next?' Agent Myers' face is plastered with a smarmy grin.

'I'll go,' says Ava.

Dylan's head swings her direction, penetrating what he once thought was the woman and now suspects is a mask. She gives Joanne a set of hurried goodbye kisses before her legs carry her away, hand smoothing her skirt as she goes. By the prowl in her step you'd think that she was a panther going to meet her prey.

'It can't be that bad if Barry's still laughing.'

'I'm a survivor,' Barry jeers. 'You'll be coming out of there in handcuffs.'

As she's being frisked down, Agent Myers, Joanne, Barry, everyone but Dylan in fact, politely look away. The detective is studying her, following every line of the body which the hands move over. She turns her head, sees him looking and displays her white gleaming teeth, pairing them with a wink when he doesn't smile back. The officer at her ankles stands up for Agent Myers to allow her into the conference room, and then, just as Dylan realises his mouth has been hanging open, the agent locks him out.

21

Ava, primly sat on a stool across the table from Agent Myers, chastises herself for forgetting the cup of coffee. Still, she says, 'Déjà vu.'

Agent Myers, prepping the software, does not turn from his screen.

'Excuse me?'

Two clicks and a rattle of typing. Ava waits for him to look up, using quiet to wrest his attention. The social agent, however, is not to be drawn, so she's forced to continue without a hold.

'Oh, just, it doesn't seem so long ago Agent Mullen was sitting on the other side of the desk. He only got a closet out of Joanne. You've got yourself the whole conference room.'

The friendly comment is read by Agent Myers as a respectful warning. Furrowing his brow, he concentrates on his work, clicking about the screen in front of him, making it clear that he can pick and choose the remarks he responds to and that he's the one in control. Ava accepts this with all the joy of someone sat waiting in a dentist's office, only it's worse, because there aren't any magazines to flick through as she anticipates the examination. To provoke a reaction, she sighs audibly. The agent looks up at her, taking his time to select what he wants to say.

'This is not like your interview with Agent Mullen. It's going to be a bit more invasive than that.'

'So I've heard,' says Ava. 'One step away from shock therapy?'

'Not quite,' he replies, his face shifting into a grin that says, 'Just you wait and see.'

The laptop is thin and sleek like most others and has a hand sized pad set beside it, linked wirelessly, for all appearances. Beside these two objects is a cardboard box containing smaller plastic packages. The setup holds no interest for Ava. Instead she allows herself a pass over the social agent's body, admiring the cut of him, the relaxed but confident way he holds himself, a man accustomed to being in this position of power. Francis, she remembers, always sat in his suit like it was a turtle shell. His pudgy head would poke out of the collar on a pencil-thin neck, the tie loosening throughout the day of its own accord. What a silly man he was, she goes sentimental, he couldn't even get his tie to do what he wanted. This social agent though has had his clothes tailored. Each piece of dress has been selected and refined to his own taste, knowing exactly his strong and weak points. She wonders how different things might have been if he had been the man investigating their newsroom in the first place. His tapping on the keyboard seems aimless to her. Resigned to the wait, one moment she absently checks for her phone and, remembering that she left it on her desk, the next she folds her arms on her lap and lets her eyes glaze over. Only when her mind has floated out the door does Agent Myers talk again, the hand sized pad in front of her humming now.

'I think we're all set.' Reaching into the box, he removes a plastic wrapper to hand her. 'Open one of these. They're sterilised and disposable, we can throw it away when we're done.'

Ava does as she's told and finds a dense putty substance small enough to be held in her fist. 'I'm not much of a sculptor.'

Agent Myers doesn't respond to the banter. Keeping a wall between them, he explains, 'It's for your mouth.'

Ava laughs but stops at his blank expression, though she keeps a distraught smile on her face. 'My mouth?'

At this the social agent launches into a short explanation of the scan. 'We're observing reactions in the brain. UPD have certain impairments in the orbitofrontal and ventrolateral cortex. I'll be measuring the responses to certain imagery as well as observing theta wave activity. I'm going to get you to place your hand on the pad and put that in your mouth to bite down on. Together they'll send information to the laptop which will create a detailed map of the brain and its reactions to the pictures that will be displayed on the screen to your right.

Not long ago we used to measure reactions based on more disturbing shots. Holocaust photos, gruesome deaths, explicit pornography, that kind of thing. I'd seen so many stupid horror films when I was a kid I don't know what effect they thought it could have had on me, but anyway, it's much more refined these days. You shouldn't be distressed at all. All you have to do is sit and look. It should only take a minute.'

Ava guffaws and squeezes the putty in her hand.

'Where does the electric shock come in?'

'The synthetic clay you're holding will release a slight electrical charge. Unless you have a lot of fillings you'll barely notice it.'

'I'm sure,' she says, doubting him as her tongue runs around her mouth.

'Shall we begin?' Agent Myers gestures to the putty. 'Place it carefully and bite down.'

Reluctant, she follows his instructions. Her lips only just touch as she closes her mouth, after which she feels a slight tingling sensation that numbs her tongue.

'Beautiful,' the social agent looks at his screen. 'Bite down a little harder, please.'

Ava clenches her jaw, annoyed at being put in this position. A round of electric shock treatment would have been preferable. Sitting here, being made a fool of, is more than she can take. Though Agent Myers has soundproofed the room and set the window to frosted, she feels like all her subordinates in the office know what position she's been put in. It doesn't help that they'll be going through the same thing. It's more humiliating for her because of her rank. This isn't something somebody with the term editor in their title should have to go through, even if it is preceded by the word assistant. She's sure she can hear them outside, finding excuses to walk by and steal looks at the door. The only thing stopping them standing with their ears up to it is an embarrassed sense of voyeurism. What's worse for her though, than the feeling of being humbled in front of these people in her moment of vulnerability, is now that she's been immobilised, so to speak, unable to comment in a coherent manner, Agent Myers has become chatty. Her face is charged with heat as he talks and she doesn't know if it's from her anger or the putty. Either way, the social agent ignores it as he launches into a monologue.

'It's ridiculous, I know. Funny how people react to it. I remember one guy I had, oh, years back, when we were only processing civil servants. He was sketchy as soon as he sat down. People get nervous, you know, untouched or not, nobody likes to be picked apart. God knows I didn't. Social agents get tested too. It'd be crazy if we didn't, wouldn't it? The guy who did me was a right nervous plonker, dropped the box of putty all over the place. Had to help him clean it up. Anyway, this civil servant I was processing, a social welfare operator, he hiccuped when I was about to start the process–' Agent Myers cuts himself off and clicks an alert on the laptop, the story brought to an abrupt halt as some feedback on the screen grabs his attention. Ava is only relieved that she doesn't have to listen to the rest of it until he speaks up again, chuckling. 'You don't need to bite down that hard. What was I saying? The guy hiccuped. Made a real show of it too. Swallowed a chunk of the synthetic clay and got it stuck in his throat. Actually choked on it, almost got himself killed. And once he coughed it up he was panting for a good ten minutes, had people bringing him cups of water, patting his face down with hankies. You should have seen him, hamming it up big time, going for the Oscar he was. And to top it off, what does he do? Starts pretending it set off some fictional heart problem. Sure we have medical histories on file. The man was fit as a fiddle. All of this nonsense to get out of the scan.' Agent Myers shakes his head in a pantomime reaction to the story. 'I don't stand for that. I didn't stand for it. We gave him a half hour to recover. Had some paramedics give him a clean bill of health. That's why we've got an ambulance here today actually. Types like that trying to waste time. Well, we went ahead with the scan anyway,' the social agent winks at her, making a show of the fact he's about to make a bad joke, 'so don't even try it.'

Ava waits for him to say if the guy turned out to be untouched or not, but she doesn't get an answer, and rolls her eyes, irritated at not being able to ask. Agent Myers reads her expression as a request to speed up the process.

'Yeah, you're right, let's get this started. Place your hand on the pad please.'

She does so.

'You'll feel a slight humming.'

In a puzzled moment, Ava doesn't feel anything of the sort and wonders where the sensation is supposed to be coming from. She's about to ask, but before she can grunt the question, she feels it in her teeth, the faint buzz, like she's biting down on a radio that's tuned to static. It starts in her mouth and moves through her skull, loud in her inner ear. Agent Myers appears to up a dial on the screen. She can feel it throughout her body, not an unpleasant sensation, but nothing she'd want to last long.

'Look at the screen on the right please. A slide show of images will appear. Give it your full attention. If you look away from it we'll have to start again.'

Ava nods and does as she's told. As she turns to it she concentrates on the blank screen to wait for an image to appear. A zigzagging line intersecting a circle. It displays for five seconds or so until it switches to another geometric shape, a hexagon. She can feel Agent Myers' probing curiosity, and is more relaxed when he looks away from her to his laptop. The hexagon changes to a circle and as the humming from the putty becomes slightly more intense, her breathing becomes that much harder. What follows over the course of the rest of the scan feels like a long index finger uncurling in her head, worming about and prodding at her brain tissue. When the hexagon changes, a spinning triangle takes its place, the very same image Francis had shown her that day in his office. At the sight of it, some reflex in her warns that her mind is being read and she wonders how detailed the scan actually is, if it can read the words that are playing, the images, the memories of everything that has happened. The things she has done. Her heart is racing and her body almost shaking from a charge of adrenaline, but before she can worry about it too much, everything comes into sharp focus. It's as if the light of day has changed, everything now bathed in a clear white. She isn't worried about anything at all. Then, the shape is gone – just another form that was placed in front of her and will never be seen again. The slideshow finishes out. A cube and lastly a trio of rectangles overlapping each other disappear. She feels the finger in her head curl in on itself until it vanishes altogether. The screen goes black and as the humming in her body slowly fades away, the only thing she's thinking is how strange it is that a simple triangle could actually mean something to her, if only for a fleeting second.

'And that, is that,' Agent Myers confirms and, handing her a tissue for the putty, tells her she can spit it out. 'There's a bin at your feet.'

Ava wraps the substance tightly so it can't escape and disposes of it as casually as she can. Coughing as she sits up on the stool, she inspects Agent Myers' face for any hints on how she might have done.

'Well,' she says.

'Well,' he repeats, hidden behind an expressionless mask.

Ava can see through it. She is, after all, somewhat of an expert on masks. What she sees underneath the man's neutral stance is that she's being weighed like a slab of steak. Crossing her leg, she breathes, confident that he'll find whatever it is he wants to see. Enjoying the tease, she meets the man's gaze and asks in her own suggestive way, 'Do I get a report in the post or are you going tell me all about it now?'

22

As the door opens, all the apprehensive eyes that have been awaiting her return are on Ava. They want their suspicions to be confirmed and she hates them for it. The jealous ingrates want Ava O'Dwyer knocked from her pedestal. Every one of them were assuming the same result from her scan. In the style of Barry Danger, she stands dramatically quiet, casts her sights over them and meets their expectations with a scowl.

'Don't you people have work to be doing?'

She glares at the baffled detective.

Arriving like an old friend, Agent Myers stands at her side. The collection of heads turn as one, a ripple of switches all set by the same fuse, to the social agent who tested her. He jumps at their attention, as though he's only just remembered that they're waiting for him.

'Don't worry,' he reassures the room. 'She's clear.'

Nobody lets go of their breath. They're waiting for the other shoe to drop. Slowly, they begin to glance at each other, checking to see if anybody believes what they're being told and reluctant to voice their own disbelief until somebody else does it first. All they find in each other though, are carefully guarded expressions that reveal little to hide their initial confusion. They're stuck there, paralysed, waiting for something more to be said. If a single voice among them speaks up in shock, now, before the day goes any further, it could make all the difference.

Instead, it's Agent Myers who moves things forward.

'Any volunteers for the next slot or will we start going alphabetically?'

A murmur of two conclusions trickle into one another: If Ava is safe, I must be too. And counter to this, If Ava is safe, god only knows what that means for me. Never have their suspicions of the woman been more certain than now when they've been revealed to be absolutely groundless. Some try to make themselves invisible by returning to their work while others remain, waiting to see what will happen next. Dylan's head is pumping with blood, his sight sharpened to a pin.

'I'll go,' Joanne says. 'It's not too bad is it sweetie?'

'No, it's not,' Ava assures her. 'It was interesting actually. You'll be fine.'

She places a supportive hand on her editor as they cross paths, and Dylan who watches the exchange, sees Ava disappear into Joanne's office. As he waits for the woman's results to come back from Agent Myers, Dylan quietly calls for Barry, but finds he has to hiss the name three times before the journalist realises someone is asking for him.

'Got the whole force in one place,' Barry says of the collective Garda and firemen scattered about. 'If I was UPD I'd blow up the whole building. Wouldn't be a cop left in Dublin.'

Dylan ignores the comment and steps closer to address Barry. He is quite aware that people have clocked his revived interest and are adjusting their attention to hear the exchange.

'What was that you said about the fire alarm?'

'I was just having a laugh,' Barry says, not sure if he's being accused of something.

'About what?' Dylan asks. 'Something happened recently?'

Barry's journalist instinct comes to the fore as he hears a suspicious note in detective's questioning. 'Yeah. A week ago somebody set off the fire alarm. Caused a bit of a disruption for the whole building. Why? You know something about it that I don't?'

'Agent Mullen was here when it happened,' Dylan mumbles to himself.

Barry nods, not knowing where this is going.

'You said Ava did it.'

At this, Barry pulls the reigns in on where he's being led, chuckling like he's trying to halt a horse. Then, guardedly, he says, 'I don't know about that.

It's just a joke. You shouldn't take everything I say so seriously. Nobody else does.'

Jaw clenched, Dylan begs the man to give him more than that.

'Alright,' Barry relents, dropping the character he's made of himself. 'Maybe she did. She was my number one suspect anyway. The alarm that was pulled was on the bottom floor. Nobody in our office did it. We were all up here. She was running late, apparently. When we got outside she was already there, having a smoke and buzzing for a chat.'

'That's all? No proof?'

'Oh yeah. Security dusted the place for fingerprints. Had a few detectives in here to work it out,' Barry's personality quickly snaps back to its base mode. 'Come on mate, there's enough going on here without worrying who pulled a bloody fire alarm. It was forgotten by lunch.'

'Bollocks,' Dylan grunts.

'Does it make a difference?' Barry raises his arms up and lets them flop to his side. Falling into the chair at his desk, he spins away from Dylan. 'I don't know much about your case, but they're not going to put someone on trial for pulling a fire alarm. The world isn't that bad a place, well unless,' he looks at the door of the testing room, 'unless Ava'd come out of there in handcuffs. Anyway, that would have just been icing on the cake, wouldn't it?'

Icing on the cake? It was one of the only solid leads he's gotten in this damned investigation and it's dangling in front of him in the closing hours of the race to finish it all.

'Barry,' Dylan says, trying to lick his lips but finding that his mouth has gone dry.

He wants to tell him he knows who killed the social agent. Barry looks at him quizzically, and realises from the determination on the detective's face that he knows indeed that the murderer was Ava. But neither of them say it. With no evidence and no other lead to follow, all the man can do is stare it into Barry, and confirm from the mirrored expression that in their midst is a human being who killed another human being. Dylan rests on the desk behind him, sure there's a solution to all of this somewhere but too exhausted to find it. Between all these good people are pieces to a puzzle that can be solved, but they won't help him do it. The fact is this it's easier for them not to.

After all, no matter what happens, Agent Mullen won't be any less dead.

'Detective Wong,' a voice calls apologetically.

Dylan ignores it, an idea is solidifying.

'Detective Wong,' the voice goes again.

Barry Danger, who has noticed the detective is zoned out, nudges Dylan and nods to the man who's been calling. Dylan follows his gaze to the Garda and in turn follows the Garda's sight over to Agent Myers. The social agent is standing at the door of the conference room, his face contorted in a demonstration of concern, skin gone grey as ash. The first thought that occurs to Dylan is that there's been another murder.

Dylan walks over. 'What's up?'

'Are you kidding me?'

'What?'

'Well why do you think you're here?'

Dylan, stubborn, waits for the situation to be explained.

'To make arrests,' the social agent says, mirthful.

'I know that,' snaps Dylan.

'So it's time to do your job.'

He is about to ask exactly what that means when it dawns on him and three words escape his mouth.

'Oh god no.'

He couldn't have stopped himself from saying them if he'd tried.

'Joanne has tested positive. She's in the higher range. Upper UPD.'

The weight of the entire office is on his back as Agent Myers confirms the bad news. He looks into the room where Joanne is sat, e-smoke dropped to the ground and resting at her feet. Her hands are gently linked in her lap, legs pressed together, head locked straight ahead and in another world. The woman is aware of everything about her, though she's incapable of thinking or saying anything about it. In a word: catatonic.

'Is she okay?' Dylan quietly steps into the conference room and closes the door behind him. 'Joanne?'

'I think she's just in shock,' Agent Myers says. Correcting the note of sympathy in his voice, he goes on dryly, 'When a UPD is caught they can become very difficult. If dramatic protests don't work it's not unusual for them to fling accusations until they give up, and well, sit like this one, just holding out for the next chance to cast some doubt.'

'She was difficult?'

'This one seems to have skipped a stage I suppose,' Agent Myers wears his half smile, repulsed by the thing that's taking up a seat. 'What a UPD does isn't entirely predictable. Anyway, It's the end of the road.'

Dylan, who has stood over many dead bodies in his career, is overwhelmed by compassion for this living woman. Like a deer that has struggled in the wild all its life, she has finally found herself in a rusty trap, and too exhausted, she's laid down, white eyed as she waits for the end.

'Joanne,' Dylan kneels at her side. 'We're going to be taking you out of the office now. We're going to have to handcuff you. It's just the procedure...' Dylan apologises, wanting to reassure her but not knowing how or even why.

Contempt makes the social agent appear drowsy. 'Just get her out of here, there's a lot more people left to scan.'

'Can I get you to stand up, Joanne? Joanne?'

Joanne's head jerks in a nod of agreement, and she rises, steadying herself on the table. Dylan crouches to pick up her e-smoke but they bump heads as she reaches for it at the same time, her hand snatching and pocketing it before he can get to it. As they go, he tells her to put her hands behind her back and puts her in plastic cuffs – loose, just for show, like he said. Standing at the door, Agent Myers in front of them, Dylan and Joanne both take deep breaths as if a rush of water is going to burst through when it's opened and they'll be pulled along with a current they can't fight. Instead what meets them is a wall of stunned faces. Seeing the monster, they can't believe it's real. Still, they leave a wide circle of space around the officers and Joanne – so this is what a UPD looks like. A girl puts her hand over her o-shaped mouth and another makes a small whimpering noise. Good god, is heard. Barry's face is set in stone. Ava is at the front of the bunch, tearing up.

'Oh no, Joanne,' she chokes out a sob that stops her from saying anything else.

One of the Garda leans over to Dylan, 'You going to say anything?'

'There's nothing to say,' he responds coolly. 'Let's just get her out of here.'

After a beat, they move. A puppet in Dylan's hands, Joanne is led from the door of the conference room to the glass doors of the office she built, an honour guard of aghast faces accompanying her expulsion.

As she reaches the exit, it occurs to her for the first time that this doesn't just mean losing her job, her business, her life as she knows it. It's a lot worse than any of that.

'I didn't do anything,' she twists in Dylan's arms to shout at her staff. 'I didn't do anything wrong! Not to Agent Mullen, good lord!' her shout is squeezed into a piercing scream. 'Don't just stand there! You have to help me! This is all wrong!'

'She's right. This is all wrong,' Ava suddenly speaks up and begins to step forward until she's held back by one of the Gards. 'Joanne we'll get this sorted out.'

'Alright let's go.' Dylan presses down on Joanne's arm to hint that she should move forward but finds it has no effect.

'I didn't do anything,' she screams again.

Agent Myers, gloating, says, 'What'd I tell you?'

'I don't understand, it was just a triangle. What was I supposed to feel about it?!'

Dylan moves her more forcefully now, counting the steps to the elevator, hoping he can get her there without having to restrain her more vigorously, but she's wriggling to pull out of his grip.

'Ava you have to help me!'

Stunned tears run from Ava's eyes, leaving black slug trails on her cheeks. 'I will!' she says, then quickly changes the statement to include all of the employees. 'We will Joanne!'

Barry Danger is speechless as he witnesses Ava's determined resolve.

'We'll have you home by the end of the day, Joanne.' A voice joins Ava's and some words of support chime in from the others. 'We'll get you out of this!'

Joanne doesn't hear them though. 'I didn't do anything,' she insists again. 'Why are you taking me away?!'

Feeling the situation getting out of hand, Dylan directs her as best he can but finds he has to shove, hating himself when he does so. As they leave through the door, a group of the emergency workers cram into the elevator with them. Joanne, stood in the middle, her hands tied behind her back, sinks down to the ground, surrounded by cops, a detective, a bureaucrat and four firemen, before being led to a waiting police car. From the car park she looks up to the office windows where she sees the line watch as her head gets pushed into the back seat.

Now, as the cops, the firemen, Dylan and Agent Myers return to the newsroom, Ava has gathered her strength to rally the crowd.

'We won't let this go. Anybody who thinks Joanne did anything wrong, even if she is untouched, should... they should leave now,' she stutters out. 'She's not a murderer and every line that comes out of this office has to reflect that. I don't know what's going to be happening with the running of this organisation in the meantime, but until a replacement is found I'm going to make sure of it.'

'Alright, alright,' Dylan says, 'that's enough excitement for now. She hasn't been accused of anything yet. She's just going in for questioning.'

'Ha!' someone says.

'Why did she have to be handcuffed?'

The mutters of agreement grow loud and more panicked questions work their way to the surface.

'We went through this at the start of the day,' Dylan shouts over them, exhausted. 'It's just procedure,' he says, and repeats with the supplement, 'It's just procedure for someone tested positive as UPD.'

A deathly silence falls over the office as the result of Joanne's scan sinks in, and someone makes a desperate request for comfort, 'It just doesn't make sense, does it?'

Not wanting the dissipating crowd to be left with that as the final note on the subject, malleable as they are in their shock, Ava weakly slams her hand down on a desk in an attempt to unite them under her flag once more. 'We'll get this sorted out. Something must have gone wrong. She can't be, she just can't be UPD. If she is–' her hand shoots up to her mouth to cover a sob, cutting off the end of her sentence. Somebody consoles her and offers a tissue to wipe away her spoilt make-up, and she thanks them as she walks away to take her seat, the one now vacated, the one that has been waiting for her throughout all the drama. The seat behind the editor's desk.

23

Detectives always return to the scene of a crime. The sombre fact, all the truer for Dylan Wong, is that a good investigator never leaves an unsolved case behind.

Once, when his wife was pregnant, in a conjunction of events, he had been assigned to the murder of a five year old child, a contrast which instilled the need for resolution with desperate urgency. The child was found at the back of a fruit picking warehouse, wrapped in an oily sack, cut from its privates up to its neck in a surgical attack. The most horrifying thing was how slow the ordeal must have lasted, how long the child would have been alive, confused, scared and suffering, as the perpetrator knelt over the boy, ignoring the cries he made. Nobody was ever convicted for the crime. Dylan had never managed to put the mystery to rest and, so far as he was concerned, the child remained laying there, listless, waiting for the case to be solved. It was one of the reasons he never left homicide and why fourteen months after the arrest and prosecution of Joanne Victoria, he has yet to push through his transfer papers. Having access to the case histories allowed him a ritual he needs. Without Dylan, these unsolved cases, these people that once existed, were just lines of code in a computer that represented absolutely nothing. It was only in his reading of them that there was any meaning to it all. On the late shift, he would sit in the empty office, manning the phones where murders were reported, studying the old files.

The child was on top of the stack. Cut by a skillet knife that left a flake of salmon skin in the wound and dumped in a sack stinking of fish, a pock faced scumbag in Smithfield, a fish monger, had been Dylan's number one suspect. He'd questioned the man relentlessly and called him into the station on three separate occasions for interview. He'd canvassed the neighbourhood for weeks, begging for something other than grudging suspicion from the locals, only to get nothing in return. And once a month in all the years since, Dylan would visit the fish shop to order fillets of pomfret for his family. Steamed whole with ginger and spring onion and bathed in a specially mixed soy sauce, the recipe had travelled from Hong Kong with his grandmother. It stank up the house for days. They hated fish, Dylan most of all, but it was a routine he forced on his wife and child under the guise of keeping some cultural tradition alive in his home. Really, it was a reminder to himself of the boy who would never have peace. Most of all, Dylan needed an excuse to visit the monger. Once a month, he needed to see there was absolutely no guilt in the guilty man's blotchy face, that the only justice in the universe was that created by a collection of individuals who served to protect people from each other and that he, Dylan Wong, was one of these men who worked to uphold the law. When he didn't do his job well enough there was no karmic balance to make up for it.

With this in mind, sitting among the empty desks of the homicide office, Dylan has put the boy's file aside and is scrolling through ChatterFive's articles. He had never been one for keeping up with the news, but since the arrest of Joanne, he's read every piece the media conglomerate has published. Have so many months really passed? He wouldn't have thought his wife would let him dig his heels on the transfer this long. He supposed time was meaningless to them. They were just existing together as their boy grew older, surprised once in a while by an event like Christmas or another Halloween. On the website tonight is a summation of the court case that led to its disgraced editor's downfall. He revisits the circumstances of it as often as he revisits the fish monger.

When the urgency of Joanne's cry for help dissipated, Ava had took to the editor's chair, leaving the words of her broken speech to linger in the minds of the staff. The firemen and Garda remained on hand to oversee the remaining hours of processing, though their jokes had dried up and they felt for the first time that their presence was justified.

Dylan remained too. He was as conflicted as ever regarding the reasons for it. One by one, the journalists took their turns in the social agent's hot seat and in time came out relieved, if a little agitated as they returned to their slots feeling violated but happy that it hadn't been any worse. Four hours went by. When it was finished no other UPD were found – Joanne was the only one. The Garda dribbled out of the newsroom with an idle word of permission from the detective. The firemen had left of their own accord an hour before. Agent Myers met Dylan with an exhausted look, who doggedly stood to meet him.

'Long day,' Agent Myers said. 'I could use a drink. What do you think?'

'The day's not over for me,' Dylan answered. 'I have to head to the station.'

Joanne was waiting in a cell. He was going to leave the social agent with that. What little cordiality that had grown between them over the days previous was gone now, extinguished by the reality of the situation. Dylan would have been happy never to see the man again, but Agent Myers, he seemed intent on drawing out their goodbyes. When Dylan was in the elevator, his back to office, he could barely hold up his arm to wave farewell. Escaping wasn't so easy. When he heard his name being called, he was forced to face the social agent. 'Dylan,' Agent Myers said, and showing a flare for dramatics, bowed to the detective, holding an imaginary top hat in his hand as he bent over. He was a grateful performer, thanking his audience from the bottom of his heart. Then, like curtains falling from either side of a stage, the elevator doors closed over Dylan's view of the man. He would never forget the sight.

Ava was true to her word. Before there had even been wind of a trial in the death of Agent Mullen, she had united the ChatterFive organisation behind their fallen editor, both in their office and within their community pages, outrage directed at the idea that Joanne might be UPD and that there must have been a mistake in the scan. In regards to Francis Mullen's death – a social agent presented to the public as a fumbling, clumsy, though good natured type – their coverage compared it to that of a man who crossed the street without looking both ways first. He certainly didn't deserve to die, but it was his own lack of mindfulness that brought it on him. A tragedy, and one that could happen to any of us, something accidental and completely separate to the possible plots against his life. How did the readership react to this line?

The editor of a leading media outlet had been found to be UPD. The woman whose articles that brought all these reforms to the fore was now being dissected by them. Either they had all been fooled by her, or she was the victim of a grievous mistake. As such, the argument initiated with the death of Agent Mullen and the arrest of Joanne was reduced to a binary issue which had but two possible answers. Was Joanne really UPD? Without a doubt, her naysayers insisted. And how could anybody be shocked by that? Over pints in pubs across Ireland there were grunts that anybody at the top is likely untouched, and before allowing themselves to think any further about it, glasses would be clinked and the drinks guzzled down. The UPD reform was already in place, after all, and was clearly doing the job it was meant for.

'What if she isn't UPD and still murdered him? Or if she is UPD and didn't? What if nobody in the newsroom killed him? What if Detective Wong was UPD and was framing her? What if the miserable drip of a social agent killed himself? He didn't seem like the happiest guy to me. And they called it a murder because why? A second glass of wine was in the room? Why wasn't Ava questioned more? Why weren't any of us after the scans? And why am the only one asking these things?'

Barry Danger hollered the flurry of questions from his desk over the course of a long Monday. The cubicle he occupied had shrunk since Joanne's removal, and under the influence of the stand-in editor, he was starting to feel the walls close in on him. Once, his anarchic attitude was indulged, now it was being suffocated. During Joanne's rule, his colleagues would cautiously welcome his dissent, knowing that his staunch contrariness was a valuable reminder that however flat their screens might be, at the very least, it was a three-dimensional world they were reporting on. Not so under Ava's supervision. There was a battle to be fought, their editor's name to be cleared. His questions, asked with no small amount of obnoxious glee, was an attack from within. The embittered journalists around him pretended not to hear, and Ava O'Dwyer, who quietly approached his work space, stopped at the bobblehead on his cubicle wall and flicked it over with a finely manicured nail.

'We are not writing a political science thesis, Mr. Danger. Save the multiple angle shots for a retrospective ten years from now. We have a very simple mission and thoughts counter to it are for our competitors to express, not us.'

Barry, obstinate in his refusal to acknowledge the shift in atmosphere since Joanne's departure, cackled and asked, 'Isn't that what got us into this mess in the first place?'

It was the last dispute any of them heard from the Englishman. Within the week, he handed in his resignation and moved back to London, wearily giving up on the plague ridden community he had been a part of for so long, choosing instead to hope his own people would find a better route through the existential mire. There were problems with the world and they were only being dealt with one at a time, issues chosen not by an informed population but in knee jerk reactions just as likely to cause more grief. As ever, in seeing this, he had no qualms about describing it as the burden it was. The last article he submitted to ChatterFive's newsdesk was a satirical piece which carried the title – Damned If You Do – and covered a long series of pets he had as a child, that try as he might, kept on dying, one dead dog piled atop another in the mass grave his garden had become. Worse still, despite all of his best efforts, each one died in pain, riddled with disease that played out over extended years. There is no good death, he concluded. The article ended with the question of why he would put himself through the suffering of replacing the animals full in the knowledge that having his heart broken was inevitable, and suggested that he didn't have a choice in the matter, and that trapped as he was, all he could do was laugh. Ava refused to publish it, citing numerous spelling errors as an extra irritant heaped onto her day. In his final hope to have it read by the local public, he posted it himself in the ChatterFive community where it was lost in a bonfire of inflammatory reactions to the trial of Joanne Victoria that was set to begin within a matter of weeks.

She was of course, as Ava demonstrated, being judged in the press long before her court date. It was a dress rehearsal for the main event. Since ChatterFive became a beacon of support for Joanne it was inevitable that other media outlets came to vilify her. Given that other newsrooms were full of people who had known her, worked with her, been fired by her, there was plenty of fuel for the fire, and though most people who read and watched the analysis of the woman agreed with the ugly portrait, ChatterFive sustained a growth in numbers from its support of her. There was an opinion in the community that the loyalty the organisation had to their commander and chief was admirable enough to reward it with their own loyalty to the brand.

She was a bully, yes. What news editor in the world wasn't? It was what the job called for. And most of all, in ChatterFive's denouncement of the system that was punishing their editor for a crime she didn't commit, there was a rally point for all those who disagreed with the belief in the UPD reforms. The unspoken understanding was that people were afraid: the woman who had broken the stories that led to the reforms so many years ago was now on trial, and if she was untouched, anyone could be. As such, they continued to follow the issue through the Ava-tinted glasses ChatterFive had adopted since she took the editor's chair. The set goal their substitute editor had set for them was to get Joanne a second scan. In agreement with her defence attorney's advice, no element of the actual murder case was concentrated on in their articles at all. The details of Francis Mullen's death were secondary, and not without reason. In Joanne's words, spoken then by Ava, the public could only concentrate on one point at a time. The more detail they attempted to add to her defence, the less outrage could be provoked. She was not UPD. All the fervour that stirred was used to this end – if Joanne got a second scan, the case would fall through and she could go home a free woman.

Dylan Wong's chief had fumed when he heard that she'd actually have it granted. If she proved to be clear on the second scan, the entire system would be shown up as a shambles, and worse, for his department, there would still be a murder to solve. Luckily for the tetchy man, when she finally got the scan it only confirmed what they were already told – the woman was untouched, incapable of empathising with all the grief she caused. Deflated from this, Ava's PR campaign could not regain its momentum. The public court had reached its verdict. Now there was but the formality of a trial.

Murder was the charge. There were no discussions of whether she should be trialled as a moral agent with full faculties and by extension, subject to standard acts of punishment and reform. That had been decided the day she was proven UPD. Though she had been listed as untouched and banned from working in certain areas of society, she was not treated as an insane person who's guilt would be excusable. The UPD hold a unique place in Irish law, somewhere in a hopeless desert between the polar ends of sane and insane. When an untouched was found to be guilty of a particular crime, rehabilitation was not considered possible.

If it was decided that Joanne had murdered the social agent, she would be sent to Inishvickillane, the closed facility for violent UPD, with no chance of remand or bail. A life sentence, for all intents and purposes, stranded with the vicious anathema of Ireland.

On the first day of the trial, though she appeared stern behind square rimmed glasses, she dressed in light silks with rounded collars, the pastel shades of her outfit chosen to give her a motherly air. Her legal team insisted that she not look upset by the proceedings as it might be interpreted as an attempt at emotional manipulation of public perception. When this was read as cold and indeed, untouched, a woman unfazed by the stranglehold of a countries law gripping her throat, she was told that maybe she should look down at the ground more, be humble, let a single tear fall for the social agent who died so young. And this in turn was read how they originally expected. There was no hope of being able to control how she was seen once the scarlet letters were draped around her neck.

The judge didn't have to worry about his own court dress. It was decided long before he was born. Black robes and a dusty grey wig, the uniform had been kept for centuries to demonstrate that this was not a man deciding the fates of those who stood in his chambers, rather, by some method of transubstantiation, he was the law incarnate, a concept literally taking human form. Evidently prepared for the nation's watchful eye, he had a speech prepared to open the proceedings. He took to the bench like a man trained in classical acting.

'It's a hefty matter we'll be dealing with over the course of these weeks, one which, though it exhausts our optimism, and thins our hair, we are lucky enough to understand as an assault on the fabric which we define ourselves by. What we're here for today is to decide if this woman is responsible for a despicable deed, the taking of Francis Mullen's life. This burden, necessary as it is for us to function as a whole, will fall to the representatives of the citizens of our state: the jury assembled to my right. It is these people I address now.

'There are conventional transgressions and moral ones. If an onlooker from the press should happen to interrupt me as I speak, try as I might, I would not be able to lock them away for it. There is the argument that there are no absolutes in morals. In this way, what is wrong in one culture may be acceptable in another.

In our reform of the law, in our acceptance of the UPD act, we defined a moral transgression for ourselves as one which engages our sense of empathy, a quality which may come naturally to us but which the boundaries of are learned. This is important, because no matter the country they are raised in, no matter the continent, the UPD have shown extreme difficulty in understanding the local differences between moral and conventional transgressions. How do we react to this? In order to be considered an agent responsible for one's actions, one must have a full understanding of their own choices that led to what they did and the implications of those choices. The UPD are aware of all these things, but do not comprehend the abstract results because they are incapable of giving the thought the weight required to do so. In our system, unequal treatment is justified when it allows for good or bad fortune. Some people are born lucky – beautiful and talented – others unlucky – disabled and sick. This is neither just nor unjust. They are merely facts of the world. The law is not as cold and detached as that. As a sentient species we come together as institutions to deal with these matters, compensating for the injustices that we perceive. We are a people who interpret each other's movements as demonstrations of intention and choice. The social contract we enter into is a concept that allows for acceptance of responsibility and possibility of guilt. One must see oneself as a cause of events in the world whose actions should be analysed and judged.

'Keeping that in mind, when we go through the process of deciding whether or not Joanne Victoria committed the killing of Francis Mullen, we are not asking if she is guilty. Having been processed, we know she is incapable of experiencing this gift. Since the untouched personality is beyond cure or reform all we can do is isolate those who suffer from it. Ms. Victoria has already been removed from the work environment she might have polluted. The process we have at hand now is to decide if she also committed the most heinous of moral transgressions: Murder, a crime which would have her removed from our culture altogether.'

The trial was not broadcast. A single sketch artist was permitted to create pieces for news outlets and historical posterity. Her eyes in all the drawings were black. When Ava received them, she ordered that they be altered to the deep wavering emerald green that they remembered in Joanne so well, infringement laws be damned.

Joanne was not allowed contact with her former colleagues, though Ava was sat behind her every day of the trial. She had waved hello and snuck sympathetic words to her any chance she got, her hand even reaching out to Joanne's shoulder on occasion to buoy her spirit during some of the more difficult stages, though she was always ignored by her former boss. Joanne had retreated inside herself and she wasn't coming out. In the drawings that were made, Ava's features were rarely visible. All that could be identified of her was a dark shadow behind the woman who had become so knotted in those strings that attached them all.

Dylan talked to Joanne that first night in her cell after the scan in ChatterFive. Her arms were folded around herself as if she were cold, though the chamber was dry with acrid heat from an electric radiator on the wall. Despite this, she was much more composed than she'd been when they'd taken her out of the newsroom in handcuffs. She met the detective's greeting with a steady glare.

'You're not smoking,' he said

'I didn't know I was allowed.'

Dylan said that she was welcome to and waited for her to light up, but instead, she'd wrung her fingers.

'There's something very wrong,' she informed him.

Did he agree with her at the time? He can't remember now. Everything is muddied as he looks back. 'Joanne,' he asked tentatively, 'what were you doing at Agent Mullen's home on the night of the 22nd?'

'I was there was I?' Her eyes lit up and then sank, like a fish jumping out of water and falling back in with a splash. 'I suppose you'll have to talk to my solicitor about that. He might have a different idea than you.'

The line between them was drawn.

There was no direct evidence linking Joanne to the crime. The witness report of the landlord, who confirmed under oath that she arrived at the social agent's apartment drunk and upset some days previous to the murder, was the strongest weapon the prosecution had in its arsenal. But what of the poison accounted for in SimperP's records and used in the medical trials of Doctor Alistair Evans? Dylan was adamant that the corporation and its lethal drug needed to be linked to Joanne for any kind of prosecution to hold water, at least, for any man with good conscience. His chief had raged at the idea.

Not only was his lead detective on the case making more work than needed, but he was trying to drag a megacorporation that had just set up in the country months ago into the most controversial court case of the past decade. Not only would it cost the state more effort and money than they cared to spend on a single dead man to bring SimperP to trial, the current government had worked for years courting the pharmaceutical business into the country, basing any number of campaign promises on the potential for jobs and revenue they would generate, and here was Dylan the scruffy Garda trying to scare them away. It would be career suicide for all involved. No, his chief informed him. The drug used on Mullen would only be mentioned if the defence brought it up. They had a suspect, now it was time to prosecute her as efficiently as possible.

'If that's all that's important then our job is a farce,' said Dylan.

Give them a pass just so they could provide employment? It was blood money. He insisted that he would not take the stand as lead officer on the case if a link between Joanne and SimperP could not be established.

As it happened, his stance had little effect. Shortly after the confrontation with the chief, their department received another case file from SimperP. Sometime after Dylan's visit to Doctor Evans' office, the corporation had become concerned with possible breaches in security and began its own internal investigation. On doing so, it turned out a young woman within the building had been smuggling out small amounts of the drug in question, probably to sell on for her own profit. She had been caught on video pocketing a bottle of pills which had left the doctor's sight. She had been fired and some weeks later, in an expedited rate for the local justice system, prosecuted, now serving time on bail. Watching the video, Dylan was shocked to see that he recognised her. It was the medical clerk, the doctor's secretary. Immediately, he proclaimed that she was a patsy, only stealing medication at the instigation of her superior and set up in advance to take any legal ramifications that he might run into. The detective cut himself off, aware that his boss was ready to hand him a tinfoil hat. Ignoring the theory, the chief was quick to explain to Dylan that they could spend their time trying to establish a link between Joanne and the black marketer, but that it could easily be a waste of effort – who knew how many hands those pills passed through before getting to the editor, and all that besides, it still wouldn't be worth the hassle of bringing the corporation into the matter.

Not being able to stomach the politics of it all, Dylan walked away from the chief, stubborn in his refusal to agree with the reasons. He was not asked to testify at the trial, neither by the defence or the prosecution. The chief, dismayed at his officer's naiveté, found a loophole to prevent it. As the body of his department had pressed the original charge when Joanne arrived at the station, the testimony of the officer on scene was not needed. The chief, that career driven type, had worked it out so that he would be on hand to illustrate some of the more technical details of the investigation and was all too happy to take the stand and explain the conditions that led to Joanne being arrested and charges being pressed. It wasn't very complicated. Between him and the prosecution, she was portrayed as a vicious drunk who'd interfered with processing from the first day. She kept alcohol in her office, was addicted to painkillers, and as a final insult to Dylan, it was hinted that she had arranged for a fire drill during the social agent's initial presentation. Though the defence objected to the supposition, the idea had been planted into the jury's collective consciousness. If Dylan had been up there, he would have only been too happy to express his opinion of this happening, and yet he remained silent, mortified that by telling the truth he would only have cast suspicion on one of the few people who was going to take the stand to defend Joanne: Ava O'Dwyer.

But really, what could ChatterFive's stand-in editor say to save the old one? She denied Joanne was an alcoholic but didn't rule out the fact that she did enjoy a few more drinks than others she knew. She couldn't deny that she'd been witnessed on numerous occasions as the head of a supply line of painkillers for Joanne. When asked if she had ever thought Joanne Victoria could be UPD, Ava insisted that no, she was a wonderful woman, an amazing mentor who had given her tremendous opportunities in life, and then, fluttering her eyes shut, her voice cracked. She broke into tears on the stand. She never saw it coming, she said. Though she couldn't deny the facts. She was UPD, the scan had twice proven it. 'How could I not have known?'

Some defence, Dylan had thought. Others forgave her for it. It was an emotionally charged time. In the end, it came down to the opinion of the jury as to whether she committed the crime.

When Dylan Wong joined the Garda Síochana all those years ago, he had been assigned to the riot squad, a force in demand, to be on call at the drop of a hat, sent into the city to douse the flames of a people full to bursting with suppressed thoughts.

The triggers identified: misworded news items, viral fictions let loose on social networks, policy changes regarding the dole, UPD manipulation, or any standard smug smile from a disgraced politician, were incidental so far as he could tell. Being called out was like jumping through a portal into another world where all rationality disappeared in a riot as disgruntled office workers readied to hurl bricks alongside youths who were only too happy to mug them after. In these brief flashes, they joined as one and destroyed all that was in their path. The contributing factors were so many and so intertwined that finding a single rationale for it was an exercise in futility. In an ouroboros of events the tail end of one incident was the beginning of the next. If there was a flare point to subdue it was long before anything illegal had happened. The role of the police, he suspected, was simply to brush the evidence of a faulty system under the rug. Dylan joined the force to make a difference, and in that squad, no single officer seemed capable of doing as much. Transferring out, he worked up to his posting today, where he could at least put a face to the irrationality in the shape of his murder suspects – one person at a time, categorising reason and choice, cause and effect. But here, all these years later, the crowd were back to haunt him.

Try as the system might, the jury was not immune to the public mood, which had come to its conclusions long before they were chosen and isolated. She was the murderer they needed. The UPD reforms had been created to protect the people. An upholder of them was dead. Who else would kill him but the untouched?

And so it was.

It had been decided before the trial, before the murder, before the law. And her sentence too was written in stone. With blindfolds on, the firing squad took aim and let their ammo loose on the wide-eyed condemned.

'I'm sure that you don't understand why this has happened to you,' the judge proclaimed. 'That you have no shame whatsoever in the committing of this crime. All I can say to that is, we would be the guilty party if we did nothing to balance the matter. The jury has done their duty today, they've decided it. The wolf must not be allowed walk among the sheep.'

When Joanne received the verdict, she edged around to Ava, who had her hands outreached to the editor, ready to catch her as she fell crying into her arms.

Seeing Ava tear up in sympathy, Joanne took her only chance to strike, and slapped the skinny bitch's face with what remaining strength she had leftover from the long ordeal. The sound echoed through the courtroom and not long after, followed by the gasps of onlookers, was heard around the country – That's the UPD for you, lashing out at the only woman who came to her defence.

After this, in her stoic support of Joanne, Ava was close to sainthood. Regarding the slap received, she was silent, apparently taking it to heart and still reluctant to betray the person she once thought was Joanne. On the matter, she remained composed, astutely picking up from where the judge had left off. She said in an editorial that, 'If as a people we're defined by our ability to place value where none exists, then the woman I thought Joanne Victoria to be, was, and always will be, real. The person who murdered Francis Mullen is someone else entirely.'

In this way, Ava's temporary position at the head of ChatterFive became a permanent one, Joanne Victoria was imprisoned, and the key which locked her up was thrown away.

It had been raining then. Towns were drowned. Despite the country being destroyed by a similar storm six years earlier, there was no disaster prevention set in place when the worst of it struck. Cork was devastated. The dams had burst. People were evacuated and their houses were flooded. Firemen and Garda were moving the population. The army reserves were in place, setting up walls of sandbags in a futile show of holding back the deluge. In time, the waters receded, the walls rebuilt, and the people returned to their flood damaged homes. All was well until next time. Dylan can't remember when the clouds had dispersed, so lost was he in the unfolding events. He felt powerless to stop any of it and tried to ignore the feeling. It remained in his chest as a damp patch, a murmur he would feel in deep breaths and neglect, counting on the problem to cure itself. He picked up smoking again and took more late shifts. The nights he spent at home were more often on the couch than in his bed and in spite of this, he didn't leave homicide, but sits now, awake in the night, reading reports issued by ChatterFive. A phone interrupts his thinking. There's nobody on the other end and the dial tone goes flat.

'Francis,' Dylan mumbles.

The sun has come out. This late shift has come to end, an uneventful one, thank god. In the morning light outside Pierce Street Garda Station, the roads are covered with vomit and urine. City cleaners are milling about, picking up the discarded packages of burgers and chips, littered by nameless drunks.

'He must have swallowed his teeth,' the realisation comes to the detective now, after everything that's happened. 'He swallowed them, and what? How does he get them back in? If a man is willing to practice regurgitating his own false teeth for the sake of a magic trick...'

It's the second revelation he's had tonight. Some hours ago, as he trawled through the articles on ChatterFive, Dylan found a piece of interest. It was a lifestyle profile on a man who found some success abroad and was now bringing the luck home to this country he felt was so starved of it. In a spread of photos he sat in his apartment, charmed and boyish looking, smiling at the camera. They seemed to be setting him up as a future medical consultant for the media's ever hungry schedule gaps. It was Doctor Alistair Evans. The byline, unsurprisingly, was Ava O'Dwyer's, contributing editor of ChatterFive. It's building is an hour in the opposite direction of Dylan's house, where his wife and child are no doubt awaiting his return. The detective grabs his coat as he punches out, determined. What's one more place to add to his list of monthly visits? It couldn't hurt anyway. All it could take from him is time.

24

Crumpled packages are scattered across the editor's desk. The paper bag which the meal had been delivered in is ripped in two, spread under the eggshell casings that carried the food. Once, it all held the promise of treats to come, but since it was scoffed down in the privacy of her office, Ava is now irritated by the mountain of rubbish. She hates seeing waste, and though her new work space is twice the size of her old cubicle, the area seems to get littered just as fast.

'Who is this guy anyway?' A pad displaying the piece on Doctor Alistair Evans is pushed through the discarded packaging. 'Why lower yourself to writing a puff piece for him?'

'Don't remind me,' Ava coughs at the sight of it, dodging a lengthy explanation as to her previous relationship with the doctor. She can't comprehend what she ever saw in the man. Superficial good looks and a path easily paved into the spotlight with him on her arm, it made a certain amount of sense at the time. All the trouble he exposed her to though. He was so uncouth and so coarse. Thank god she managed to find a more elegant fit in the end. Getting this far though, she supposes, was in small part thanks to Alistair. For those few weeks they partnered he was like a rocket she had strapped herself to and jumped from right before it exploded. She thought she'd gotten away with it. As breaks go it seemed a fairly clean one. If only. After the dust on the court case had settled, the doctor got around to calling her out on the fib of a recording, and reminded her of the suggestion she'd made.

His violent tantrum having subsided, he didn't seem upset about how things panned out, just interested in whatever last benefit he could gain from their history. When Ava trusted he wasn't looking for anything more than that, she'd kept the promise she made in jest, and permitted her old lover the carefully designed introduction to their readership he so desired, setting him on the way to public fame. 'I owed the guy a favour. Besides, he's got the face for it. You build these people up so you can report on them some more. I'm sure we'll knock him down one day. Meanwhile we'll have earned back our work given with interest. It's all business.'

An alert chimes on her screen, saving her from going into further detail. It's the new assistant, whats-his-name? She can never keep track of the people that come and go, mere avatars that appear as faint blips on her radar.

'That detective is still waiting.'

'Detective?' she asks the screen. 'Oh that's right. Give us a minute.'

He arrived at the office unannounced some while ago, but lunch had been served, and well, the day just got away. Embarrassed by the rubbish in front of her – it looks like she'd eaten a family sized meal – she glances about for a dustbin in the sparsely furnished office and hurriedly sweeps the packaging into an empty drawer of her desk instead. She's just caught a scrap of noodle on the side of her lip when the door opens and quickly guzzles it down before Detective Wong has a chance to notice. She can feel the meal swelling the stomach on her slender frame. Conscious of bulge, she walks over to cordially welcome him. 'Dylan Wong. I didn't think we'd be seeing you again.'

'Ms. O'Dwyer,' he says, cautious.

'What a nice surprise.'

'I was in the neighbourhood. Feels like I never left–' he stops himself.

By the desk, Agent Myers has risen.

'Long time,' the social agent smiles. 'What brings you here?'

Dylan, surprise manifest in a stunned moment of silence, finds himself wondering if he should be reaching for a gun. In a double-take, he sets his feet apart, bracing himself for the impact of whatever's to come. Slowly, he comments, 'I could ask you the same thing.'

Hostess skills in full effect, Ava covers the lull that follows. 'It's like a little reunion.'

'It's certainly unexpected,' Dylan fails to recover his cool.

'Well, I'm glad you dropped by,' and she remains unflappable in hers.

Pleasantries exchanged, they stand, door ajar so that the sound of the newsroom trickles through a gap. Agent Myers, strolling over, ignores Dylan, explaining to Ava that he has a meeting to get to and will leave them alone to catch up. Leaning toward her, he finds the curve of her waist as he kisses her goodbye, then he shakes hands with Dylan, 'Sorry I have to rush off. You know how it is,' and winks, as if he's just let the detective in on a delicious secret.

Dylan finds himself nodding in agreement. The room spins around him when he turns to watch the social agent depart. His hand feels oily after the shake and he wipes it on the side of his coat. As they're left alone, Ava looks over Dylan's shoulder to an intern, who understands the signal and closes the door. Twitching as it's shut, Dylan is suspicious that with the sound of the latch he's been caught in a trap.

'Let me take your coat,' Ava suggests.

'I shouldn't be here long,' he stares at her.

Ava wonders if there's another piece of food stuck to her cheek, or perhaps ink from a pen. 'It's roasting in here,' deftly stepping behind him, her hands go up to his shoulders to pull the coat off. 'Sit down. Make yourself at home.'

'You said we should have a chat sometime...'

Did she? It would have been months ago if she had. Another life, before she was editor. Hanging the coat on a hook behind her desk, Ava tries to recall when it might have been. Dylan follows the journey the rag of a thing makes, feeling all the more cornered now that it's in her possession. He won't be able to leave without having to ask for it.

'I suppose Agent Myers took you up on the offer before I did.'

Feigning a blush, Ava replies, 'I don't know, things just seemed to have worked out this way. He's a nice guy. A real gentleman.'

Dylan flinches. 'I see you've made some changes.'

'Changes happen,' Ava looks around the room. 'I can't take credit for them all.'

'You've got yourself a bigger office than Joanne had anyway.'

There's an accusation in the way he makes the remark.

The office they're conversing in is what used to be the conference room.

When Ava was promoted to editor she'd claimed it for herself, giving the smaller office that Joanne once occupied to the new assistant editor. That was the pretence for it. An AE should have their own space, she insisted, I worked for years keeping this newsroom together sat amongst the chaos and it's a miracle I managed anything at all. If that meant taking the conference room for herself, well, they could just talk around the water cooler if need be. 'Joanne was always dashing about on her feet. You'd be lucky to get a sit down with her. She didn't really need an office at all.'

'The cubicles are gone too.'

Another accusation.

Ava doesn't reply. The entire newsroom has had a makeover. Gone are the walled boxes in which Joanne kept her people. In their place, bean bags and an open plan, desks that nobody can claim as their own. A shared work space, but for the segregation of boss and employee. The carpets are a startling bright red. On the wall are spreads of photos from popular stories ChatterFive has broken over the past decade. The young girl from the riot article proudly hangs among them, accepted as the victim of a flash mob as Joanne was accepted as the agent of Francis Mullen's demise. Behind Ava, her office window overlooks the distant city where the spire rises among a spread of low buildings, the peak of it at level with her sprawling view. She was right about the heat. The sun blasts over her shoulders so the detective has to squint as they talk.

'And Barry Danger. Gone back to London, isn't he?'

Amused, Ava teases, 'You don't seem to deal with change very well. We were actually thinking of moving the whole setup. Seems a little silly having a news service operating on the outskirts of town. Joanne liked cheap rent. I think we could afford something a little closer to the centre though.'

The topic has no traction. The detective seems unsettled by the suggestion. There's an awful stickiness in the air. Neither of them rush to find a point of conversation to justify their sitting together.

'Agent Mullen's anniversary mass is coming up,' Dylan informs her. Is that spite in his voice? 'I told his family I'd be there.'

'It really crept up on us. I'll be there too.'

'You will?' he asks, tiredly bewildered.

She wants to snap at him for it. Why shouldn't she be there? She knew the man better than anyone else involved. Dylan never even met him. He couldn't even solve the case! And here he is making a vulgar show of mourning. Hiding these thoughts, she says instead, 'I think Francis was a bit lost. I tried helping him find his way, but, well, it's pointless to regret things that can't be altered. I don't know if we should cover the mass for his anniversary or not. Would that be tasteless? I feel like we owe it to him. He was doing his work for us, for ChatterFive, when he died.'

Still, the detective looks at her, trying to see something. Can he smell the lingering scent of the food she'd been eating? She'll have to get one of the interns to bin it for her when he leaves. She can't think of anything to prompt him with, to find what it is he wants. The nicest social protocol to get her out of the situation is to stand and explain she's busy, that they should have a chat again sometime. He's only been here a minute, so it might seem rude, but really, he's the one who's acting strangely. She'd be justified in walking him out. Not convinced of this herself, she wanly sits, waiting for him to get to whatever issue it is that's bothering him.

'It must have been difficult, taking over under those circumstances...'

Referring to everything that led to Ava becoming editor.

'I always knew I'd get the job someday. It's not the route I would have taken, given a choice,' she says sadly. 'But we're here now.'

'Yes,' Dylan agrees, 'we are.'

As he goes to rub the stubble under his nose, his hand seems to get lost along the way.

'Would you like a glass of water, Dylan?'

Not responding, he considers her suggestion as though it were a puzzle, some riddle from which he has to decipher a hidden meaning. Scrutinising her, he's struggling to see to the back of her head and doesn't notice that she's addressed him.

'Detective Wong?'

Ava has seen the look he wears before, that night on the steps of Francis Mullen's building. She'd thought that it was desire but she gathers now, in the face of the detective, that it is something completely different. Like the man who came before him, she expects him to keel toward her, until, as his lips peel apart like old wallpaper, a thought seems to pull him back from the edge.

Whatever it is that's been bothering Dylan Wong, she's about to find out. Peeved that it's taking so long to get to it, she fixes her hair, preparing on herself the appearance of a person who listens with a compassionate ear.

'You know, my wife and I have had our fair share of problems,' taking a deep breath, he readies himself to expel his thoughts. 'My work really gets to me. More than most cops I think. The other guys, they seem to be able to shut down a part of themselves just so they can get on with the job. I don't know how to manage that. I can't get past the horrible things people do to one another. Finding out the motive seems to help. It's a way for me to make sense of it all. Usually people have their reasons, even if they don't know it themselves. I almost hit her one time, you know. My wife. We were arguing and I raised my hand. I stopped myself before I did anything. But the damage was done, she'd seen it. Ever since then we've both lived in separate rooms. Went through the motions of marriage. The fights are just scripted, like we actually care that things are falling apart. I don't think she hates me. But she sees I hate myself. The only reason we stay together is for the boy and sometimes I even wonder if he'd be better off if we separated. I don't know. Is what I do worth it? There have been eighty murders in Dublin since that social agent died and I have to ask myself would the world be a different place if I wasn't the one who was on those cases? I really don't know.'

That's it. All he wanted to say. Ava is flabbergasted, not knowing what she's supposed to do with the information or why it's been given to her. She could console him, she supposes, say the world isn't a horrible place, good things happen, after all, look at the lovely office she's gotten. But that doesn't seem to be what he's seeking. She could ask him to leave now. He's made things uncomfortable enough, that's for sure.

'Did you like Francis Mullen?' he asks. 'Did you think he was a good guy?'

Feeling that she's threading on thin ice, Ava tiptoes into a reply. 'He was a caring man. Confused maybe, but always had the best of intentions.'

Dylan recognises the sentiment from ChatterFive's obituary for the social agent and can't figure out whether it's something she believes, or just an idea that lets her get on with her day. By the way she talks, you'd think that Francis had been dodging falling piano's unawares and was simply a fool for not having noticed them.

'Well,' he relents, rubbing his eyes, ' I'm going to go home now. My family will be wondering where I've been.'

The detective swallows, and Ava shifts in the black leather chair, waiting for him to explain why he told her all of this. There's nothing more to say though. It was a confession, an admission of guilt, and an explanation of surrender. She doesn't understand any of it, and she despises the mystery that she's been handed.

'Everything will be fine,' she says, making sure to use the most tender smile in her repertoire. Taking his coat in her hands, she walks around the desk now and gestures for him to stand. As she slips the thing back onto him, she gives his arm an affectionate rub. 'Go home. Tell them you love them. That's all they need from you.'

Her arm is hooked with his as she guides him into the revamped newsroom.

'It's very bright,' he says, stopping to look at the carpet, so red in the tense sunlight. Regarding the journalists, he grows concerned that the garish colour might make their work environment that much harder to operate in, like they're knee deep in a pool of blood, ignoring it as best they can as they wade through the swamp it makes.

'I thought it was green when I approved it.'

'Green?'

'I'm colour blind, Dylan,' she takes some perverse joy in telling him this.

'But you used to be a fashion writer, didn't you?'

'That's right,' she says. 'My deepest, most darkest secret. Now you know. I had to bluff about colour for years. There were a few people I could talk to about it, have them run my articles by so they were publishable. It doesn't matter now.'

'Now that you're at the top,' he says.

As he wanders away from her, Ava watches as he falls into a huddle of staff members. The man is caught in a state of fight or flight.

He asks himself, Is this actually an office? Or is it a movie set? Is that coffee one man drinks or a brown stand-in liquid? If Dylan read their screens would he find a collection of gibberish made to look like news? It all feels so real. Confused at first, the journalists about the detective follow his line of sight, then land on an understanding – they see their editor and recognise the anomaly which has the man so paralysed.

Ava, she returns the gathering's skittish look, and steeling herself against the accusation they represent, dares any of them to let her know what's on their minds. Of course, none of them do, and with a coy flick of her hair, she shows them her back and closes the door.

25

Arriving at the spread of gravel, ground stones that make up the oblong driveway crunch under the wheels of Dylan's car as it comes to a stop. The last thing he remembers on leaving ChatterFive's building is getting into the driver's seat. Now, the engine runs expectantly and a notification hums to announce its arrival at the keyed in destination. Dylan might have slept the entire way. Just another vehicle carrying its passenger from one lane to the next. He can only hope that the car didn't bring him anywhere unexpected during his apparent blackout, had him driving on the wrong side of the road, knocking over pedestrians, or performing frantic drug runs. Though he doesn't remember setting it to automatic, the fact of the matter is evident – he's home. The hum stops after a final warning and the engine shuts off. He's supposed to get up now. He's supposed to go into his house. Obeying the custom, his legs move as mindlessly as the car drove. Above, the sky is a pale sheet. In the distance, outside the walled estate, traffic on the N7 rushes in a torrential wind which, as Dylan finds himself in his hallway, is replaced by the obnoxious blare of cartoons. Admiring his son, whose face rests an inch from the blinking screen, he ruffles the mesmerised head. He'd been left in this position almost a day ago and Dylan is nonplussed to find he has not been uprooted from the spot. Draped around the room are the half hung paraphernalia of party decorations. In the kitchen go the voices of his wife and her sister, chattering happily in overlapping chirps.

His son laughs at a senseless animation on the screen. Dylan can't remember the last time he felt joy as freely as that. To become a shrivelled old man, able to count on his left hand the amount of times in his adult life he lost control of himself in a fit of giggles, is not a future he desires. Watching the ludicrous animals annihilate each other in a race to reach some ever moving goalpost, he tries for one, but his throat clogs and he falls into a coughing fit instead.

'Dad!'

Dylan slaps the boy a high-five.

'It's my birthday,' his son informs him. 'You're supposed to help us decorate.'

'I know, I know.'

Balloons waiting to be inflated droop over the coffee table. Taking one, he blows and knots it, and bats it away before reaching for the next. Two minutes pass this way until his wife, clenching a buttered piece of toast between her teeth and holding a steaming mug of tea in her hand, enters the room

'Look who it is,' she mumbles over the toast.

Splayed on the couch, Dylan is about ready to pour out of his policeman clothes and into a puddle on the floor. 'I'm home,' he says, and raises a hand in the air.

His sister-in-law is pacing in the kitchen, arguing with somebody on the phone. Flustered, his wife looks for somewhere to put her mug and toast without sprinkling crumbs on the ground, eventually deciding to place the toast on top of the mug and the mug on top of a dog-eared magazine. When her lips are free, she tells their son to get his auntie to make Daddy a cup of tea, and perching beside Dylan, her legs cross toward him. 'Where have you been?'

Dylan waves her away, 'Work stuff.'

'You look wrecked,' she says. 'You're supposed to be the party planner, remember?'

'I need to lie down for a bit. I want to help. Really, I do. Just let me get changed,' he leans forward, and takes another breath, mentally preparing himself for the climb upstairs. Like a man at the foot of Everest, he imagines each step he'll have to mount. Before long, his son stands at attention and holds out a cup of tea. Dylan takes a token sip to satisfy the boy.

'Thanks Robbie.' And to his wife he also says, 'Thank you, Cheryl.'

As he stands, he lets his coat fall from his arms, loosens his tie, drops it to the ground, and is about to unbuckle his belt when he remembers his sister-in-law is present. Along the way his wife travels behind him, picking up the offensive items. She's cleaning away his policeman life from sight. Sitting on the side of their bed, Dylan watches as she unbuttons his shirt and obeys as she tells him to pull off his trousers, tugging them in two jerks, then hands them over to be stuffed into a wicker basket on the other side of the room. At the open door, his son worries a spot on the frame, looking on with a novice mask, trying to measure the mood between his parents. Dylan winks at the boy to coax a charitable smirk.

'You can't keep doing this,' his wife says, little menace in her voice. She is only describing the state of their marriage. 'Coming and going as you please. I know it's work. I trust you on that. But it's no excuse.'

Not having the energy to appease her, Dylan merely watches as she empties his coat pockets of the job's remaining evidence. His phone is laid out, his ID, a handful of sticky copper change is dropped into an ashtray and receipts are scrunched up, thrown into a dustbin by the closet. Almost as an afterthought, her hand slips into his pocket one more time and comes out with something unexpected, a card, which she examines quizzically and looks at her husband, who she never took for a gambler.

'And after me saying I trust you,' she says.

'What is it?' he manages to ask, though at this stage he doesn't really care.

She flips it around for him to see.

It's the queen of hearts.

'Where did it come from?' she asks.

Shocked, Dylan considers reaching out for the card, but the weak effort is barely noticed. His fingers hover mindlessly. He's not sure that he wants the thing. With it comes a responsibility he doesn't know he can bare. The years it would take off his life, if not the remaining bulk of them in a misjudged step. His hand falls, then with a cracked smile on his face, he bursts into a spasm of laughter, a fit of giggles he can't stop. It's about to die away when he sees the look of dread on his wife's face, who must think he's hallucinating when it bursts out again and it erupts to the surface until his chest aches from the reels of it.

There's a problem Dylan could spend his life digging to the bottom of. Systematically, he could unearth all the desecrated truths he saw buried in the trial of Joanne Victoria, madly hoping all the while he wouldn't be entombed along with them. If Ava placed that card in his pocket, there's more than a murder to uncover. There's corruption in a service designed to rid the world of it, a social agent who said that red was green and a woman who doesn't know the difference between the two, lecturing all on the matter through ChatterFive and having the audience nod along in dull agreement. The queen of hearts and all it stands for, gloats. The masses Dylan would work to protect are asking that he do one thing – Investigate – while telling him to do just the opposite – Let us be at peace. Shocked he is, only at the arrogance of Ava. The card is but a confirmation of what he already knew. The role he had been asked to play in the events he examined was that of an accomplice, and two of the people asking it of him are those steadfast by his side.

Their son, dangling on his wife's leg, paws at her until she absentmindedly hands him the card, and forgets it as the boy disappears around a corner of the landing. If only Dylan could let go so easy. The grubby hands will soon have wiped away any fingerprints that might be on the thing, but he can't muster the strength to ask for it back. His wife lies down beside him, running her hand over his hedgehog crop of hair. Faced with the option of chasing the boy or laying here to let the world revolve around him, he admits, 'I don't want to sleep on the couch anymore.'

'Well,' his wife offers, not sure if now is the time to discuss the matter, 'I don't want you to either.'

What she means to say is that nothing changes unless you do, Detective Wong. No more late shifts and disappearing on long walks. No more reading case files over breakfast and making promises that can't be kept. There's a bubble to maintain and you need to start doing your share of the work.

'I'll get that paperwork pushed through. I mean it. It's you or the job and the job doesn't make life any better. Not for us. You guys are all that matter. I promise. I don't care about the card,' he tries to tell himself. 'I'm getting out. It doesn't change anything. She knew it wouldn't. But I don't know how. I don't know how to forget.'

'Just close your eyes,' his wife instructs, ignoring his delirium to impart the advice like a spoonful of honeyed medicine. 'Just close your eyes and everything will be better.'

On the one hand, Dylan is faced with the task of righting a wrong, on the other, renewing the life he has built with his wife and child. Pursuing the crime and the enormous collaboration from all involved would be perilous for his family. Remember the children. The slogan had once sounded to him a reminder of obligations. Now it seemed like a threat. Though it crushes him, it is a thing of beauty that he can choose his family at all. There are bonds between them, woven into the fabric of their reality. Love exists, that much Dylan knows now, but so long as every bit of it he has is to be for these two people, and not a stitch for those outside their home, the untouched, hollow as their joy may be, will prosper.

'It's so hard,' he whispers.

His wife hushes him. 'Never mind that. Just enjoy today.'

With this, she takes his hand, and leading him downstairs, she will gently direct he set a table with jellies and other assorted treats, the bowls to be laid atop a cloth, spangled and glittering for the celebration. At place mats, noise makers will be left. Dylan was supposed to have prepared a treasure hunt, with clues and a clever map, but they'll make do by hiding tiny prizes in nooks for the children to stumble across. Together, with her sister and their boy, they'll sing along to silly tunes, hang streamers and prepare the sitting room floor for dancing toddlers and their blundering parents. Goodie bags will be packed, pink for the girls, blue for the boys, and later, a tantrum will be thrown by the girl who wants blue but finds that none remain. Eventually, sweets will make all of the children hyper, so there's a healthy supply of alcohol and Disprin in the kitchen for the parents who'll suffer the fallout. The games and giddiness will subside and a child will fall asleep in an armchair. Others will get grumpy. A fight or two will happen among them, over a toy or a game, and the parents will begin to trickle off, sensing the end of festivities by the sad quiet that gathers. Dylan and his wife will put their boy to bed, sighing in relief – another day survived. And sitting up with a glass of wine, they'll guardedly discuss their future, what department Dylan might go to, and the bounty of things to come, when this time next year their boy will be yet a year older and their marriage at a new stage, all dependant on Dylan being able to forget a card.

Enjoy today, she says, go along with it all, live in this plastic dollhouse with us, make-believe the figures in white coats are there to help and that there's a system, impossible to subvert, of suits and badges and judge's wigs to make certain that they do. Dylan is sure that he can join her. He need only check there are no fingerprints so that, finally, he can resign. Trying to tell his wife this, he finds the lilt of her voice too soothing, and the thought remains bottled, oscillating frantically within.

'Smile,' she says.

Her sister has met them by the stairs and has nudged their son into frame. Her camera takes them in its grasp and it won't let go until they comply with her demand. If he doesn't do what he's told, the picture will be ruined.

'Smile,' his wife sings it again, playfully scooping their boy into her arms and embracing Dylan, whose mouth, caught on two fish hooks, contorts his cheeks, almost splitting the skin of his face as he tries the grin. Just smile, they instruct, say cheese, and let the bulb go flash. Through the multicoloured spots the light leaves in his eyes, for a moment, Dylan sees that out there, at the centre of it all, is a singularity, which relentless in its consumption of the intangible qualities that exist between persons, grows nothingness in return. Francis Mullen had dared himself close and was killed in the venture. Tipped into the centre where he was torn apart and spaghettified, it had been called murder, but Dylan knows it for what it was. Francis Mullen is one of the sacrificed, his death a concession so folk by the outskirts can go on existing where the cost of living is cheap, and all they have to pay are mouthed words of condolence. So, here he is among them, Dylan Wong, trapped on the event horizon, offering his apology and tending a memory of the extinguished, when over there, is Ava O'Dwyer, flitting about like gravity doesn't exist.

THANK YOU, FRIEND

If you enjoyed People in Season, don't forget to subscribe to my newsletter or add me on Twitter – www.simonfayauthor.com.

As a self-published author every supporter I get means a lot to me, so I hope you check out my other books. One is about robots and the other is about a bodybuilder.

Cheers,
Simon @simonfayauthor

Printed in Poland
by Amazon Fulfillment
Poland Sp. z o.o., Wrocław